Please return on or before the latest date above.
You can renew online at www.kent.gov.uk/libs
or by phone 08458 247 200

CUSTOMER SERVICE EXCELLENCE

Libraries & Archives

Kent
County
Council

ASK FOR RONALD STANDISH
THE BLACK GANG
BULLDOG DRUMMOND
BULLDOG DRUMMOND AT BAY
CHALLENGE
THE DINNER CLUB
THE FEMALE OF THE SPECIES
THE FINAL COUNT
THE FINGER OF FATE
THE ISLAND OF TERROR
JIM BRENT
JIM MAITLAND
JOHN WALTERS
KNOCK-OUT
MUFTI
SERGEANT MICHAEL CASSIDY RE
TEMPLE TOWER
THE THIRD ROUND

SAPPER

Bulldog Drummond

THE RETURN OF
BULLDOG DRUMMOND

HOUSE OF
STRATUS

This edition published in 2001 by House of Stratus, an imprint of
Stratus Books Ltd., 21 Beeching Park, Kelly Bray,
Cornwall, PL17 8QS, UK.

www.houseofstratus.com

Typeset, printed and bound by House of Stratus.

A catalogue record for this book is available from the British Library
and the Library of Congress.

ISBN 1-84232-556-6

CHAPTER 1

Slowly but relentlessly the mist was creeping over the moor. It moved in little eddies; then it would make a surge forward like a great silent wave breaking on the shore and not receding. One by one the landmarks were blotted out, until only some of the highest tors stuck up like rugged islands from a sea of white.

As yet it had not reached Merridale Hall, which stood on highish ground, some hundred yards from the main road to Yelverton, though already it was drifting sluggishly round the base of the little hill on which the house was built. Soon it would be covered: it would become a place cut off from the outside world, a temporary prison of stones and mortar whose occupants must perforce rely upon themselves. And it is possible that a dreamer standing at the smoking-room window, and gazing over the billowing landscape of cotton wool, might have pondered on the different dramas even then being enacted in all the other isolated dwellings. Strange stories of crime, of passion; tragedies of hate and love; queer figments of imagination would perhaps have passed in succession through his mind, always provided that the dreamer was deaf. For if possessed of normal hearing, the only possible idea that could have occupied his brain would have been how to preserve it.

Twice already had the butler entered, only to retire defeated from the scene. The cook, who had been trying to obtain a little well-earned rest herself, had then advanced into the hall and dropped a fusillade of saucepans one after another on the tiled

1

floor without the slightest success. And finally, in despair, the staff had barricaded itself in the pantry and turned on the gramophone.

There was something majestic about the mighty cadence. The higher note caused the window to rattle slightly: the lower one seemed to come from the deep places of the earth and dealt with the rest of the room. And ever and anon a half-strangled snort shook the performer with a dreadful convulsion. In short, Hugh Drummond was enjoying a post-prandial nap.

His hands were thrust deep in his trouser pockets, his legs were stretched out straight in front of him. Between them, her head on one knee, sat Bess, his black cocker spaniel. Unperturbed by the devastating roars that came from above her, she, too, slept, trembling every now and then in an ecstasy of dream hunting. And the mist rolled slowly by outside, mounting nearer and nearer to the house.

Suddenly, so abruptly that it seemed as if a soundproof door had been shut, the noise ceased. And had the mystical dreamer by the window been really present, he would have seen a rather surprising sight. For the man who the fraction of a second before had been sound asleep was now sitting up in his chair with every sense alert. The dog, too, after one look at her master's face, was sitting rigid with her eyes fixed on the window. Volleys of saucepans might be of no avail, but the sound which had caused this instantaneous change was different. For from the direction of the main road had come the crack of a rifle.

Still with his hands in his pockets, the man got up and crossed to the window. The mist was not more than twenty yards away, and for a while he stared down the drive. Who could be firing on a day like that? And yet he knew that he had not imagined that shot.

Suddenly his eyes narrowed: the figure of a man running at top speed came looming out of the fog. He raced towards the house, and on his face was a look of abject terror. And the next moment he heard the front door open and shut, and the sound of footsteps in the hall outside.

"Down, girl!" he ordered quietly, as Bess began to growl. "It would seem that there are doings abroad."

Drummond strode to the door and stepped into the hall. Cowering in a corner was a young man, whose breath still came in great choking gasps, and whose trembling hands gave away the condition he was in. For a moment or two he stared at Drummond fearfully; then, getting up, he rushed over to him and seized his arm.

"For God's sake save me!" he stammered. "They're after me."

"Who are after you?" asked Drummond quietly, and even as he spoke there came a ring at the door, accompanied by an imperative tattoo on the knocker.

"Quick: tell me," he went on, but he spoke to empty air. For with a cry of terror, the youngster had darted into the smoking-room and shut himself in.

There came a further loud knocking, and with a shrug of his great shoulders Drummond crossed the hall and opened the front door. Outside stood two men in uniform, each with a rifle slung over his back, and he recognised them at once as warders from Dartmoor.

"Good afternoon," he said affably. "What can I do for you?"

The senior touched his cap.

"Do you mind if we search your outbuildings, sir?" he said. "A man we're after disappeared up your drive, and got away in the fog. But he must have come here: there ain't nowhere else he could have gone."

"Who is this fellow you're looking for?" asked Drummond.

"A mighty dangerous customer, sir," said the warder. "You look as if you could take care of yourself all right, but there are a good many people round here who won't sleep happy in their beds till we've got him under lock and key again. It's Morris, sir, the Sydenham murderer: escaped in the mist this morning. And a more brutal devil never breathed."

Drummond raised his eyebrows: anyone less like a brutal murderer than the frightened youngster who had taken sanctuary in the house it would have been hard to imagine.

"Very near killed a warder this morning," went on the officer. "And then dodged away across the moors. Of course, with a face like his he never had a chance from the beginning, but if he is here, sir, as we think, we'll take him along with us."

"What is the peculiarity about his face?" demanded Drummond.

"He's got a great red scar down one cheek," said the warder.

"I see," said Drummond. "Look here, officer, there has evidently been some error. It is perfectly true that a man dashed into this house just before you arrived and implored me to hide him. But it is equally true that from your description he is not Morris. So we will elucidate the matter. Come in."

He crossed the hall to the smoking-room, with the two warders at his heels.

"Now then, young feller," he cried, as he flung open the door, "what's all this song and dance about? I presume this is not the man you want."

He turned to the warders, who were staring in a bewildered way at the panic-stricken youth cowering behind a chair.

"Never seen the gentleman before in my life, sir," said one of them at length.

"Get up, man!" remarked Drummond contemptuously. "No one is going to hurt you. Now then," he continued, as the youth slowly straightened himself and came out into the room, "let's hear what happened."

"Well, sir," said the one who was obviously the senior of the two officers, "it was this way. My mate and I were patrolling the road just by where your drive runs into it. Suddenly behind the gatepost we saw someone move, someone who it seemed to me had been hiding there. In this fog one can't see much, and it wasn't possible to make out the face. But when he sprang to his feet and rushed away it naturally roused our suspicions. So I fired a shot wide, as a warning, and we followed him up here."

"But surely you could have seen he wasn't in convict's kit," said Drummond.

"The first thing an escaped man does, sir, is to steal a suit of civvies. He either lays out some bloke he meets and strips him, or he breaks into a house. And a man like Morris, who is as powerful as they make 'em, and is absolutely desperate into the bargain, wouldn't stick at either course. I'm sorry, sir," he continued to the youngster, "if I've given you a fright. But you must admit that your behaviour was hardly that of a man who had nothing to fear."

"I quite agree," said Drummond tersely. He was covertly examining the youngster as he spoke, and there were times when those somewhat lazy eyes of his could bore like gimlets. But his next remark gave no indication of his thoughts.

"A drink, my stout-hearted sportsmen," he boomed cheerfully. "And good hunting to you. By the way," he went on, as he produced glasses and a tantalus, "you say this man is a murderer. Then why didn't they hang him?"

"Don't you remember the case, sir? About four years ago. An old man was found with his head bashed in, in some small street in Sydenham. They caught this fellow Morris and they found him guilty. And then at the last moment the Home Secretary reprieved him and he got a lifer. Some legal quibble, and he got the benefit of the doubt."

The warder smiled grimly.

"It's not for the likes of me to criticise the decision," he went on, "but I'd willingly bet my chances of a pension that he did it."

"That's so," agreed his mate.

"A more callous brutal swine of a man never drew breath. Well, sir, we must be getting along. Here's your very good fortune."

The two warders raised their glasses.

"And if I might make so bold as to advise you, sir, I'd have a pretty sharp look round tonight. As I said before, from the looks of you Mister Morris would find he'd met his match. For all that, he's a desperate man, and he might get at you while you were asleep."

He put down his empty glass.

"And as for you, sir," he went on, turning to the youngster, into whose cheeks a little colour had returned, "all I can say is, once again, that I'm sorry. But it's a dangerous thing to run from an armed warder, in a fog, down these parts, when a convict has escaped that very day. Good afternoon, gentlemen: thanking you very much again."

The two men picked up their hats, and Drummond went with them to the front door. Then he returned to the smoking-room, and having lit a cigarette, he threw himself into an armchair, and signed to the youngster to do likewise.

"Now, young feller," he said quietly, "it strikes me that there is rather more in this affair than meets the eye. You wake me from a refreshing doze by dashing into the house with a remark that they are after you, and it then turns out to be a completely false alarm. Why should you think that two warders were after you?"

"In the mist I didn't realise they were warders," stammered the other.

And once again Drummond stared at him thoughtfully.

"I see," he remarked. "Then who, may I ask, did you mean by 'they'?"

"I can't tell you," muttered the other. "I daren't."

"As you will," said Drummond casually. "I must confess, however, to a certain mild curiosity as to the identity of people who can reduce anyone to such a condition of pitiable funk as you were in. Also as to why you should anticipate meeting them on Dartmoor in a fog. Incidentally, my name is Drummond – Captain Drummond: what's yours?"

"Marton," said the other, fumbling in his pocket for his cigarette case.

For a while Drummond looked at him in silence. The youngster was clearly a gentleman: his age he put down at about twenty-one or two. His face was good looking in a weak sort of way, and though he had the build and frame of a big man, he was obviously in rotten condition. In fact, it would have been impossible to produce a better specimen of the type that he utterly despised. If fit, Marton would have been big enough and strong enough for anything on two legs; as he was, one good punch and he would have split like a rotten apple.

Drummond watched him light a cigarette with a trembling hand, and then his glance travelled over his clothes. Well cut: evidently a West-End tailor, but equally evident West-End clothes. And why should a man go careering about Dartmoor dressed as he was and in fear of his life? Was it just some ordinary case of a youngster absconding with cash, whose nerves had brought him to the condition he was in? Or could it be that there was something more in it than that? And at the bare thought of such a possibility his eyes began to glisten.

Life had been intolerably dull of late: in fact, since the affair with the masked hunchback on Romney Marsh nothing had happened to make it even bearable. He had shot, and fished, and consumed innumerable kippers in night clubs, but beyond that nothing – positively nothing. And now could it be possible that as the result of a sudden whim which had caused him to spend a week with Ted Jerningham something amusing was going to happen? The chances were small, he reflected sadly, as he again looked at Marton: still, it was worth trying. But the youngster would have to be handled carefully if anything was to be got out of him.

"Look here, Marton," he said, not unkindly, "it seems to me that you're in a condition when it will do you no harm to shoot your mouth to somebody. I'm considerably older than you, and I'm used to handling tough situations. In fact, I like 'em. Now what's all the trouble about?"

"There's no trouble," answered the other sullenly. "At least none where anyone else can help."

"Two statements that hardly tally," remarked Drummond. "And since the first is obviously a lie, we will confine ourselves to the second. Now, might I ask what you are doing in that rig down here, hiding behind the gate-post of this house?"

"I tell you I saw them looming out of the fog," cried the other wildly. "And I thought – I thought – "

"What did you think?"

"I just lost my head and bolted. And then when one of them fired – " He broke off and stared round the room. "What is this house?"

"Merridale Hall," said Drummond quietly. "Now out with it, young feller. What have you been up to? Pinching boodle or what?"

"I wish it was only that." He lit another cigarette feverishly, and Drummond waited in silence. If he was trying to bring himself up to the point of telling his story, it would be better to let him do it in his own way. "God! What a fool I've been."

"You're not the first person to say that," Drummond remarked. "But in what particular line have you been foolish?"

His curiosity was increasing now that any question of money was ruled out. However poor a specimen Marton might be, there must be something pretty seriously wrong to produce such a result on his nerves. So once again he waited, but after a while the other shook his head.

"I can't tell you," he muttered. "I daren't."

"You damned young fool," said Drummond contemptuously, losing his patience. "What on earth is there to be frightened of? Your affairs don't interest me in the slightest, but you've made a confounded nuisance of yourself this afternoon, and frankly I've had enough of you. So unless you can pull yourself together and cease quivering like a frightened jelly, you'd better push on to wherever you're going."

He had no intention whatever of turning him out of the house, but it struck him that the threat might produce some coherence in the other. And his surprise was all the greater at the unexpected answer he received. For the youngster for the first time pulled himself together and spoke with a certain quiet dignity.

"I'm sorry, Captain Drummond," he said. "And I apologise for the exhibition I've made of myself. I know my nerves are all to hell, and though it was my fault in the beginning, it hasn't been entirely so since. And so, if I might ask you for a whisky and soda, I'll be getting on."

"Now," said Drummond cheerily, "you're beginning to talk. I was trying to get you into some semblance of coherence, that's all. There can be no question whatever of your leaving tonight: you'd be lost in this fog in half a minute. And I know that my pal Jerningham, whose house this is, will agree with me when he gets back – that is, if he gets back at all: with this weather he'll very likely stay the night in Plymouth. So here's a drink, young feller, and again I tell you candidly that if you're wise you won't bottle this thing up anymore. Whatever it is, I won't give you away, and, unless it's something dirty, I may be able to help you."

Marton drained his glass, and into his eyes there came a look of dawning hope.

"Good Lord!" he cried, "if only you could. But I'm afraid it's beyond anyone: I've got to go through with it myself. Still, it will be an awful relief to get it off my chest. Do you go much to London?"

"I live there," said Drummond.

"And do you go about a good deal?"

"I trot round," remarked the other with a faint smile, "the same as most of us do."

"Have you ever run across a woman called Comtessa Bartelozzi?"

Drummond thought for a moment, and then shook his head.

"Not that I know of: she's a new one on me. Hold hard a minute: we'll have the other half-section before you go on."

He rose and crossed to the side table, carrying Marton's glass and his own. So there was a woman in the situation, was there? Name of Bartelozzi. Sounded a bit theatrical: might be real – might be false. And as for the title, Comtessas grew like worms in a damp lawn. In fact, he was so occupied with his thoughts and the mixing of two drinks, that he failed to see the hard hatchet face of a man that for one second was pressed against the window. And Marton, who had his back to it also, sat on in ignorance that, in that fleeting instant, every detail of the room had been taken in by the silent watcher outside.

"Now then," said Drummond, returning with the glasses, "we've got as far as the Comtessa Bartelozzi. Is she the nigger or rather negress in the wood pile?"

"If only I'd never met her!" said the other. "I was introduced to her one night at the Embassy, and… Great Scot! what's that?"

From outside had come the sound of a crash. It was some distance away, but in the still air it was clearly audible. And it was followed almost immediately by a flood of vituperation and loud shouts of 'Hugh.' Drummond grinned gently, and going to the window opened it.

"Hullo! Peter," he shouted. "What has happened, little one?"

"That perishing, flat-footed idiot Ted has rammed the blinking gate-post," came an answering shout. "We've taken two and a half hours to get here from Plymouth, most of the time in the ditch, and now the damned fool can't even get into his own drive."

The voice was getting nearer.

"What's Ted doing, Peter?" demanded Drummond.

"Sitting in the car drinking whisky out of my flask. Says that God doesn't love him, and that he won't play anymore."

Peter Darrell loomed out of the fog and came up to the window.

"Hullo!" he muttered, "who is the boy friend?"

"We'll go into that after," said Drummond. "Does Ted propose to sit there the whole night?"

"He says he wants you to come down and help," answered Darrell. "The car is half stuck, and you can barely see your hand in front of your face."

"All right, I'll come. You wait here, Marton, and carry on with your yarn later."

"Bring a torch, old boy," went on Darrell. "Not that it's much use, but it might help to pilot him up the drive."

"There's one in the hall," said Drummond. "I'll get it. And, Marton, you'll find cigarettes in the box there."

He got the torch and joined Darrell outside. And as they disappeared into the mist, their feet crunching on the gravel, two dim figures crouching near the wall began to creep slowly towards the open window. Their footsteps were noiseless in the earth of the flowerbed that bordered the wall, and the youngster sat on in utter ignorance of the fate that was threatening him. A good sort, this Captain Drummond, he reflected: was it possible that he would be able to help him? And even as the dawn of hope began in his mind there came a sound from behind him. He swung round in his chair: his jaw dropped: wild terror shone in his eyes. Not a yard away stood the man he had seen only once before – but that once had been enough.

He gave a hoarse, choking cry and tried to get up. And as he moved he felt his neck held in a vice-like grip. He struggled feebly, staring into the cruel, relentless eyes of his assailant. And then there came a roaring in his ears: the room spun round until at length everything grew black.

"Take his hat, Steve, and then give me a hand with the young swine. Those guys may be back at any moment."

"Have you killed him?" asked the second man.

"No. But we'll have to carry him. I guess it's the first time I've been thankful for this darned fog."

And a few moments later the only moving thing in the smoking-room was the mist that eddied in through the open window, whilst all unconscious of what had happened, Drummond and Darrell were groping their way down the drive.

"All sorts of excitement here, Peter," said Drummond. "There is an escaped murderer wandering about at large – "

"We heard in Plymouth that a convict had got away. Poor devil! I'd sooner be tucked up in my cell than wandering about this bit of the country on a night like this."

"And then the arrival of that youth."

"He seems a rather leprous-looking mess, old boy."

"Nothing to what he was when he first appeared. He's just beginning to tell me the secret of his young life. Evidently got into the deuce of a hole somehow, and probably wants the seat of his pants kicked good and hearty. However, Ted will have to give him a shake down: can't turn him out in this fog. And we'll hear what the worry is."

"Doesn't sound a particularly absorbing evening's entertainment," remarked Darrell dubiously.

"Probably not," agreed Drummond. "But there's just a bare possibility it might lead to some amusement. And, by Gad! Peter, anything would be welcome these days."

"A drink most emphatically would be," said the other. "Here is the car."

The sidelights suddenly showed up a yard in front of them, and Darrell demanded his flask.

"Finished, dear old lad," came Jerningham's voice happily. "Quite, quite finished. What an infernal time you've been! Now if you'll both push hard I'll get her into reverse, and we ought to do it!"

The wheels skidded on the greasy turf, but with Drummond's great strength to help they at length got her into the road.

"The gate is open, Ted," he said. "Wait a moment now until I mark the right-hand pillar with the torch."

He stood beside it, throwing the light down on the ground, and as he did so a piece of paper lying at his feet caught his eye. It was clean and looked like a letter, and almost mechanically he picked it up and put it in his pocket as the car went slowly past him. Then, leaving Darrell to shut the gate, he piloted Jerningham up the drive until they got to the house.

"Parker can put her away," remarked the owner, getting out. "Jove! old boy, we've had an infernal drive."

"I thought you'd probably stop in Plymouth, Ted," said Drummond.

"It wasn't too bad when we started," said the other, "was it, Peter? Let's get into the smoking-room, and I'll ring for someone to get your kit."

"Wait a moment, Ted," said Drummond. "There's a visitor."

"A visitor! Who the devil has rolled up on an evening like this?"

"Fellow by the name of Marton," went on Drummond, lowering his voice. "He's a pretty mangy piece of work, and he's in a state of mortal terror over something or other. He'd just begun telling me about it when you arrived. I'll tell you the beginning of the thing later on, but treat him easy now. He's as frightened as a cat with kittens."

He opened the smoking-room door.

"Now then, Marton, here's the owner – "

He broke off abruptly: the room was empty. And for a while the three of them stared round in silence.

13

"Have you got 'em again, Hugh?" demanded Jerningham.

"No. I can vouch for the boy friend," said Darrell. "I saw him."

Drummond stepped into the hall, and shouted. And the only result was the arrival of the butler.

"Jennings, have you seen a young gentleman lying about anywhere?" he asked.

"No, sir," said the butler, looking slightly bewildered. "What sort of a young gentleman?"

"Any sort, you old fathead," said Jerningham, and once again Drummond shouted 'Marton' at the top of his voice.

They waited, and at length Jerningham spoke.

"Your young friend has apparently hopped it, old boy," he remarked. "And if, as you say, he's a bit of a mess I shouldn't think he's much loss. Get Mr Darrell's kit out of the car, Jennings, and tell Parker to put her in the garage."

He led the way back into the smoking-room and Drummond followed slowly. To the other two the matter was a trifling one: a youngster whom neither of them had met had come and gone. But to him the thing was much more puzzling. Even if Marton's terror had finally proved groundless, it had been very real to him. And so what had induced him to leave a place where he knew he was safe? And why had they not met him going down the drive?

"There's something damned funny about this, you chaps," he said thoughtfully. "I'll tell you the whole tale."

They listened in silence as he ran over the events of the afternoon, and when he'd finished, Jerningham shrugged his shoulders.

"It seems pretty clear to me, old boy," he remarked. "When you left him and he began to think things over he came to the conclusion that he'd been talking out of his turn. He realised that, having once started, it would be difficult for him not to continue. Possibly, too, what he might have been prepared to tell to you alone he funked giving tongue to before a bunch of us.

And so he decided to beat it while the going was good, which would get him out of his dilemma. And that answers your query about not meeting him as we came up the drive. Naturally he didn't want to be seen, so he just stood a couple of yards in on the grass as we went past. In this fog we'd never have spotted him."

"That answers it, Ted, I agree," said Drummond. "And yet I'm not satisfied. Don't know why, but there it is. By the same token, do either of you blokes know this Comtessa Bartelozzi?"

They both shook their heads.

"Not guilty," said Darrell. "Did he give any description of her?"

"No," answered Drummond. "He'd only just started to tell his little piece when you arrived."

"Anyway," said Jerningham, "I don't see that there is anything to be done. He's not here, and that's an end of it. And the point that now arises is what the deuce we're going to do tonight. I'd ring up the doctor and ask him round for a rubber, but I doubt if he'd get here. What are you staring at, Hugh?"

Drummond had his eyes riveted on a spot on the carpet, and suddenly he bent down and touched it with his fingers. Then he gave a low whistle and straightened up.

"I knew I was right," he said quietly. "It's earth. And more there – and there. Somebody has been in through the window, Ted."

"By Jove! he's right," said Darrell, peering at the marks on the floor.

"And look at those two close by the chair Marton was sitting in. Whoever it was who came in stood by that chair."

"Come here," called out Darrell, who, with the electric torch in his hand, was leaning out of the window. "There are footmarks all along the flowerbed."

"Let's get this clear," said Jerningham. "You're certain those marks weren't there before?"

"Of course I'm not," cried Drummond. "I don't spend my time examining your bally carpet. But that mud is still damp. Well, I was asleep here after lunch until young Marton arrived, and all that time the window was shut. In fact, it was never opened till I heard Peter shouting."

"What about the two warders?"

"Neither of them ever went near the window. Nor did Marton. Lord! man, it's as clear as be damned. It's a definite trail from the window to the chair the youngster was sitting in."

"There's no sign of a struggle," said Darrell.

"Why should there have been one?" demanded Jerningham. "It may have been some bloke he knew with whom he toddled off all friendly like."

"Seems to me there are two pretty good objections to that," said Drummond. "In the first place, how did anyone know he was here? Secondly, if it was a pal who, by some extraordinary fluke, arrived at the window, why did he bother to come into the room? Why not just call out to him?"

He shook his head gravely.

"No, chaps: as I see it, there's only one solution that fits. The visitor was Morris – the escaped convict. He was lying hidden in the garden and seized his chance when he saw Marton alone."

"By Jove! that's possible," said Darrell thoughtfully.

"But, damn it – why should he go off with a bally convict?" demanded Jerningham.

"Probably Morris dotted him one over the head," said Drummond. "Then dragged him outside, and, hidden by the fog, stripped him. It's the very point the warders mentioned: the first thing an escaped man does is to try to get civilian clothes."

"Then in that case the wretched bloke is probably lying naked in the shrubbery," cried Jerningham. "We'd better have a search-party; though our chances of finding him, unless we walk on top of him, are a bit remote."

16

"Doesn't matter: we must try," said Drummond. "Got any lanterns, Ted?"

"I expect Jennings can produce something," answered the other. "Though I'm afraid it's pretty hopeless."

He rang the bell, and as he did so there came from outside the sound of footsteps on the drive. All three stared at the window expectantly: was this Marton coming back? But it was one of the warders who materialised out of the mist, to be followed a moment or two later by his mate.

"Beg your pardon, gentlemen," he said, "but as I was passing I thought I'd let you know that Morris was seen about a quarter of a mile from here an hour ago. So warn your servants to keep the windows shut and the doors bolted."

"I'm rather afraid it's a bit late, officer," said Drummond. "Unless I'm very much mistaken, Morris has been here within the last quarter of an hour. And those" – he pointed to the marks of mud – "are his tracks."

"But what were you doing, sir?"

"Helping Mr Jerningham to get his car out of the ditch. You remember that youngster who was here? Well, I left him in this room, and when I came back he was gone. And the only possible solution that I can think of is that Morris laid him out in order to get his clothes. We're just going to have a search through the grounds now."

"I've told Jennings to get lanterns," said Jerningham.

"Possibly you're right, sir," said the warder. "He'd seize a chance like that. But there is another thing that may have happened: the young gentlemen may have joined his friends."

"What friends?" demanded Drummond.

"Well, sir, just after me and my mate left you this afternoon and got into the main road we ran into two gentlemen walking along. So we stopped them and warned them about Morris. One of them, a great, big, powerful-looking man he was, began to laugh.

" 'Thank you, officer,' he says. 'But if this guy Morris tries any funny stuff with me he won't know whether it was a steam hammer or a motor lorry that hit him.'

" 'No, sir,' I answers, 'you look as if you could take care of yourself – same as another gent I've just been talking to.' Meaning you, sir, of course." He turned to Drummond. "Well, he seemed interested like," went on the warder, "and so I told him what had just happened – about the young gentleman being in such a panic and all that.

" 'Can you describe him?' says he, and when I done so he turns to his friend.

" 'Quite obviously it's the boy we were expecting,' he says. 'The poor lad must have lost his way in the fog. Up there, is he, officer? And what is the name of the house?'

" 'Merridale Hall,' I tells him. 'You can't miss it: you are only thirty yards from the entrance gate.'

"And with that he says good afternoon and walks on. So I should think, sir, that in this case that is what happened: the young gentleman went off with his friends. Not that what you thought wasn't very probable: Morris would stick at nothing. And, of course, you didn't know anything about these two gents."

"No," said Drummond slowly, "I didn't. They did not, by any chance, say where they were stopping?"

"No, sir, they didn't. Well, good night, gentlemen: we must be getting along."

"The plot thickens," said Drummond, as the footsteps of the two warders died away. "And, boys, it seems to me it thickens in a rather promising manner."

"I don't see much ground for optimism at the moment, old lad," said Darrell.

"Don't you, Peter? I do. It seems to me that we have at any rate established the fact that Marton's story was not entirely a cock-and-bull one: nor was it mere groundless panic."

"I'm darned if I see why," said Jerningham. "Anyway, we shan't want those lanterns now, I take it."

He went to the door and shouted the fact to Jennings: then he came back to his chair.

"Those warders," went on Drummond quietly, "met these two men just outside the gate. Now it would have taken them, at the most, two minutes to walk up the drive. At a conservative estimate it was at least twenty minutes after when you two rammed the gate-post. What do you suggest they were doing during the gap? Why, if they were friends of Marton, didn't they ring the front door bell and inquire if he was here? Why, when they finally did come in, did they come in through the window? No, my boy – it's a fiver to a dried orange pip that those two men are the 'they' he was so terrified of. And now, owing to the mere fluke of that warder meeting them, they've got him."

"I'll grant all that, old lad," said Jerningham. "But what I want to know is, what the deuce you propose to do about it. You don't know where these men are living: you don't know anything about 'em. All we do know is that your boy friend's name is Marton, which cannot be called a very uncommon one."

"Afraid I'm rather inclined to agree with Ted, old boy," said Darrell. "Doesn't seem to me that we've got anything to go on. True, we know about this female – Bartelozzi or whatever her name is – but as she is presumably in London, that doesn't help much."

Drummond gave a sudden exclamation, and pulled out of his pocket the piece of paper he had found on the drive.

"I clean forgot all about this," he said, opening it out. "Picked it up by the gate-post."

"Anything interesting?" cried Darrell, as he watched the other's face.

Without a word Drummond laid it on the table, and they all three stared at it. It was an ordinary piece of office notepaper with the name and address of the firm stamped at the top.

MARTON, PETERS & NEWALL, 134, *Norfolk Street*,
Solicitors.   *Strand, WC2*

Underneath was written in pencil the two words: Glensham House.

"At any rate that establishes something else," remarked Jerningham: "a point that does give us a foundation to work on. Glensham House is about half a mile down the road towards Yelverton."

"The deuce it is," said Drummond, his eyes beginning to gleam.

"It's a big house, and it's been empty for some years. They say it's haunted, but that is probably poppy cock. It has recently been let to a wealthy American, who has installed a housekeeper, and is, I believe, shortly coming to live there himself."

"Things are marching," remarked Drummond. "It is, I take it, a fair assumption that Glensham House was Marton's objective."

The other two nodded.

"It is also, I take it, another fair assumption that the Marton who seems to be the senior member of the firm is this fellow's father or uncle."

"Go up top," murmured Darrell.

"Why, then, my stout-hearted warriors, should the junior bottle-washer of a firm of respectable lawyers be wandering about Dartmoor in such a state of abject terror?"

"Wait a moment," said Jerningham suddenly. "Where have I heard or seen the name of that firm recently? By Jove! I believe I've got it."

He crossed the room and picked up the morning paper.

"Here it is," he cried excitedly. "I knew I wasn't mistaken."

"TRAGEDY AT SURBITON
"LONDON LAWYER'S DEATH

"A shocking tragedy occurred yesterday at 4, Minchampton Avenue, Surbiton, the residence of Mr Edward Marton, senior partner of the well-known firm of Norfolk Street solicitors – Marton, Peters and Newall. Mr Edward Marton, who was a very keen sportsman, went into his smoking-room after dinner with the intention of overhauling his guns. A few minutes later his wife and daughters, who were sitting in the drawing-room, were alarmed by the sound of a shot. They rushed into the smoking-room, and were horrified to find Mr Marton lying on the carpet with a dreadful wound in his head. A gun was by his side, and some cleaning materials were on the table close by. A doctor was at once summoned, but the unfortunate gentleman was beyond aid. In fact, the medical opinion was that death had been instantaneous. It is thought that Mr Marton, who frequently shot during the weekend, must have taken down his gun for the purpose of cleaning it. By some fatal mischance a cartridge had been left in one of the barrels, which went off, killing Mr Marton immediately. The deceased, who was a very popular member of Surbiton society, leaves one son and three daughters."

Drummond lit a cigarette thoughtfully.

"The Marton family don't appear to be in luck," he remarked. "Ted," he went on suddenly, "have you ever left a cartridge in a gun?"

"Can't say I have, old boy. Why?"

" 'Well-known sportsman,' "quoted Drummond. " 'Frequently shot over the weekend.' I wonder: I wonder very much. Confound it, you fellows, when you clean a gun you break it first, don't you? And when you break a gun you can see the blamed thing is loaded. Mark you, I'm not saying it wasn't an accident, but, once again, I wonder."

"You mean you think he shot himself?" said Darrell.

Drummond shrugged his shoulders.

"I can understand a gun being loaded and a man fooling about with it and by accident potting somebody else. I can understand a man climbing a fence, and through not holding his gun properly or forgetting to put it at safety, getting peppered himself. But I find it deuced difficult to understand it in this case."

"And supposing you're right – what then?" said Jerningham curiously.

"Son in a condition of abject terror: father committing suicide. Surely there must be some connection."

"Do you think the son knows what's happened?"

"Can't tell you: he said nothing about it to me. But in the account in the paper it specifies Mrs Marton and her daughters only, so possibly he doesn't. Anyway, Ted, your question as to what to do tonight is now answered."

The other two stared at him.

"We pay a little visit to Glensham House. You say the new owner is not yet in residence."

"As far as I know, he isn't," said Jerningham doubtfully.

"Splendid! And if by chance he is, we'll swear we've lost our way in the fog. Great Scot! chaps, think of the bare possibility of having stumbled on something. Admittedly it may prove a hopeless frost, but it would be nothing short of criminal to neglect such an opportunity."

"That's all right, old bean," said the other, "and no one likes a bit of fun and laughter better than I do. But don't forget I live in this bally locality, and what you're proposing is nothing more nor less than housebreaking."

"I know, Ted." Drummond grinned happily. "Maximum penalty ten years. But we'll plead we're first offenders."

"Confound you, Hugh," laughed Jerningham. "What do you expect to find there anyway?"

Drummond waved a vast hand.

"What about a perfectly good ghost? You say it's haunted. Honestly, chaps, I've got a feeling that we're on to something. And whatever you two blokes decide to do – I'm going."

"That settles it, Peter," said Jerningham resignedly. "Tell mother that my last thoughts were of her."

CHAPTER 2

Glensham House was a large, rambling old place. It stood on low ground surrounded by trees, about halfway between the main road and the deadly Grimstone Mire. For generations it had belonged to the Glensham family, but increasing taxation and death dues had so impoverished the present owner that he had been compelled to let.

Legends about the place abounded, and though some of them were undoubtedly founded on fact, many were merely local superstitions. For the house was an eerie one, set in eerie surroundings: the sort of place round which stories would be likely to grow – especially in the West Country.

But whatever the truth of some of the modern yarns – strange lights seen without human agency, footsteps when there was no one there to make them – certain of the older legends were historically true. The house was honeycombed with secret passages, and there was documentary proof that it had sheltered many of the Royalists during the Civil War with Cromwell.

For the last two years it had been empty, the tenants having left abruptly because, so they said, of the servant troubles. An old woman who lived in a cottage not far away had aired the place and kept it more or less clean, but there was a dark and unlived-in atmosphere about the house as it loomed up that made the man who was feeling his way cautiously forward along the edge of the drive shiver involuntarily and hesitate.

He was cold and hungry: for eight hours, like a phantom, he had been dodging other phantoms through the fog. Once he had butted straight into a woman, and she, after one glance at his clothes, had fled screaming. He had let her go: anyway there would not have been much good in attempting to follow her in that thick blanket of mist. And in some ways he was glad she had seen him. Already he was regretting bitterly the sudden impulse that had made him bolt, and she would most certainly say she had seen him, which would localise the hunt. In fact, only a certain pride and the knowledge that he was hopelessly lost prevented him from going back to the prison and giving himself up.

Sheer chance had guided his footsteps to Glensham House. He knew the dangers of the moor in a fog: he knew that the risk he ran of being caught by a patrol of warders was a lesser evil far than a false step into one of those treacherous green bogs, from which there was no return. But he also knew that the main road was more dangerous than a side track, and when he had accidentally blundered off the smooth surface on to gravel he had followed the new direction blindly. Food and sleep were what he wanted: then perhaps he would feel more capable of carrying on. Perhaps he might even do the swine yet, and make a clear get away. Other clothes, of course – but that would have to wait. It was food first and foremost.

And now he stood peering at the house in front of him. He could see no trace of a light: not a sound broke the silence save the melancholy drip, drip from the sodden branches above his head. And once again did Morris, the Sydenham murderer, shiver uncontrollably.

Like most men of low mentality, anything at all out of the ordinary frightened him. And having been born in a town, and lived all his life in crowds, the deadly stillness of this gloomy house almost terrified him. But hunger was stronger than fear:

where there was a house there was generally food, and to break into a place like this was child's play to him.

He took a few steps forward until he reached the wall: then he began to circle slowly round the house in the hope of finding a window unlatched. To save himself trouble had always been his motto, and in case there should be anyone about it would minimise the risk of making a noise. But ten minutes later he was back at his starting point without having found one open. He had passed three doors, all bolted, and he had definitely decided in his own mind that the place was empty.

And now the question arose as to what to do. If it was empty there would probably be no food: at the same time it was shelter – shelter from this foul fog. He would be able to sleep: and, he *might* find something to eat. Perhaps the owners were only away for the night, in which case he might even get some other clothes. Anyway it was worthwhile trying, and a couple of minutes later there came a sharp click, followed by the sound of a window being gently raised.

Inside the room he paused again and listened: not a sound. Once a board cracked loudly outside the door, and he waited tensely. But there was no repetition, and after a while he relaxed.

"Empty," he muttered to himself. "I guess we'll do a bit of exploring, my lad."

He turned and softly shut and re-bolted the window. Then he crept cautiously towards the door. There was a carpet on the floor, but except for that it struck him the room was very sparsely furnished. And hopes of food drooped again, only to be resurrected as he tiptoed into the hall. For close beside him in the darkness a clock was ticking. Another thing struck him also: the temperature in the hall seemed appreciably warmer than in the room he had just left.

He paused irresolutely: he was beginning to doubt after all if the house was empty. And then the clock began to strike. He counted the chimes – eight: why, if there were people in the house, were they all upstairs or in bed so early?

The darkness was absolute, and if he had had any matches he would have chanced it and struck one. But matches are not supplied to His Majesty's convicts, and so he could only grope forward blindly and trust to luck that he would not kick anything over.

He wanted, if he could, to locate the kitchen, as being the most likely place to find food. And so, guessing it would be at the back of the house, he tried to move in a straight line directly away from the room by which he had entered. And he had taken about ten paces when his foot struck something. All too late he knew what it was – one of those rickety little tables which are specially designed to upset on the slightest provocation. He felt it going, and his hand shot out to try to save it, with the result that he gave it the *coup de grâce*. It fell with a crash, and a thing that sounded as if it must be a brass bowl went with it.

In the silence the noise was appalling, and the convict, with the sweat pouring off his forehead, stood motionless. He'd find out now sure enough if the house was empty or not. Was that somebody moving upstairs, or was it his imagination? He waited for what seemed an eternity: no further sound came. And at length his heart ceased to race, and with a sigh of relief he wiped his forehead with the back of his hand. Safe, so far.

Once more he went cautiously ahead, and a few moments later he bumped into a door. He tried the handle: it was unlocked, and he opened it. And at once he knew that he had struck lucky, for there came to his nostrils the unmistakable smell of food. Another thing, too – and this time there was no doubt at all about it – the room he was now in was much warmer. He groped his way forward, until his hands encountered a table – a solid, substantial table. Very gently he moved them over the surface. What was that? A cup and saucer, a loaf of bread, and last but not least a candle. And if there was a candle there might be matches.

He went on feeling with his fingers: a knife, a plate with meat on it, and – but that seemed too good to be true – a bottle with a screw stopper: a bottle of a shape he had only seen in his dreams for years: a bottle of beer. And then, when he had almost decided to begin to eat, he touched a box of matches.

For a while he hesitated: was it safe? There was still no sound from outside, and he decided to risk it: he wanted to gloat over that wonderful bottle. The next moment the candle illuminated the repast in front of him, and like a famished wolf the convict fell on it.

He tore the bread in hunks from the loaf, beautiful white bread the taste of which he had almost forgotten. He crammed his mouth with beef – beef cut in thin slices. And finally he washed it down with great gulps of beer.

At last the immediate pangs were appeased, and he began to think things over. The room he was in was apparently the servants' hall, and since the meal had obviously not been prepared for him, there must be someone in the house. Then why had nothing happened when he upset the table in the hall?

After a while a possible solution dawned on him. The owners of the house were clearly away, and had left the house in charge of a caretaker, who had gone out and been unable to get back owing to the fog.

The point was, would he or she return that night? And even as he cogitated over it, his throat turned dry and he froze into a rigid block of terror. A mirror was hanging on the wall in front of him, and in it he could see the reflection of the door behind his chair. And it was slowly opening. He watched it with distended eyes, unable to move or speak: what was coming in? And nothing came: as silently as it had opened, it closed: almost he might have imagined the whole thing.

But he knew he hadn't imagined it: he knew that the door had opened and shut. Who had done it? Who had peered in and seen him sitting there? He had heard no sound: he had seen nothing. But that silent watcher had seen him!

At last he forced himself to get up from his chair and turn round. The movement caused the candle to flicker, and the distorted shadows danced fantastically on the walls and ceiling. The only sound in the room was his heavy breathing as he stared fearfully at the door. Who was on the other side?

He took a step forward: another. And then with a sudden run he darted at it and flung it open. The passage was empty: there was no one there.

He rubbed his eyes dazedly: then, going back into the room, he got the candle, and holding it above his head once again examined the passage. No sign of anyone: no sound. The door which led into the hall was shut: so were two others that he could see. And suddenly a thought occurred to him that drove him back into the room almost frantic with fear: supposing there had never been anyone there, supposing it had been a ghost that had stood in the passage?

Almost gibbering with terror, he shut the door again and fumbled wildly for the key. It was not there: if there was one at all, it was on the other side of the door. But not for a thousand pounds would Morris, brutal murderer though he might have been, have opened it again. All the horrors of the unknown were clutching at his heart: he would have positively welcomed the tramp of heavy hoots in the hall, and the sight of a warder with a gun.

Keeping the table between him and the door, he crouched on the floor, staring with fascinated eyes at the handle. Was it going to turn again or not? And after a while his imagination began to play him tricks: he thought it was moving, and he bit his hand to prevent himself crying out. And then it didn't: nothing happened.

Suddenly he straightened up: for the moment the ghost was forgotten. A sound had come from above his head – the unmistakable sound of a footstep. It was repeated, and he stood there staring upwards, listening intently. No ghost about that, he reflected: somebody was in the room above him, and by the heaviness of the tread it sounded like a man.

He leaned forward to blow out the candle: then he paused, torn between two conflicting fears. If he left it burning it might be seen, but if he blew it out the room would be in darkness. And darkness with the thing outside in the passage was impossible to contemplate: if the door was going to open again he felt he must see it. And even as he hesitated there came a strange, half-strangled cry from overhead followed by a heavy bump that shook the ceiling.

He began to tremble violently: things were happening in this house that he could not understand. Give him a squalid slum, the lowest of boozing dens with murder in the air, and he was as good a man as anyone. But this was something he had never met before, and it was making him sweat cold. That noise upstairs – it wasn't normal: and now there were other sounds, for all the world like the flounderings of some huge fish on the floor above. Gradually they died away, and once again silence settled on the house.

After a while, as the silence continued, he grew a little calmer: he must decide what he was going to do. On one thing he was absolutely determined: clothes or no clothes, nothing would induce him to go upstairs. And the only point was whether he should go through the window now and out into the foggy night, or whether he dared to wait a few more hours. He opened the shutters, and found the point was settled for him: there were bars outside, and so that means of exit was cut out. And the bare idea of going through the hall until daylight came was out of the question.

He sat down once more in the chair by the table, and tilted up the bottle of beer to see if by chance a drop remained. Then he spied a cupboard in the corner, and crossing the room he looked inside. And there, to his joyful amazement, he found five more. He greedily seized one, and turned back towards the table to get the glass. And the next moment the bottle fell from his nervous fingers on the carpet. For the door had opened again.

He stared at it, making hoarse little croaking noises in his throat. He was in such a position that he could not see into the passage. All he knew was that it was open wide enough to admit a human being, or whatever it was that was outside. And now it was opening wider still, and he cowered back with his arm over his eyes. In another second he felt he would yell: his reason would give. And then suddenly the tension snapped. He heard a voice speaking, and it was a woman's voice, though curiously deep and solemn.

"My poor man, do not be frightened. I am here to help you."

He lowered his arm: the door was now wide open. And framed in the entrance was a grey-haired woman dressed in black. She stood very still. Her features were dead white, her hands like those of a corpse. But for her eyes, that gleamed strangely from her mask-like face, she might have been a waxwork model.

The convict swallowed twice, and then he spoke.

"Gaw lumme, mum, you didn't 'alf give me a start opening that there door like that. The fust time was bad enough, but this time I thought as 'ow I was going to go barmy."

"The first time?" she said, still in the same deep voice. "This is the first time that I have been here tonight."

"Then 'oo was monkeying with that blinking door quarter of an hour ago?"

She came slowly into the room, and the convict backed away. There was something almost as terrifying about this woman as if she had actually been a ghost.

"Strange things happen in this house," she said. "It is not wise to ask too many questions."

"There was a norful row going on above 'ere a few minutes ago," he said nervously.

"So you heard them too, did you?" she answered gravely. "Every foggy night the curse must be fulfilled: such is the penalty that even in death they must carry out."

"Spooks!" he muttered. "Is that wot you mean?"

"Thirty years ago my son killed a man in the room above. He deserved to die if ever a man did, but they took my son, and they hanged him. Even, Morris, as they might have hanged you."

He took a step forward, snarling, only to stand abashed before those glowing eyes.

" 'Ow do you know my name is Morris?" he muttered sullenly.

"There are many things that I know," she said: "things that are whispered to me in the night by those who live around my bedside: those whom you could never see."

He shivered uncomfortably.

"But it was not they who told me about you," she went on. "This afternoon a warder came and warned me to be on my guard against you. I listened to what he had to say, and when he had gone I laughed. For I knew you would come, Morris: I willed you to come to me through the fog: it was for you I prepared the meal."

"Very nice of you, I'm sure, mum," he said, scratching his head in a bewildered way. "But I don't quite – "

"Listen," she interrupted imperiously. "I have told you that they hanged my son, and I have sworn to be revenged on them. Then perhaps the curse may be lifted."

He stared at her, and for the first time noticed that she was carrying a suit of clothes over her arm.

"And for that reason, Morris, I have brought you these."

She laid the clothes on a chair.

"I am going to help you to escape so that I can revenge myself on those who hanged my son. They are my son's clothes, which I have kept against such a day as this. When I leave you, you will put them on. In the pockets you will find money, and cigarettes. Leave your own clothes on the floor here: I will dispose of them tomorrow. Do not thank me." She held up her hand to stop him. "I do this not for you, but for my son: so that the curse may be lifted. One thing, and one thing only, do I say to you: as you value your life, and more than your life, do not go upstairs. For when the fog is on Dartmoor, there is death in this house."

The convict stared at her fearfully and the hair on the back of his scalp began to tingle and prick. Her eyes seemed to be glowing more than ever: her right arm was outstretched, with finger pointing directly at him. And even as he watched her she appeared to recede through the doorway: a moment later he was alone. The door was shut: the candle still flickered on the table, but of his mysterious visitor no trace remained save the clothes lying on the chair.

"Barmy," he muttered to himself. "Clean barmy. But, strewth, the old gal guessed right."

His nerves were still on edge, and the sound of his own voice comforted him.

"Suppose them ruddy clothes are real," he went on. "Not ghost clothes, are they, like everything else in this blinking spookery?"

He crossed to the chair and picked them up: no ghost about them. He ran his fingers eagerly through the pockets: notes, silver, cigarettes were all there.

"Lumme!" he chuckled, " 'ere's luck to the old geyser. May 'er curse be lifted. But if ever I sees 'er again, I'll ask 'er to wear glasses. Luva-duck, them eyes of 'ers were 'orrid."

He lit a cigarette, and blew out a cloud of smoke luxuriously. Then he poured out the beer, and bringing the other four bottles he ranged them on the table.

"If the meal was for me," he announced, "I'll show the old gal that I appreciates it."

He finished his cigarette, and then began to change his clothes. His convict rig he threw into the cupboard, and to his joyful amazement he found that the others fitted passably well. A little tight round the shoulders, and a little long in the legs, but not too bad, he considered, as he toasted his reflection in the mirror. The hat was a bit small, which was a pity, but by ripping out the lining he could just get it on.

Anyway, what was a hat? He had already counted the money – fifteen pounds odd: he would buy another at the first opportunity. And having by that time lowered the third bottle of beer, he decided that it was time he made some plans. Here he was with clothes and money, full of good food and good drink – in fact, in a position that would have seemed impossible half an hour ago – but he was not out of the wood by any manner of means yet. He poured out the fourth bottle, and began to think.

Presumably he could wait there till the morning if he wished to – the beer had produced a certain contempt for such trifles as spooks. And if he went now he would undoubtedly again lose his way in the fog. Of course daylight was dangerous: he knew that his description would have been circulated everywhere. But even if he went now, daylight would still come, and he would have the intense discomfort of wandering about in the fog all the night.

And then another idea struck him which was so wonderful that he promptly broached the fifth bottle. Why should he go at all – at any rate for days? If the old trout really wanted to lift the curse from her son, the best thing she could do would be to hide him until the hue and cry had blown over. Give him his half dozen, or dozen bottles of beer a day, and three or four good square meals, and he'd be perfectly happy. In fact, he'd do all he could to help the poor old thing with regard to her son.

A righteous glow was spreading over him: of course he'd help her. A shame, he reflected, that the old girl should be haunted like that every foggy night. Lucky thing he'd come here, instead of wandering about on the moor, where he might have fallen into a bog. Which brought a sudden idea to him of such stupendous magnificence that he bolted the last half of the fifth bottle and seized the sixth.

The bogs! Why in Heaven's name hadn't he thought of them before? The next morning he would give her his convict's cap, and tell her to take it to the nearest one. She could there place it on a tuft of grass at the edge where it was bound in time to be discovered. Everyone would immediately think that he had fallen in, and the search would be given up. Then in due course he would leave comfortably and go overseas: the old lady was sure to have a bit of savings put by. The least she could do if he was going to help her over this curse business was to pass them across. If she wouldn't – well, there were ways of making her. And at that stage of his reflections anyone looking at his face would have realised the truth of the warder's remarks that afternoon about his character. The features bloated with the unaccustomed beer, the great red scar on his cheek standing out the more vividly for it, the small vicious eyes, the heavy jowl – all combined to show the murderer through instinct. And between him and the murderer through sudden passion a gulf is fixed which is immeasurable...

He finished his glass, and lit a final cigarette. Having decided on his plans for the future, a desire for sleep was beginning to make itself felt. And after a while his head began to nod, and he was on the verge of falling right off, when a bell began to ring in the passage outside. The sound brought him scrambling to his feet. His head was feeling fuddled and muzzy, and for a while he stood staring stupidly in front of him. Who on earth could be ringing that infernal bell? Was it someone in the house, or was it someone outside at the front door? Again it pealed, and he began to curse foully under his breath. Could it be that the warders had got on to him?

In a panic of fear he blew out the candle and stood listening intently. Would the old woman answer the door? If she did, the swine might insist on searching the house, and they would be bound to find him. And then as the seconds went by and the ring was not repeated, he began to breathe freely again. There was no sound in the hall, and he knew that if the warders had come in they would not trouble to walk quietly. So she hadn't answered the bell, and with luck they would go away, believing the house to be empty.

But what if they broke in – the same as he had done? The thought set him trembling again: surely luck couldn't be so cruel just after he'd thought out this wonderful scheme. Warders wouldn't dare to break into a house: it was against the law. A minute passed: two – still no sound. And he was on the point of sitting down again when he saw a thing that turned him cold with fright. A light had shone for a moment under the door.

He strained his ears, though all he could hear was the heavy thumping of his own heart. And then above it came the sound of muffled voices just outside the room. He backed away into the corner farthest from the door, and crouched there. There were men outside in the passage. Who were they, and how many?

Suddenly the door opened, and a voice came out of the darkness.

"Look out, chaps. The place reeks of cigarette smoke, and a candle has just been blown out. Stand away from me: I'll switch on the torch."

Came a little click, and the beam travelled round the room till it picked up the snarling figure in the corner: then it checked.

"Hullo! Hullo!" came a quiet voice. "What have we here?"

Slowly Morris straightened up, his great fists clenched by his sides. He could see nothing behind the torch, but he could hear. And by the voice he knew that this was no warder, but a blasted toff. Trouble was there was more than one, but – Gawd! he'd learn 'em.

"Light that candle, will you, Peter?" went on the voice, and someone stepped into the circle of light. He was a youngish man, and he didn't look too big. And as he took a box of matches out of his pocket, with a grunt of rage the convict sprang at him.

What happened then was not quite clear to him. It seemed that the torch wavered for a moment, and then a thing like a battering-ram hit him on the point of the jaw. He had a fleeting recollection of being hurled backwards: he felt his head strike the wall: and then for a space he slumbered.

When he came to himself again, he lay still for a moment or two trying to collect his thoughts. The candle had been relit, and he saw that there were three men in the room. They were standing by the table regarding him dispassionately, and he particularly noticed that one of them was quite the largest individual he had ever seen. And it was this one who spoke.

"Don't do that again, Morris: next time I shall really hit you."

The convict scrambled sullenly to his feet.

" 'Oo the 'ell are you calling Morris?"

He knew he was caught, but there was no harm in trying the bluff.

"You," said the large man quietly. "I had an accurate description of your face given me by one of your kind warders this afternoon. And I must admit I had not quite anticipated finding you here. But if you will smoke cigarettes in an empty house, you must expect to be discovered. However, the point that now arises is what the devil to do with you. You seem to have done yourself pretty well, judging by the table: and, not to mince words, you're an infernal nuisance. What do you say, Ted?"

"Well, old boy," said the third individual, "I don't know. If there's a 'phone here we ought to ring up the prison, I suppose."

"But that means sitting and mounting guard on the damn fellow," remarked the big man peevishly.

A ray of hope dawned in the convict's mind.

"Give us a chance, guv'nor," he cried, coming into the centre of the room. "Give us a chance. If they cops me, I won't never give yer away. I swears it. But yer don't know wot it's like up in that blarsted place. Give us… Gaw lumme, guv'nor, wot are yer looking at me like that for?"

He cowered back, staring at the big man, whose face had suddenly changed from being almost good-natured, to an expression that the convict couldn't understand.

"Where did you get those clothes from, Morris?" he said in a terrible voice.

"Strewth, guv'nor," he stammered. "I… I…"

"Where did you get them from, damn you? Answer me."

"The old woman – she give 'em to me, sir. Belonged to 'er son, wot was 'anged."

"You're lying, you scum. If you don't tell me the truth, I'll smash your face in."

"I swear to Gawd, guv'nor, I'm telling yer the truth," he said earnestly.

"What's the great idea, Hugh?" said the man called Peter.

"That suit is the one young Marton was wearing this afternoon. As soon as he came nearer the light I recognised it at once. Now listen to me." He took a step forward, and stood towering over the convict. "Those clothes belong to a young man whom I was talking to this afternoon. Where is he, and what have you done to him?"

"I ain't seen no young man, sir," answered the convict quietly. "They was given to me by the old woman in the 'ouse 'ere, and she told me they belonged to 'er son 'oo murdered a man in the room above thirty years ago."

He looked upwards and pointed, and the next instant every drop of colour had left his face.

" 'Oly 'Eaven, look at that!" he screamed. "It's the mark of wot 'e did, and I ain't noticed it before."

A circular crimson patch stained the white ceiling, and for a space they all stared at it – stared at it until, with a yell of terror, the convict made a dart for the door. For the patch was growing bigger.

The three men hurled themselves on him, and he struggled like a maniac till another blow from Drummond's fist knocked him half silly.

"Lemme go," he whimpered. "I can't abear it. I'd sooner be copped, strite I would. It weren't there when I came: I swear it weren't. And I 'eard 'em, guv'nor: I 'eard the ghosts a-murdering one another. And now there's ghost blood too. It ain't real: Gawd! it cawn't be real. It just comes every foggy night, like wot the old woman said, and then goes away again. Let's get out of the 'ouse, guv'nor: it's 'orrible."

The man was almost mad with fear, and Drummond watched him curiously. Then once again he looked at the ceiling. The patch had grown enormously, and now a dark central nucleus was visible, in which great drops formed sluggishly and fell to the floor.

"Come here, Morris," he said quietly. "Put out your hand: hold it there."

He seized the convict's arm, and forced it into the line of falling drops.

"Is that ghost blood?" he demanded.

Like a crazy thing Morris stared at the palm of his hand: then at the three men.

"I don't understand," he muttered helplessly. "This 'ere is real blood."

"It is," said Drummond even more quietly. "Real blood. And now we're all going upstairs, Morris, to see where that real blood is coming from."

But that was too much for the convict. He flung himself on his knees, and literally gibbered in his terror.

"Not me, guv'nor: for pity's sake, not me! I dursn't do it – not if you was to let me off the rest of me sentence. There's death in the 'ouse on foggy nights: the old woman said so. As you values yer life, she says to me, don't go up them stairs. I cawn't understand about this 'ere blood, but it's ghosts, don't yer see? – ghosts wot are upstairs. I 'eard 'em."

"And now you're going to see them, Morris," answered Drummond. "There's no good protesting, my man: you're coming upstairs with us. Get his arms, you two fellows, and bring him along. I've got a pretty shrewd notion what we are going to find. I'll go first with the torch."

He led the way to the stairs, while Darrell and Jerningham forced the struggling convict to follow. Once or twice he almost threw them off in his frenzied endeavours to escape, but between them they half pushed, half carried him up the stairs.

"Stop that damned noise," snapped Drummond, when they reached the top, "or I'll lay you out. I want to listen."

But no sound broke the silence, and save for his torch there was not a glimmer of light anywhere. And after a while he led the way along a passage, the end of which was barred by a green baize door.

"Through here," he said, "and it should be the first room on the left, if my bearings are correct. Ah!" He drew in his breath sharply. "It's what I expected. Bring that man in here."

He had flung open the door of the room, and the others followed with the convict between them.

"Stay there, Peter, till I see if this gas will light. And mind where you put your feet."

He had turned his torch on the gas bracket, so that the floor was in darkness. But a moment later the light flared up, and Darrell and Jerningham gave a simultaneous gasp. Sprawling on the boards was the body of a man, clad only in a shirt and underclothes. It was obvious at a glance that he was dead; his head had been battered in with inconceivable ferocity. But his face was just recognisable: the dead man was young Marton.

"Now, Morris," said Drummond quietly, "is that a ghost?"

The convict was staring foolishly at the body: his mouth kept opening and shutting, though no sound came from it.

"I don't understand, guv'nor," he said hoarsely after a while. "The old woman said as 'ow it was a ghost."

"Where is the old woman?" demanded Drummond.

"I dunno, guv'nor. I ain't see'd 'er since she give me these clothes."

"You realise, don't you, Morris, that those clothes you are wearing belong to that man who has been murdered?"

"Well, I didn't know it, guv'nor: 'ow could I? She said as 'ow they were 'er son's."

"Was there ever any old woman, Morris?" cried Drummond sternly.

"In course there were, guv'nor: ain't I been telling yer? It was she wot told me abaht the ghost."

And then suddenly the real significance of his position penetrated his slow brain.

"Gawd! guv'nor," he screamed, "yer don't think I did it, do yer? Yer don't think I croaked the young gent? I ain't never seen 'im in my life: I swears it on me mother's grave."

"How long have you been in this house?" demanded Drummond.

"It struck eight, guv'nor, as I was standing in the 'all."

Drummond looked at his watch.

"So you've been here two hours," he remarked. "Did anyone see or hear you come in?"

"I suppose the old woman must 'ave, sir. And then the door opened once in the room dahn below: opened and shut, it did. She said as 'ow queer things took place in this 'ere 'ouse."

"Was that before she gave you those clothes?"

"Yus, guv'nor – afore that."

"And before you heard the ghosts fighting up here?"

"That's right, sir," said the convict eagerly. "Yer do believe me, sir: yer don't think as 'ow I done that bloke in?"

"It doesn't much matter what I think, Morris," said Drummond gravely, "but you're in a devilish serious position, and there's no good pretending you're not. We find you in this house alone with a murdered man, and wearing his clothes. And all you can say about it is that some old woman who can't be found spun you a yarn about ghosts. It's pretty thin, my lad, and you may find the police a little difficult to convince."

The convict was looking round him like a trapped animal. Why this thing had been done to him he didn't know, but all too clearly did he realise the truth of this big man's words. The whole affair had been a frame-up from beginning to end: what he had thought were ghosts had been nothing of the sort. The noise he had heard had been the actual murder of the man who lay on the floor with his head battered in.

And suddenly his nerve broke completely. For the moment his three captors were not looking at him, and with a cry of terror he sprang through the door and banged it behind him. Then he rushed blindly along the passage to the top of the stairs. To get away from that dead man whose clothes he wore was the only thought in his brain as he blundered through the hall. And a moment later he had flung open a window and the fog had swallowed him up.

"Excellent," said Drummond thoughtfully. "Thank Heavens he decided to make a bolt for it! I was wondering what we were going to do with him. Hullo!" He paused, listening intently. "Some more people playing. This house is getting quite popular."

He opened the door, and the sound of angry voices came up from below. And then, followed by the other two, he strolled to the top of the stairs. A light had been lit in the hall, and two men were standing there who fell silent as soon as they saw them.

"Say," shouted one of them after a while, "are you the damned ginks who have eaten our supper?"

"Perish the thought, laddies," remarked Drummond affably. "We dined on caviare and white wine before coming to call."

"Well, who is the guy who rushed through the hall and jumped out of a window a few moments ago just as we were coming in?"

"He also came to call, but he didn't seem to like the house. He got the willies about it and decided to leave."

"Look here," said the other savagely, beginning to mount the stairs, "is this whole outfit bug house? What under the sun are you doing up there anyway?"

He paused in front of Drummond, a great, powerful, raking man with a nasty look in his eyes.

"We've been ghost-hunting, Percy," said Drummond genially. "Very naughty of us, but we thought the house was empty. And instead of that we find a delightful escaped convict replete with your supper, and other things too numerous to mention."

"If you call me Percy again," snarled the other, "you won't speak for a few days."

"Is that so, Percy darling?" said Drummond lazily. "I always thought it was such a nice name."

The veins stood out on the other's forehead, and he took a step forward with his fists clenched. And then the look in Drummond's eyes made him pause, while his companion whispered something in his ear.

"Well, the house isn't empty," he remarked sullenly. "So you can damned well clear out before I send for the police."

"But how inhospitable of you," said Drummond mildly. "However, I fear that anyway you will have to communicate with that excellent body of men. You must do something about the dead man, mustn't you?"

The other stared at him.

"The dead man," he said at length. "What in fortune are you talking about?"

"I told you we'd found a lot of other things," remarked Drummond. "Come along, and you shall see for yourself."

They walked along the passage to the room where the body lay.

"Holy Smoke!" cried the big man, pausing by the door. "Who's done that?"

"Who indeed," murmured Drummond thoughtfully.

"Where are his clothes?" asked the other.

"Adorning Mr Morris, the escaped convict," said Drummond: "the gentleman who left the house so rapidly."

For a while the other looked at him in a puzzled way.

"This seems to me to be a mighty rum affair," he remarked at length.

"Mighty rum," agreed Drummond.

"Since you say the convict was wearing his clothes, it looks as if he had done it."

"It certainly does," Drummond again agreed.

"What a damnable crime! Jake! if we hadn't gone out for a breather this would never have happened. I guess I'll never forgive myself."

"It sure is tough on the poor young chap," said his companion.

"A young friend of ours, Mr... Mr...?"

"Drummond is my name. Captain Drummond."

"Hardcastle is mine. And my pal is Jake Slingsby. To think that this poor young fellow should be murdered like that: I guess I can't get over it."

"The strange thing is that he should have had a premonition of danger," remarked Drummond. "I saw him this afternoon when he lost his way in the fog."

"He told us he had called in at the wrong house," said Hardcastle.

"A call is one way of describing his visit," murmured Drummond. "I gathered his name was Marton."

"That's so. Down on business about the house. Well, well! This is terrible: I don't know how I shall break the news to his father."

"Nor do I," said Drummond. "For, unless I am greatly mistaken, his father was killed last night through a gun accident."

"What's that you say?" shouted Hardcastle, and his companion seemed equally perturbed. "Old Marton dead?"

"According to the papers he is," answered Drummond. "It must be a great shock to you, Mr Hardcastle, to have a firm with whom you are doing business dying off so rapidly."

The other looked at him suspiciously, but Drummond's face was expressionless.

"Well, I suppose we ought to ring up the police," he went on after a pause.

"That would seem to be the thing to do," remarked Drummond. "And since they will probably take some time coming on a night like this, I think we might wait for them elsewhere, don't you? You must be very fond of fresh air, Mr Hardcastle," he continued as they left the room.

"How do you make that out?" demanded the other.

"To go for a stroll on a night like this," said Drummond. "I should have thought that a book and a whisky and soda would have been preferable."

"Then why don't you follow your own advice?"

"Ah! it was different in our case. You see, it is only on foggy nights that the ghost is supposed to walk."

"What is all this rot about a ghost?" said Hardcastle contemptuously. "I reckon the ghost isn't made yet that I shall ever see."

"Do not scoff, Mr Hardcastle, at things beyond your ken," said Drummond reprovingly. "What would your housekeeper say if she heard you?"

The other paused and stared at him.

"Housekeeper!" he cried. "What fly has stung you this time? If there's a housekeeper here it's the first I've heard of it."

"Really: you surprise me."

Drummond stopped suddenly and began to sniff the air.

"By the way, Ted," he remarked, "which was the room you told me was haunted? The second from the top of the stairs, wasn't it?"

And before anyone realised what he was going to do, he flung the door open.

"Most extraordinary," he said blandly. "Do you use scent, Mr Hardcastle? Or is it Mr Slingsby? But I don't see any ghost, Ted."

He let the light of his torch travel round the room, until it finally rested on the bed.

"Oh!" he cried, covering his eyes with his hand, "is that your nightie, Mr Hardcastle? Or yours, Mr Slingsby? It makes me go all over goosey."

But by this time Hardcastle had recovered from his surprise, and there was murder in his eyes.

"How dare you go butting into a lady's bedroom," he shouted furiously. "Get out of it, you damned meddling young swine."

He seized Drummond by the arms, and then for half a minute there ensued a struggle the more intense because neither man moved.

It was just a trial of strength, and the others watched it breathlessly. For to all of them it seemed that far more depended on the result than what happened at the moment. It was the first clash between the two men: the outcome would be an omen for the future.

Their breathing came faster: the sweat stood out on both their foreheads. And then, after what seemed an eternity, Drummond began to smile, and the other to curse. Slowly and inexorably

Hardcastle was forced back, and then Drummond relaxed his hold.

"Not this time, Percy," he remarked quietly. "And I must really apologise for entering the lady's bedroom. It's this confounded ghost business that is responsible for it. By the way, where is she? Did you carelessly lose her in the fog?"

"What the hell is that to do with you?" snarled Hardcastle.

"My dear fellow!" Drummond lifted his hands in horror. "As the president of several watch committees, to say nothing of societies for moral uplift, the thought of the owner of that delicious garment wandering forlornly over Dartmoor distresses me beyond words!"

The other looked at him sullenly: the type was a new one to him. Accustomed all his life to being top dog, either by physical strength or through sheer force of will, he found himself confronted by a man who was his match in both.

"You needn't worry yourself," he muttered. "My daughter is in Plymouth."

"And a charming spot it is, too," boomed Drummond genially. "I must give you the address of the Girls' Home from Home there: or is it the Decayed Gentlewoman's Aid Post? Well, well – to think of that now. The jolly old daughter in Plymouth of all places! Happy days we used to have there, didn't we, Peter, prancing along the Hoe?"

His torch, in apparently a haphazard way, was flashing about the room as he rambled on, and suddenly it picked up a box of cigarettes lying open on the dressing-table.

"But how careless of her, Mr Hardcastle! he cried. "They will all get stale. I must really close it up."

He crossed the room and shut the box: then he calmly returned and strolled towards the top of the stairs.

"Daughter or no daughter, duty calls us, Mr Hardcastle. We must ring up that fine body of men, the Devon constabulary."

"A thing that ought to have been done ten minutes ago, but for your infernal impertinence," said the other furiously.

He crossed the hall to the telephone, and rang up the exchange. He did it again: then a third time, and gradually a smile spread over Drummond's face.

"Most extraordinary!" he murmured. "I expect the telephone girl is in Plymouth too. Or can it be that you aren't connected up, Mr Hardcastle?"

"The damned line must be out of order," grunted the other.

And Drummond began to shake with laughter.

"You sure are out of luck tonight, aren't you?" he remarked. "A dead man in the house: a daughter painting Plymouth red: a telephone that doesn't function: and last but not least, three interfering ghost-hunters. However, don't be despondent: the darkest hour is always just before the dawn."

He paused for the fraction of a second, and only Darrell saw the look that flashed momentarily into his eyes. He had noticed something, but his voice as he went on was unchanged.

"We'll do the ringing up for you, Mr Hardcastle, from Merridale Hall, and tell the police all your maidenly secrets. And as your next-door neighbours, welcome to our smiling countryside. Which concludes the national programme for this evening: a depression over Iceland is shortly approaching us: good night. Good night."

CHAPTER 3

The fog had lifted a little as they left the house, though it was still sufficiently thick to make progress slow. And they had only gone some thirty or forty yards down the drive when a cry came echoing faintly over the moor. They stopped abruptly: it was repeated again and again. It sounded as if someone was calling for help, and then as suddenly as the shouts had started they ceased.

"That's the direction of Grimstone Mire," said Jerningham gravely. "Surely no one could be such a damned fool as to go near it on a night like this."

"Dangerous, is it?" said Drummond.

"Dangerous, old boy! Why, it's a death trap even by day. And in the dark, and foggy at that, it would be simply suicide. No one who lives round here would go within half a mile of the place."

"No good going to have a look, I suppose?"

"Not the slightest, Hugh. Whoever it is has either scrambled out by now, or it's all over, with the odds on the latter."

"Then let's get back," said Drummond. "We've got to put on our considering caps, you fellows, but it darned well can't be done till I've lowered some ale. For unless I'm much mistaken we've stepped right into one of the biggest things we've ever handled. And the first thing to be considered is what we're going to do about Mr Morris."

"You think he did in Marton?" said Darrell.

"I'm damned certain he didn't," answered Drummond shortly. "But they'll hang him all the same. It's one of the most diabolically clever bits of work we've ever butted into, comparing quite creditably with the deeds of our late lamented Carl. Thank the Lord! here's the house. Ale, Ted, in buckets. Then you, as the resident, get on to the police. Tell 'em a man has been murdered at Glensham House, and say that we shall be here to give 'em all the information we can. And one other thing, old lad. Ask the exchange if Glensham House is disconnected or not."

"What was the sudden brainstorm in the hall, Hugh, just before we left?" said Darrell curiously.

Jerningham was telephoning, and Drummond's face was buried in a tankard, which he drained before answering.

"A little matter of dust," he remarked. "But all in good time, Peter: we've got to get down to this pretty carefully."

"The house hasn't been connected up for two years," said Jerningham, coming back into the room, and Drummond nodded thoughtfully. "I've told the police, who darned near fused the wire in their excitement. They'll be round as soon as they can."

"And before they come we've got to decide exactly what we are going to say," remarked Drummond, lighting a cigarette. "I'll take the chair for the moment: you stop me the instant you disagree with anything. Point one: was the story told us by Morris true? I unhesitatingly maintain that it was, for one very good reason. That man at the best of times hasn't got the brains to *invent* such a wildly fantastic yarn and stick to it. And half screwed as he was when we found him, the thing is an utter impossibility. No – he was speaking the truth the whole way through; I watched him closely."

"I agree," said Jerningham. "Or else he is the most consummate actor."

Drummond shook his head.

"He wasn't acting, Ted. What do you say, Peter?"

"I agree with you, old boy. Which brings us to point two: if Morris didn't murder Marton, who did?"

"Exactly. But let's go back a bit farther, and see what we can build up on the assumption that Morris' story is true. Clearly there were people in the house when Morris broke in. There was a woman, young Marton, and another man or men. Right! They hear him come in, or someone – they don't know who. The woman comes down, sees the glint of the candle and opens the door just enough to see who the visitor is. A convict: must be Morris. And it's at this point, you fellows, that I maintain we get a line on to what we are up against which gives one pretty furiously to think. Because without the smallest hesitation they seized on a thing that had happened by the merest fluke, and had turned it to advantage with a brutality that is damned near unprecedented. Common or garden murder we know, but they don't stick at butchery. I'm not often serious, as you know, but, 'pon my soul, this show is a bit over the odds. For some reason we haven't got, they wanted young Marton out of the way: behold the unsuspecting scapegoat all ready to hand. Morris can be hanged for what they've done. But in order to make it doubly sure, they asked themselves the safest way of killing Marton. A revolver? Out of the question: Morris wouldn't have one. A knife means fingerprints on the shaft, which Morris could prove were not his. And so these beauties, remembering that in the Sydenham case he was reputed to have bashed his victim's head about, and acting on the well-known truth that a murderer rarely changes his methods, went and did likewise. They deliberately killed young Marton by battering his head in."

"Sounds OK so far, Hugh," said Jerningham.

"Hold hard, old boy, for a minute: we've got to go a bit farther. Down comes this woman with Marton's clothes and pitches Morris a yarn which was exactly the kind to impress and frighten an ignorant man. Ghost and foggy night: just the stuff to scare the fellow stiff. And then she disappears, intending in all probability to come back later and get his convict's uniform, so that there shall be no chance of his not putting on Marton's clothes. And from that moment Morris would have been a doomed man. Supposing we hadn't heard his yarn under the circumstances we did, should we have believed it? No: and that is the only point where their plan miscarried. No one was ever intended to hear it under such circumstances. It rang true tonight; it wouldn't have rung true two or three days from now, when Morris was found wandering about. He would not have had a dog's chance. The woman would either have disappeared, or she would have denied his story *in toto*. And then, unfortunately for them, we came barging in, which necessitated a considerable change in their plans. For my own belief is that if we had not arrived, they would merely have left, with the absolute certainty that it was only a question of time before Morris was caught. Our arrival altered matters, and completely forced their hands, so that we were treated to the theatrical performance we've just had. They knew we should have to ring up the police, and the instant the police arrived they were in the soup. What were they doing while this wretched boy's head was being bashed in by Morris? It can't have been a silent proceeding: why didn't they hear it? They could only pretend they were out of the house, and if they were going to do that, the sooner they took the bull by the horns the better."

"You think they were in the house the whole time?" said Darrell.

"My dear old Peter, who goes for a walk on a night like this for fun? Of course they were, though there is no denying that that swine Hardcastle's acting was damned good. Probably to the police they will say they were walking back from Yelverton, which sounds feasible, because the police won't be able to get beyond the point that Morris is the murderer."

"You think those two did it?" said Jerningham.

Drummond shrugged his shoulders.

"There, old boy, we're getting into the region of guesswork. From what I saw of Hardcastle I should think he's quite capable of anything. But it was either them or pals of theirs."

"And what about the housekeeper?" said Darrell.

"Housekeeper, my aunt, Peter! Who ever heard of a housekeeper with a nightdress like that? Who ever heard of a housekeeper who smoked expensive cigarettes with purple-tipped mouthpieces? It's just possible that the woman who fooled Morris was really Hardcastle's daughter made up for the part, but there was never any housekeeper."

"And where was she all the time?"

"In the hall, just as we were going, I happened to look at the floor close by the wall. It was very dusty, and I saw the marks of a woman's footsteps going up to a big piece of panelling. There were none coming away from it."

"There undoubtedly are secret passages in the house," said Jerningham thoughtfully. "So you think the fairy was there, and not in Plymouth?"

"Do we or do we not accept Morris' story? That's the answer, Ted. If we do, she was there."

"In which case she is there now. Are we to tell the police?"

Drummond refilled his tankard thoughtfully.

"I think we must tell the police the entire story that Morris told us. I don't think any good will be done by putting in any comment on it: we must leave them to form their own conclusions. You see, a mere statement on our part that we believe the yarn cuts no ice anyway. At the same time, I think it's going to be a little awkward for them. There are a whole lot of points they will have to explain away which would never have cropped up but for our arrival on the scene. Jove! they must have been as wild as civet cats when we appeared."

He rubbed his hands together and began to grin.

"Boys, we're going to have some fun. What is that galaxy doing there at all? Why do they know so little about it that they don't even realise the telephone is not connected up? Why do they want to murder young Marton? Why does the old man have a gun accident? And I'm just wondering how much will come out when Morris is caught. Nothing – if we hadn't come into it. But we have, and we're damned well not going out."

He paused as a ring came at the front door bell.

"Is that the police already? They've been pretty quick. Now don't forget, you fellows, we were ghost-hunting, believing the house to be empty. And, for the rest, we give Morris' story without expressing any opinion."

"It's not the police," said Jerningham, who had gone to the door. "It's a woman's voice."

A moment or two later Jennings entered the room.

"A lady, sir, has lost her way. She is looking for Glensham House."

"Have you directed her?" asked his master, glancing at Drummond.

The butler hesitated.

"She seems very tired, sir. I was wondering if I should offer her a glass of wine. She is, if I may say so," he continued confidentially, "distinctly – er – worthwhile."

"Bring her in, Ted," said Drummond. "Tell Jennings to bring some champagne and sandwiches. Peter," he went on, as they left the room, "the rush on Glensham House is making me giddy."

"But it is too kind of you," came a woman's voice from the hall. "I really am quite exhausted. If I could rest a little before continuing it would make all the difference."

She entered the room, and paused in momentary embarrassment on seeing the other two.

"Of course," cried Jerningham. "I have ordered some sandwiches for you. May I introduce Captain Drummond and Mr Darrell? My own name is Jerningham."

He pulled up a chair, and she sat down with a charming smile that embraced all three. And, as Jennings had remarked, she was distinctly worthwhile. Dark and of medium height, she had a complexion that was simply flawless. Her eyes, of which she knew how to make full use, were a deep blue: in fact, the only thing that struck an incongruous note was her frock, which was more suitable for Ascot than Dartmoor.

"I have been over in Plymouth," she explained, "and had intended to spend the night there. And then I suddenly decided to return. If only I had realised what a fog on Dartmoor was like, nothing would have induced me to. No taxi at the station: not even a cab. So I started to walk, and when I got to your gates I thought it was Glensham House. Luckily my father thinks I'm still in Plymouth, so he won't be worried."

"Have we the pleasure of meeting Miss Hardcastle?" asked Drummond.

She laughed merrily.

"It is some time since I was called that," she said. "I am Comtessa Bartelozzi." And then she gave a puzzled little frown. "But how did you know my father's name?"

"Your father and we have been having a lot of fun and excitement this evening," explained Drummond genially. "I feel we're quite old friends."

"But I didn't know that he had met anyone round here," she said. "You see, we're only newcomers. My father has rented Glensham House, and we just came down for a night or two to see what furniture was wanted."

"Well, I'm afraid your preliminary reconnaissance has not been devoid of incident, Comtessa," he remarked. "It's a merciful thing for you that you were in Plymouth; otherwise I fear the shock would have been considerable. A young man has had his head battered in at Glensham House."

She stared at him in speechless amazement.

"Head battered in! A young man! But who?"

"I gathered his name was Marton," answered Drummond. "Ah! here is the champagne."

"Marton! But he's our solicitor. Captain Drummond – please explain."

With a completely expressionless face, he told her the story, which she listened to with ever-increasing horror.

"But how dreadful!" she cried as he finished. "Poor, poor boy! What a brute that convict must be!"

"It certainly is one of the most brutal murders I have ever come across," he agreed. "And we are expecting the police at any moment to hear what we have to tell them about it."

"Oh! I hope they catch the brute," she cried passionately. "What a pity you ever let him escape! I can't understand how you could have been taken in for a moment by such a story."

"You mean with regard to the housekeeper?"

"Of course. There's no such person in the house. Why, if there had been you would have seen her."

"That is true, Comtessa: perhaps we were credulous. Anyway, Morris is bound to be caught very shortly, and the whole thing will have to be thrashed out in court. Are you proposing to stay long at Glensham House?"

He poured her out another glass of champagne.

"It all depends on my father," she answered. "Mr Hardcastle is very interested in cinema work, and he wants a place where he can work undisturbed at a new invention of his which he thinks is going to revolutionise the whole business."

"Indeed," murmured Drummond. "Then we can only hope there are no more diversions of the sort that occurred tonight. It will have a most upsetting effect on his studies. By the way, you know it is your room, don't you, that is reputed to be haunted?"

"What: my bedroom!" she cried. "Is that really so?"

"My host, Mr Jerningham, is quite positive about it," he answered. "We didn't see anything, I must admit, but perhaps your father and Mr Slingsby have an antagonistic aura for ghosts.

Fortunately we did one good deed in shutting up a box of your cigarettes, which would otherwise have got dreadfully stale."

She stared at him thoughtfully.

"Do you think it's possible," she remarked at length, "that the woman this man Morris said he saw was a spirit?"

"My dear Comtessa," said Drummond gravely, "I have reached the age when I never think anything is impossible. And there is no doubt that the amount of beer he had consumed might have rendered him prone to see things. However, those surely are the fairy footsteps of the police I hear on the drive. After we have talked to them, you must allow us to see you home."

It turned out to be a sergeant, who stood in the door with his helmet under his arm.

"Mr Jerningham?" He looked round the group, and Jerningham nodded.

"That's me," he said.

"It was you that telephoned, sir, wasn't it, about this murder at Glensham House? Well, sir, the Inspector has gone straight there, and he gave me orders to ask you to go round there at once and the other gentlemen that were with you."

"Of course," cried Drummond. "We'll all go. And you too, Comtessa."

"He didn't say nothing about any lady, sir," said the sergeant dubiously.

"The Comtessa is living at Glensham House," said Drummond. "Fortunately for her, she has been in Plymouth today, and lost her way in the fog coming back."

"Then that's a different matter, sir," answered the sergeant. "It's much clearer now: we shan't have any difficulty in getting there."

"Good," said Drummond. "Let's start."

The sergeant proved right: a few isolated stars were showing as they left the house. Pockets of mist still hung about the road, but they grew thinner and thinner each moment. And in a few minutes they could see the outline of Glensham House in front of them. There were lights showing in several of the downstair rooms, and finding the front door open, they walked straight in.

An inspector, with a constable beside him, was seated at the table: opposite him were Hardcastle and Slingsby and a third man who was smoking a cigar.

"Gee, honey," cried Hardcastle, springing to his feet, "what under the sun are you doing here? I thought you were in Plymouth."

"I suddenly decided to come back, Dad," she said, "and in the fog I went to this gentleman's house by mistake. What is this awful thing I hear?"

He patted her on the arm.

"There, there," he cried soothingly. "It's just one of the most terrible things that's ever happened. An escaped convict has murdered poor young Bob Marton."

"Are you the gentleman who telephoned?" asked the Inspector, rapping on the table for silence.

"I telephoned from Merridale Hall," said Jerningham.

"I've explained that our instrument was disconnected," said Hardcastle.

"Please allow me, sir, to do the talking," said the Inspector firmly. "Now, sir, would you be good enough to tell me exactly what happened? But before you begin, would you, sir" – he swung round in his chair and addressed Drummond – "be good enough to stop walking about?"

"Sorry, old lad," boomed Drummond, coming back into the centre of the room. "Carry on, Ted."

"One moment," interrupted Hardcastle. "I'm sure you don't want to ask my daughter anything, Inspector, and she must be tired. Go to bed, honey: go to bed."

"Well, if the Inspector will allow me, I think I will," she said.

"Certainly, miss," he said. " If I do want to ask you anything I will do so tomorrow. Now, sir" – he turned to Jerningham as Hardcastle led the Comtessa upstairs – "will you fire ahead?"

He listened to the story, taking copious notes, whilst Drummond studied the third man covertly.

"By Gad! Peter," he whispered after a while. "Number Three looks, if possible, a bigger tough than the other two. What's that you say, Inspector?"

"This gentleman says that it was you who identified the man as Morris. How did you know him?"

"By the red scar on his face," said Drummond. "Two warders this afternoon described him to me. And afterwards he admitted it."

"And you knew the clothes were the clothes of the murdered man. How?"

"Because I saw them on Marton this afternoon, when he lost his way in the fog and came to Merridale Hall instead of here," answered Drummond. "They were so obviously London clothes that I noticed them particularly. When you catch him you'll see what I mean."

"I guess the Inspector will have to take it on trust," said the newcomer shortly. "That was the guy right enough: the scar proves it. Say, mister" – he turned to Drummond – "when he bolted was he wearing a hat?"

"He was not," remarked Drummond.

"Then that settles it. He's cheated the hangman all right. He went bathing in Grimstone Mire."

"What's that?" said Drummond slowly. "You say he fell into Grimstone Mire?"

"Yep," answered the other. "There can't be two birds like him loose. I was in the garage tinkering with the car when I heard someone crashing about in the bushes near by. So I went out and flashed a torch around. Suddenly I saw him: a wild-looking fellow without a hat and a great red scar on his face. He bolted like a hare towards the Mire, and I went after him to try to stop him, but I couldn't do anything in the fog. And in he went – splosh. Let out one yell, and then it was all over."

"An amazing development, isn't it, Captain Drummond?" said Hardcastle, who had rejoined them.

"Most amazing," agreed Drummond. "However, as you say, it saves the hangman a job."

And at that moment the constable let out a yell.

"Look at the top of the stairs, sir!"

They all swung round and stared upwards. Standing motionless in the dim light was a woman dressed in black. Her hair was grey; one arm was outstretched, pointing towards them. And the only thing that seemed alive in her were her two eyes that gleamed from her dead-white face.

For a few seconds they all stood rooted to the ground; then very slowly, almost as if she was floating on air, the woman receded, and disappeared from sight.

"What the devil?" cried Hardcastle, and the next instant he dashed up the stairs, followed by the others. For a scream of terror had come from the Comtessa's room.

It was Hardcastle who reached it first, to find that the door was locked.

"Honey," he shouted. "Honey: open the door. Are you all right?"

There was no reply, and in a frenzy he beat on the door with his fists. But the wood was stout, and it was not until they had all charged it several times with their shoulders that it began to show signs of giving. At last the bolt tore away from its fastening and in a body they surged into the room.

The Comtessa was lying on the bed clad in pyjamas. She was motionless, and Hardcastle rushed to her and picked her up.

"It's only a faint, boys," he cried. "Get some brandy."

But even as he spoke, with a shuddering sigh the Comtessa opened her eyes. For a moment she stared in bewilderment at the group of men; then suddenly they dilated with terror.

"Where is she?" she screamed. "What is she?"

"There, there, honey," said Hardcastle, "it's quite all right now. Tell your old Dad what frightened you."

"Oh! it was horrible," she moaned. "I was just getting into bed when a hand touched me on the shoulder. A woman was standing there – a woman in black with grey hair. Her arm was stretched out pointing at me – and her eyes – "

She began to shudder violently.

"They seemed to shine like balls of fire. And then, while I was looking at her in amazement, she just vanished. She was standing just where you are, Captain Drummond, and she disappeared."

Hardcastle looked significantly at the other men; then he turned soothingly to his daughter.

"Perhaps you imagined it, honey: maybe it was a trick of the light."

"But it wasn't," she cried wildly. "And Mr Jerningham said this room was haunted, didn't you?"

She appealed to him, and he nodded.

"That's right, Comtessa," he agreed.

"It was a ghost," she went on. "It must have been a ghost. It must have been her the convict saw. Oh, let me get out of this room! I can't stop here another moment. And never again after tomorrow will I set foot inside this house."

"Honey, don't take on so," implored her father. "Even if it was a ghost, the poor thing didn't do you any harm. Come into your Dad's room, and he'll stop with you till you're all right again."

He put his arm round her waist, and led her gently out, whilst the others, after a brief pause, trooped down into the hall again.

Well, if that don't beat cock-fighting, gentlemen," said the Inspector, scratching his head. "I take it we all saw the woman or the ghost or whatever it was."

"Very clearly," agreed Drummond.

"And, gentlemen, the lady's door was locked. Locked on the inside. It must have gone clean through the wood."

Slingsby lit a cigarette with a puzzled frown.

"I guess," he said, "that I'm a converted man. Up till now I've regarded any guy who got chatting about ghosts as dippy. And now, damn it, I've seen one with my own eyes. Gosh! it gave me the creeps."

"She is quieter now," said Hardcastle, coming down the stairs. "I've given her a dose of sleep dope. And the first thing that I guess I owe is an apology to you, Captain Drummond, for my sneering remark about ghosts earlier in the evening."

"Don't mention it, Mr Hardcastle," answered Drummond. "We are all of us wiser and more tolerant men, I trust, after the amazing escapade of psychic phenomena we have just witnessed."

Darrell glanced at him out of the corner of his eye, but his face was expressionless.

"Moreover, as my daughter says, it does seem to bear out part of Morris' story," went on Hardcastle. "If we saw it, so may he have done."

"That's so, sir," said the Inspector. "But there's one point we mustn't forget. A ghost can go through a closed door: we've seen it happen. But a ghost can't carry a suit of clothes through a closed door: a ghost can't carry anything at all."

He glared round the group as if challenging anyone to contradict him.

"That being so," he continued, "we still have not accounted for Morris having on the murdered man's clothes."

"That's very true," agreed Hardcastle. "Don't you think so, Penton?"

The third man rolled his cigar from one side of his mouth to the other before replying.

"I guess I don't know what to think," he remarked at length. "I'm with Jake in what he said. The whole thing is a new one on me."

"Anyway, gentlemen," said the Inspector, "clothes or no clothes, one thing *is* certain: no ghost can murder a man, certainly not by bashing his head in."

"I suppose that's a fair assumption," said Penton.

"Very well, then: let's disregard the ghost for a moment, and I think we can reconstruct what happened. Morris broke in, and in all probability thought the place was empty. All you gentlemen were out: only Mr Marton was in the house. Maybe he came downstairs, thinking it was one of you returning, and Morris attacked him. Marton fled and Morris pursued him, finally doing him to death in the room above. Then he changed clothes, came down and found the supper spread out. While he was in the room he suddenly saw the ghost, which terrified him so much that he daren't leave. And there you other gentlemen found him. To his dismay, you recognised his clothes, and the blood on the ceiling showed him the game was up. Half tipsy with beer, and with the thought of the ghost in his mind, he said the first story that came into his head."

"That sounds very feasible," said Hardcastle: "very feasible indeed."

"Another point that goes to prove it," continued the Inspector, "was his great reluctance to go upstairs and look at the body – a well-known characteristic of murderers. That's what happened, gentlemen, or as near to what happened as we are ever likely to get now the man is dead. I don't wonder, sir" – he turned to Drummond – "that you were taken in for a bit. You didn't know that there wasn't a caretaker in the house: besides, it's amazing the yarns these old lags will spin."

"So it seems," answered Drummond. "By the way, has the weapon with which Marton was murdered been discovered?"

"Not yet. He probably threw it out of the window, and I'll have the ground searched thoroughly tomorrow morning. Then we'll have his fingerprints and absolute proof."

"Look here, Mr Inspector," said Hardcastle in a rather hesitating voice, "I don't know if what I'm going to suggest is very irregular, but if it is you must put it down to my ignorance of the law. Now I take it we are all agreed that Morris murdered Marton in some such manner as you described, and then blundered into Grimstone Mire. At any rate, Morris can never be brought to trial. Wal – I've just obtained a lease of this house; I'm engaged in certain scientific researches, and I must frankly admit I don't want to be disturbed. Now what I want to know is this: is it necessary to say anything about this ghost? I quite understand that if Morris wasn't dead it would be impossible not to allude to it: he would tell the same story he told Captain Drummond. But now that he is dead, are we defeating the ends of justice in any way if we keep our mouths shut about it? It can do neither Morris nor Marton any good, and the only result that is going to happen is that this house will be surrounded with swarms of journalists and sightseers."

A faint smile twitched round Drummond's lips, but his face was in the shadow.

"In addition to that," Hardcastle continued, "though naturally such a thing will not deter us if it is our duty to speak, I'm sadly afraid we're all of us going to have our legs pulled nearly off. We have seen it – we *know*; but that's a very different thing from convincing somebody else. If we hadn't been here tonight, would we have believed it if we'd been told it? Your police are second to none in the world, but they're a hard-headed body of men. And I can't help thinking, Inspector, that you're going to come in for the hell of a lot of chaff from your brother officers. What do you say, Captain Drummond?"

"Don't you think," Drummond murmured, "that in a case of such remarkable psychic interest we ought to get in touch with that jolly old society that goes spook-hunting?"

"I do not," said the other firmly. "If, in the interests of justice, the Inspector considers we must speak – that's one thing. But I flatly refuse to have bunches of people sitting all over the place on the chance of seeing something."

"I quite see your point," agreed Drummond pleasantly. "I believe most of 'em are trained to the house, but it would be deuced boring to have an ancient professor permanently in the bathroom. Well, well – the Inspector must decide. Do we burble of ghosts or do we not?"

The Inspector cleared his throat. Until Hardcastle's remarks, that aspect of the case had not struck him. Now it did – forcibly. No one knew better than he did that there was an enormous amount in what had been said. He could imagine the headlines in the papers: "Police Inspector sees Ghost. New Scope of Activity for Scotland Yard." And even nearer ahead, the thought of telling his own Chief Constable – a retired Major of unimaginative temperament – was not one that he relished. If only the constable wasn't there it would be so much easier. And then a sudden inspiration came to him – a perfect way out of the dilemma. He cleared his throat again.

"I think we can look at it this way, gentlemen," he remarked. "The crime we are investigating began with the death of Morris in Grimstone Mire. Nothing that has happened subsequent to that can have any bearing on the crime. In other words, the fact that we saw this ghost has nothing whatever to do with the matter. It lends a certain air of truth to part of Morris' rigmarole, I agree: and, as you said, Mr Hardcastle, if he were still alive it would be our duty to say what we had seen. But as he isn't, it is a thing which it seems to me does not come within the scope of enquiry. Naturally, Captain Drummond will have to state what was said by Morris to him and his friends, but at that I think we are entitled to leave it. It is no part of the duty of the police to cause inconvenience to law-abiding citizens, and I quite understand that you, sir, would find it most annoying to have crowds of inquisitive people all round the house."

"Good," said Drummond. "The oracle has spoken: ghosts are off. And that being so, I think we might go home, Ted, and hit the hay. My kindest regards, Mr Hardcastle, to the Comtessa, and I sincerely hope that the little wanderer is laid for tonight, at any rate. But you must certainly rope her in for the cinema work your daughter tells me you are interested in. Damned good performer, and no screw to pay. Night, night, souls: we shall doubtless hear, Inspector, when and where our presence is desired."

And it was not until they reached the main road that he spoke again.

"There's no doubt about it, boys," he said, "that that little bunch of beauties is pretty high up in the handicap. It's a pleasure to have met them. There's a calm nerve about their doings which beats the band. It's gorgeous. And having shown us the damned old ghost, the subtle way Hardcastle got round the Inspector was a delight. The actual suggestion to say nothing about it came much better from the police than from anyone else."

"I gathered from your face you were a bit sceptical about the spectre," said Darrell.

"Sceptical!" laughed Drummond. "I should say. For a moment I admit I was taken in: the thing was staged so well. And I'd been going on the assumption that there was only one female in the house. But then I went back to our one basic idea – that Morris was speaking the truth. And that being so, the Inspector's profound statement that a ghost can't carry a suit of clothes on its arm assumes a rather different complexion from what the worthy warrior intended. That was the woman whom Morris saw, and who gave him the clothes. And having done her little piece at the top of the stairs, she backed into 'honey's' room, who then bolted the door and let out an ear-splitter. Meanwhile, the ghost vanishes through some secret panel, and that's that."

"Probably you're right, old boy," said Jerningham. "But for the life of me I can't see their object in doing it."

"That's what I was trying to get at, Ted, all the time we were in the hall. And I think it's this way. Their original plan miscarried owing to our being there, and so they had to amend it. They knew the police would arrive shortly, and that from then on there would always be at least one constable in the house. They knew also that we should mention the woman, which would cause awkward questions. So the first thing they do is to send the Comtessa along after us – I saw the marks of footsteps *leaving* that panel in the hall – partially to find out what we were going to say, and partially to sustain the bluff that she had been in Plymouth. Now, since that cry we heard was almost certainly Morris in Grimstone Mire, the sweet thing must have known of his death before she saw us. And, incidentally, I wonder if he fell or was pushed: his death was a godsend to them. However, to continue – back we go with the lady, who is suitably greeted by dear Dad, once more registering her absence in Plymouth. Then what about the other woman? If 'honey' was in Plymouth, what about the female Morris said he saw? Where was she? Or was it a complete invention? Great idea – stage her as a ghost; and, as I said before, they staged her damned well."

"Do you really think we ought to let them get away with it?" said Darrell.

"How can we prevent it, old boy? If Morris wasn't dead, I'd agree with you: he may have been a swine, but we couldn't have let the poor blighter swing without making an effort to save him. But now he's dead, what's the use of worrying? Put it how you will, the only thing we can say is that we believed his story. Who cares? We should merely be regarded as gullible mugs. No, our line is to pretend that we are in complete agreement with the theory put forward by the Inspector, and once the inquest is over set to work from the other end. I'm inclined to think that if there are any survivors left at all of the firm of Marton, Peters and Newall, we might be able to get on to something."

"I'm just wondering," said Jerningham, "if by chance that is one Dick Newall with whom I've played a lot of golf. As far as I remember, he is a legal bird of sorts."

"The rum thing, to my mind, is what they're doing down here at all," said Darrell, as they turned in at the gate of Merridale Hall.

"The solution of that little problem, old lad," cried Drummond, "may possibly prove to be the solace of our declining years. But don't forget that the one essential thing is to make that bunch believe that they've fooled us. We've got to do a bit in the acting line ourselves. For, unless I'm much mistaken, the situation is this at the moment. They know they've bluffed the Inspector: they're not certain about us. And it therefore behoves us to allay their maidenly fears. Even as the trout swallows the mayfly, so must we swallow their little effort. And that is going to entail a certain discretion at the inquest: I should loathe to get it in the neck for perjury."

CHAPTER 4

As was only to be expected, the affair attracted an enormous amount of attention. The escape of Morris, duly reported in all the evening papers, had already brought Dartmoor into the centre of the limelight: the subsequent development increased the interest. Reporters swarmed like bluebottles; it was unsafe for anyone even remotely connected with the matter to be seen in the open.

Two facts, one positive and one negative, came to light the next day. The first was the clear imprint of a boot of regulation prison pattern on the track over Grimstone Mire – a boot, moreover, of the size taken by Morris. The second was the complete failure of the police to discover any trace of the weapon with which the crime had been committed. And when the inquest opened at eleven o'clock the day after, there was still no sign of it.

With some reluctance Mr Hardcastle had agreed to it being held at Glensham House. At first he demurred on the grounds of the added publicity, but when it was pointed out to him how very much proceedings would be facilitated if the enquiry was held on the spot, he finally consented.

"The whole thing is most annoying, Captain Drummond," he remarked, as they met in the hall. "I particularly dislike notoriety in any form, and then a crime like this occurs, literally in my house."

"Deuced boring, Mr Hardcastle," agreed the other sympathetically. "I, too, like to blush unseen. Been worried by the jolly old newspaper men?"

"They swarm like maggots in a bit of bad meat," snorted Hardcastle.

"An apt and charming simile," murmured Drummond. "Ah, well, if you will have these regrettable incidents in the old family mansion, you must expect 'em to sit up and take notice. By the way" – he lowered his voice confidentially – "any further sign of the ghost?"

The other glanced quickly round the room; then, taking his arm, he drew Drummond on one side.

"Yes – last night. She was in exactly the same place at the head of the stairs. But not a word to my daughter about it."

"The Comtessa has remained on, has she?"

"I persuaded her to. For one thing alone, I thought it better she should be here over the inquest, in case they want to ask her any questions. Tell me, Captain Drummond, what do you make of that apparition?"

" 'Pon my soul, Mr Hardcastle, it's deuced difficult to say, isn't it? We've all seen her, and in my own mind I have no doubt that Morris saw her. It's a strange thing, this haunting of old houses. I remember a great pal of mine whose house was haunted by a little green man. Most astonishing case it was. The little fellow used to come and perch on the end of his bed. And one night, after we'd got my friend there with some trouble – I may say he suffered from another delusion, and that was that whisky didn't affect his head – we suddenly heard an awful crash outside. My poor old pal had jumped out of the window. We picked him up, Mr Hardcastle, and with his dying breath he told us what had happened. Thirteen little green men had come just after we left him, all armed with rifles. And as he'd always promised his mother he'd never be shot, he just jumped out. I cried like a child as the dear fellow passed away. Ah! there, if I mistake not, is your charming daughter. Good morning, Comtessa: I hear you have decided to risk the ghost."

"Please don't speak about it, Captain Drummond," she cried. "My father persuaded me to stay on the one more night just for this inquest, but I leave this afternoon. You only saw her in the distance, don't forget: when I saw her she was as close as I am to you."

"A terrifying experience, Comtessa," he remarked gravely. "Hullo! it looks as if the individual with the somewhat bulbous nose is about to kick off. Incidentally, who is the man talking to your father?"

"Mr Peters," she said. "He is one of the members of Bob Marton's firm."

He proved to be the first witness, and identified the murdered man as Robert Marton. He explained that no relative was available for the purpose owing to the recent death of Mr Marton, senior, and that he had therefore come down from London on hearing the news. He further added that it was he who had sent him down at the request of Mr Hardcastle, who had recently acquired the lease of Glensham House through his firm.

"When did he receive your instructions?" demanded the Coroner.

"On Tuesday afternoon – the day before he was murdered. I gave him the address on a piece of paper, as he did not know the house."

The Coroner consulted some documents in front of him.

"Am I not right in supposing that it was on Tuesday evening that his father was killed owing to an accident with a gun?" he asked.

"Perfectly right," said Peters, speaking with some emotion. "I may say that the two things coming so close together has been a very great shock to me and the other members of the firm."

The Coroner nodded sympathetically.

"I am sure that we quite understand that, Mr Peters," he said. "But there is one point that I should like to get clear. You say that you gave him his instructions on Tuesday afternoon, so that he presumably left London on Wednesday morning. Where did he spend Tuesday night? I assume he cannot have been at home; for if he had been, his father's death would naturally have prevented him coming here."

"Exactly," agreed the witness. "From inquiries I have made I find that Robert Marton did not go home on Tuesday night."

"Have you any idea where he stayed?"

"None whatever, sir. His train on Wednesday morning left Paddington very early, and he probably stopped at some hotel."

"So he was in ignorance of his father's death?"

"That I can't tell you, as he may have seen it in the papers. But I assume he did not, as otherwise he would surely have got out at the first stop and returned to Surbiton."

"And he did not telephone to his father or mother or send them any message saying he was remaining in London for the night?"

"Certainly not to his mother. With regard to his father, unfortunately I cannot tell you, but I should think in all probability not. Had he done so, I think he would have told Mrs Marton."

Peters stood down, and Hardcastle was called.

"Now, Mr Hardcastle," said the Coroner, "will you kindly tell us all you know of this distressing affair?"

The witness bowed gravely.

"Distressing is too mild a word for it, sir," he remarked. "I feel that I shall never forgive myself for having been the unwitting cause of this poor boy's death. He was down here on business for me, and then this ghastly thing happened to him."

He paused, overcome with emotion.

"However," he continued, after recovering his composure, "I will tell you all I know. My daughter, my friends and I came down here on Tuesday to have a look at the house, which, as Mr Peters told you, I have recently leased. Marton was to come down on Wednesday, as you have heard. That morning we all went over to Plymouth to see that some alterations on my yacht had been carried out. Then, leaving my daughter there, we returned here to find that a dense fog had come down. I may say," he remarked with a faint smile, "that we are accustomed to things on a big scale in my country, but that fog beat anything we've ever turned out. You gentlemen may be used to it, but it defeated us. However, as time went on and he did not appear, we realised he must have lost his way, and so my friend Mr Slingsby and I went out to look for him. And it was then we ran into two warders on the road, who told us about the escaped convict, and also mentioned that they had met a young man who was obviously lost, but who had finally reached Merridale Hall – the property of this gentleman."

He bowed to Jerningham.

"From their description of him we realised it must be Marton, and so we walked on with the idea of finding Merridale Hall. In the fog we missed it, and then we got hopelessly lost ourselves. We wandered backwards and forwards, and then there came a crash from some little distance off which sounded like a car running into a gate or a wall. We blundered on until, quite suddenly, Marton ran right into us. He told us he had had a drink at Merridale Hall, and had then come on in another attempt to find us."

He paused and blew his nose.

"I now come, sir, to the dreadful tragedy. The boy, I may say, did not seem at all himself. He was nervy, and about seven o'clock he began to shiver. Clearly he'd got fever, and so I gave him some quinine and told him to go to bed. And that" – his emotion was evident – "was the last time I saw the poor lad alive."

"Take your time, Mr Hardcastle," said the Coroner. "We all of us understand how you feel."

"I thank you, sir," continued the witness, after a moment or two. "I should think it was about eight o'clock that Mr Slingsby and I decided to go for a walk. It seemed to us that the fog had lifted a little, and we felt the need of some exercise. Mr Penton refused to come, but went to the garage instead, as something had gone wrong with the car. We thought that if we stuck to the main road we should have no difficulty, but somehow or other we got off it, and once again we found ourselves lost. And it was not until well after ten that we finally got back to the house. The first thing we found was that the whole of our supper had been eaten, and we were just blaming Mr Penton, as being the only possible person who could have taken it, when a man dashed down the stairs, rushed through the hall and vanished into the night. We stood dumbfounded, and a moment or two later we saw three gentlemen standing on the top of the stairs. And they told us what had happened in our absence."

He paused again, and sighed deeply.

"I blame myself bitterly, Mr Coroner, for having gone out and left that sick boy alone in the house. I knew about this escaped convict, but frankly the thought of such a ghastly tragedy never entered my head. Had it done so, I need hardly state that nothing would have induced me to leave the house."

He sat down, and a murmur of sympathy came from the jury.

"Thank you, Mr Hardcastle," said the Coroner. "I speak for the jury as well as myself when I say that your feelings are only natural. But I can assure you that no vestige of blame can be attached to you for what you did. There is, however, one question I would like to ask you. Did the murdered man say anything to you about his father's death?"

"No, sir: not a word. The first I heard of it was from this gentleman, Captain Drummond."

"Thank you. Then I think we may safely conclude that Robert Marton was in ignorance of the fact. And now, to keep things in their correct order, I will call Captain Drummond. My first question, sir, is to ask what brought you here at all?"

"My friends and I, believing the house to be empty, decided that we would come along and see if the rumour of its being haunted was true," answered Drummond.

"And did you see a ghost?" asked the Coroner with ponderous sarcasm.

"Other things occupied our attention, sir," murmured Drummond.

"Kindly tell us what happened?"

"The first thing was that a strong reek of cigarette smoke proved the house was not empty. And we traced it to the room in which we found Morris."

"Did you know it was Morris as soon as you saw him?"

"Yes," said Drummond. "A warder had given me a description of him earlier in the day, and I spotted him by the red scar on his face."

"And then?"

"I recognised the clothes he was wearing as belonging to a young man called Marton who had lost his way during the afternoon and come to Merridale Hall."

Briefly Drummond outlined the events of the afternoon, and Darrell watched Hardcastle covertly. But his face was as expressionless as the Sphinx.

"You, too, say that he seemed nervy," said the Coroner when Drummond had finished.

"He did."

"Did he give you any reason?"

"I think the unexpected appearance of the two warders looming out of the fog and the discharge of a rifle had shaken him considerably."

"Were you not surprised when you returned with your friends to find him gone?"

"Very. And my assumption was that he was a little ashamed of the condition of fright he had been in and had left."

"Did he say he was going to Glensham House?"

"He never mentioned Glensham House."

"Now, Mr Hardcastle stated that it was you who told him of the death of Mr Marton, senior. How did you know?"

Once again Darrell glanced at Hardcastle, whose eyes were now fixed on Drummond.

"Marton told me his name and the name of his firm," said Drummond. "And when I happened to see the account of the accident in the paper, I assumed it was either his father or his uncle who was dead."

Almost imperceptibly Hardcastle relaxed.

"I see," said the Coroner. "Now, Captain Drummond, will you please continue from the point where you found Morris hiding in the room here?"

"I first of all asked him where he got his clothes from."

"What did he say?"

"He told me that an old woman had given them to him and that they belonged to a son of hers who was dead."

"But since you knew they belonged to Marton you must have known that his statement was a lie."

"My brain was moving on those lines," said Drummond mildly, "when we saw the stain on the ceiling."

"What did you do when you saw the stain?"

"We took Morris with us upstairs and went and investigated. And we then found the murdered man."

"Did Morris show any reluctance to going upstairs with you?"

"The very strongest."

"What did he say when he saw the body?"

For a moment or two Drummond hesitated; then he shrugged his shoulders.

"He said something about a ghost," he remarked.

The Coroner smiled.

"Ghosts seem to have been popular that night. Now, Captain Drummond," he went on severely, "are you seriously asking the jury to believe that when you found a man foully murdered on the floor, and an escaped convict, with a record like Morris, wearing the dead man's clothes in an empty house at that hour of the night, you still harped on the subject of ghosts?"

"I come of a very superstitious family," said Drummond with the utmost gravity. "My mother was the thirteenth child of a thirteenth child, and I suppose I have inherited a strain of the whimsical, of the mystical, one might almost say a Puck-like, elfin streak which at times has had the strangest results in my life."

The Coroner looked at him suspiciously, while Jerningham was suddenly shaken with a bad fit of coughing.

"Would you kindly answer my question, Captain Drummond?" said the Coroner. "These family details, though interesting, are hardly relevant. Did you, or did you not, attach any importance to this story of Morris'?"

"He certainly seemed to attach a great deal of importance to it himself," answered Drummond. "And then, before we realised what he intended to do, he bolted. I knew it would be useless to pursue him in the fog, and that sooner or later he would certainly be caught. And we were just going to ring up the police when we met Mr Hardcastle and Mr Slingsby here in the hall."

"Now, Captain Drummond, I am going to put a leading question to you. You and your friends are the only people who actually saw and spoke to Morris. I dismiss the brief glimpse that Mr Hardcastle got of him as he dashed through the hall. Have you any doubts in your mind that Morris was the murderer of Robert Marton?"

"The evidence on the point appears conclusive, Mr Coroner," said Drummond, and the jury nodded their heads in agreement. They were getting bored: the case was such an obvious one. But the Coroner – a man of stern determination – was not to be baulked. First Darrell, then Jerningham, was called to substantiate Drummond's story. Then Penton deposed to what he had seen when working on the car in the garage. And finally the Inspector put forward his reconstruction of the crime.

"The only thing wanting, sir, for absolute proof," he concluded, "is the discovery of the weapon with which the murder was committed. The doctor has told us that the crime took place round about nine o'clock; he also says that in his opinion the weapon used was something in the nature of a meat-chopper. On the handle of that weapon, if we find it, will be the fingerprints – the fingerprints of the murderer: the fingerprints of Morris. But so far the most exhaustive search has failed to bring it to light."

"Is it possible that he had it with him the whole time?" suggested the Coroner, glancing at Drummond.

"An axe is a difficult thing to conceal about one's person," remarked the latter mildly. "In fact, I feel almost sure we should have noticed it."

"You have searched the grounds?" continued the Coroner to the witness.

"Yes, sir. But they are, of course, extensive, and we have not given up hope of discovering it. As Captain Drummond says, it is almost impossible that he should have had it on him, and in all probability, therefore, it is either hidden in the house, or he threw it from the window of the room in which he killed Marton."

Finally the sergeant was called, who gave evidence of his call at Merridale Hall, and the presence there of Comtessa Bartelozzi, whom the Coroner decided it was not necessary to trouble. And so the inquest ended with the verdict that had been obvious from the commencement: "Wilful murder by John Morris, subsequently believed drowned in Grimstone Mire." They further added a rider to the effect that no pains should be spared to discover the weapon with which the crime was committed.

"I think we may congratulate ourselves on the way that went off," said Hardcastle to Drummond, as the jury began to disperse. "It was most masterly the way you avoided any direct reference to the ghost, and I'm very much obliged to you."

"Don't mention it," said Drummond affably. "It is a pleasure to assist you in any way. But you'll still have to watch it. We may have finished with the inquest, but we've not got rid of the reporters yet. Here's one of the blighters bearing down on us now."

But it was not at the newspaper man that Hardcastle was looking, and following the direction of his glance, Drummond saw Jerningham, at the other side of the hall, chatting to Mr Peters.

"May I trouble you for a few moments, gentlemen?" The reporter, notebook in hand, paused hopefully.

"You may not," laughed Drummond. "Nothing on this earth is going to keep me one minute longer from the consumption of ale. My throat is like a lime-kiln. So long, Mr Hardcastle: doubtless we shall meet again in less stirring times. Are you coming, Ted? Peter is in the bus already."

"A stroke of luck, Hugh," said Jerningham as they left. "You remember my telling you about Dick Newall, whom I've often played golf with. Well, he is in the firm. He's the sort of opposite number to young Marton. There's an old Newall, and Dick is his nephew."

"What sort of a bloke is he, Ted?"

"Quite a cheery lad, and plays no bad game."

"Good! But we'll have to get hold of him on the quiet. Hardcastle had an eye like a gimlet on you when you were talking to Peters."

"And he had an eye like a gimlet on you when you were giving evidence, old son," said Darrell.

"I know he had, Peter. He's not very good at disguising his expression. I thought I was pretty hot stuff over the Puck-like elfin streak, didn't you?"

"I damned near gave it away by laughing," said Jerningham. "And as for your thirteenth child of a thirteenth child, it's seventh, you ass."

"To the great artist what is a trifle of that sort?" remarked Drummond. "It is the general atmosphere that counts. And incidentally," he continued more seriously, "there's nothing much wrong with the general atmosphere the other side have managed to produce, as far as they're concerned. What a stroke of luck for them that Morris hadn't got to be reckoned with! But, for all that, the more you look into it, the more masterly do you find the way they've extricated themselves from a very nasty position."

"What's going to happen if they do find the chopper?" said Darrell.

"Find your grandmother, Peter! Morris was not the only thing that went into Grimstone Mire that night. They aren't the type of bunch who would keep a weapon covered with fingerprints that are *not* Morris'. No: I should say that delightful creature Penton bunged the chopper into the bog immediately the thing was done, and I'm wondering how it's going to strike the Inspector when he fails to find it."

"Bring the cocktails, Jennings," shouted Jerningham, as they got out of the car.

"Because, if he only realises it, it knocks the whole verdict endways. If the original scheme had gone through, and Morris had been caught later, the point didn't arise: naturally he would have thrown it away where it could never be found. And little Willie isn't going to find it."

"It would take more than a trifle of that sort to worry him," said Darrell. "But the point now is, what's the next move?"

"The trail here is dead for the moment," remarked Drummond, lighting a cigarette. "I think we'd better try this pal of yours, Ted – young Newall."

"Right you are, old lad: there's nothing to stop us. We can easily beetle up to Town by the three o'clock train from Plymouth. But I can't promise that we'll get anything out of him. I mean, even if by chance he knows something, he may flatly refuse to pass it on."

"We can but have a dart at it," answered Drummond. "Because it's perfectly obvious that the matter can't stop where it is. I haven't enjoyed myself so much for a long while."

"It was rather interesting to hear that friend Hardcastle has a yacht," said Darrell, as Jennings announced lunch.

"The whole thing is deuced interesting," cried Drummond cheerfully. "Let's get to the stewed hash, Ted, and tell him to throw a few toothbrushes into a bag. And you never can tell: I shouldn't be surprised if we didn't find ourselves travelling up with little Pansy-face."

He paused, struck with a sudden idea.

"I say, chaps – what's Algy Longworth doing these days?"

They both stared at him.

"Algy!" said Jerningham. "The last time I saw him he was pretending to do a job of work in his uncle's office. What's the idea?"

"Algy and Pansy-face: our Comtessa. Might be rather useful if they met one another. Algy wouldn't know us: we wouldn't know Algy. Perhaps we'd get on to something that way."

"How are we going to get them to meet?"

"I haven't an earthly at the moment," admitted Drummond. "But it's a possibility that's worth bearing in mind. If we do travel up with Pansy-face – and she said she was going this afternoon – we'll try and find out her haunts in Town."

And, as it turned out, the first person they saw on the platform at Plymouth was the Comtessa. Hardcastle was with her, and she gave them a charming smile.

"Are you all going up to London as well, Captain Drummond?" she asked.

"That's the idea, Comtessa. The country is really getting so deuced exciting these days, that one has to calm one's nerves in the old Metropolis. Got rid of the reporters yet, Mr Hardcastle?"

"No, confound it!" cried the other. "That constable or the sergeant has been talking, and they've got on to a rumour about the ghost."

"Barricade the front door and bark at them," advised Drummond, as the train began to move out of the station. "So long, Mr Hardcastle: my love to your boy friends."

"How thankful I am to get away from that dreadful place!" said the Comtessa, as he sat down opposite her. "These last two or three days have seemed like an awful nightmare."

"They have certainly been full of incident," agreed Drummond. "Ted is quite jealous that it didn't happen at Merridale Hall."

"I thought it was charming of you to give your evidence about the poor boy in the way you did," she said, leaning towards him and lowering her voice.

He looked a little puzzled.

"I hope I'm not being dense, Comtessa, but I don't quite follow you. In what other way could I have given it?"

"My dear man, you're not going to tell me that you really thought the cause of his nerves was due to the fact that two warders suddenly loomed out of the fog?"

She smiled and lit a cigarette.

"No, Captain Drummond – that did well enough for the inquest, and it is much better that his poor mother should think so – but as a man of the world you cannot really believe it yourself."

"My dear Comtessa," he remarked, "you are, in our English phraseology, barking up the wrong tree. The youngster struck me as being very unfit: I should say he had been drinking too much and hitting it up generally. But more than that I frankly know nothing about."

"Do you mean to say that he didn't tell you he was in very serious trouble?"

Drummond nodded.

"My dear lady, he was a complete stranger to me. I was with him for ten minutes at the most. Would he be likely to spring an intimate confession on me in such a very short time? Now that you mention it, his condition, if what you say is true, is far more comprehensible. But it's the first I've heard of it."

She looked at him keenly, but Hugh Drummond was not accounted one of the best poker-players in London for nothing.

"I'll tell you why I thought you must know more than you said," she continued after a moment. "To be perfectly candid, Captain Drummond, I did not believe that you went to Glensham House in search of ghosts."

"It did sound a bit thin, I admit," he laughed. "And yet there was the ghost that you and I both saw. However, if it wasn't the ghost that took us there, what did you think it was?"

"I thought you were worried over Bob Marton, and that, knowing he was going to Glensham House, you came along to see if he was all right."

"At ten o'clock at night! Really, Comtessa, it seems an odd hour to pay a call. And you are ignoring the somewhat important fact that he never even mentioned Glensham House to me."

"It was such an extraordinary coincidence, wasn't it, you selecting that particular night?"

"Foggy, you see. It is then that the ghost walks. Though the story current in these parts is of a very different type of manifestation from the one we saw."

"Really! What is that?"

"Honestly I would sooner not tell you, Comtessa."

He shook his head gravely and stared out of the window.

"But I would like to know," she insisted.

"Comtessa," he said after a while, "you wouldn't think, would you, to look at me that I am at all a nervous individual? And I must say for myself that it has to be something pretty large in the human line for me to get the wind up. But when it comes to the thing that is reputed to haunt Glensham House, it's a different matter. Ted knows more about it than I do, he'll tell you."

"What's that, old lad?" said Jerningham, apparently waking up suddenly.

"I was telling the Comtessa about the horror of Glensham House," explained Drummond. "It's a thing, Comtessa – a monstrous misshapen thing."

"That's right," said Jerningham. "No one knows what it is for certain, because everyone who has seen it either goes mad or dies. Some people say it is an elemental, of incredible strength and ferocity; others say that it is some dark secret of the Glenshams. And one of the few facts that seems to be known about it is that its appearance is always preceded by a horrible vault-like smell. Whether, of course, there is any truth in it at all, I don't know. West Country people are notoriously superstitious. And it may be that occasionally on foggy nights Grimstone Mire produces this strange fetid odour, which by some means or other reaches the house."

"And that is what you came to see," she exclaimed a little breathlessly.

"That was our idea," answered Drummond. "Though probably the whole thing is a fable."

"That is what I say when sitting in a comfortable carriage on the way to London," said Jerningham. "But what was it that sent young Roger Glensham mad in the course of a single night? Was it an accident that caused his great-uncle to fall from his bedroom window and break his neck, or was that look of terror in his staring eyes due to something else? I always think that it is one thing to talk about these matters in the broad light of day, and quite another when one is in an old house at night."

"But has no one ever heard of the ghost that we saw?" asked the Comtessa.

"The Glenshams are notoriously uncommunicative about the whole thing," said Jerningham. "I personally had never heard of a woman haunting the house, but since we all saw her, the matter is proved. And for my part, at any rate, I'm glad it was that one we saw, and not the other."

The train was slowing down for Exeter, and he rose.

"What about a spot of tea?" he remarked.

"I'm with you, Ted," said Darrell, but Drummond shook his head.

"I'll come along a bit later, old boy," he said. "Now, Comtessa," he continued, as the other two left the compartment, "to revert once more to the question of young Marton. Don't say anything if you would prefer not to: naturally I don't want to pry into any secrets. But since you mentioned the matter in the first instance yourself, what was this trouble he was in?"

She hesitated: then, taking her cigarette case from her bag, she opened it. And over the match which Drummond held for her their eyes met.

"Very serious financial trouble, Captain Drummond," she said gravely. "The poor lad confided in me. I can't tell you the details: they are too complicated. And anyway, it's not my secret."

"I quite understand, Comtessa," answered Drummond. "And I shall, of course, respect your confidence. Confound it! – here are some people getting in. Why is it that certain individuals are born without tact?"

She smiled at him sweetly.

"Do you ever dance in London?" she asked.

"I periodically tread a measure and then mangle a kipper," he said. "Ciro's and the Embassy, and one or two others of the smaller places."

"Do you know the Custard Pot in Wardour Street?"

"That's a new one on me," he answered. "Is it a good spot?"

"It is a quiet one," she murmured.

"Then it shall be added to my list, Comtessa," he said. "Do you go there often?"

"*Ça dépend*," she answered. "Most young men in London today are so boring, aren't they?"

"If you dare to risk it," said Drummond, "the Senior Sports will always find me."

"I think I might – once. And my telephone number is Mayfair 0218."

He scribbled the number in his notebook, and once again their eyes met.

"What about some tea, Comtessa?" he remarked but she shook her head.

"I detest eating in a train, *mon ami*," she answered "But don't let me stop you."

"It always sounds better to call it tea," he grinned. "So, if you will excuse me, I'll join the other two for a while."

He strolled along to the dining-car, and having joined them at their table, he ordered a whisky and soda.

"Have we or have we not?" he remarked thoughtfully.

"Have we not what?" said Darrell.

"Allayed her suspicions," answered Drummond. "Since you left, chaps, I've got off with Pansy-face: we purpose dancing together at the Custard Pot in Wardour Street. But does she still think that Marton told me something while he was in the house? That is the crux."

"Didn't you think Ted was inventing the whole of that ghost stuff?" put in Darrell.

Drummond stared at him.

"Of course I did. And I thought he did it deuced well, though what he wanted to introduce the smell for, the Lord alone knows. You don't mean to say there's any truth in it, Ted?"

"No, I don't say that. But for the first time today, funnily enough – and I'd forgotten to mention it before – I heard that story. Some bloke at the inquest told me. That is the Glensham legend."

"Well, I think Pansy-face swallowed it all right. But it's the other point that is the really important one. I asked her point blank what was the trouble she alluded to, and she said he had got into a mess over money, and had confided in her."

"Possibly the truth," said Darrell.

"He said to me that afternoon, 'I wish it was only that,'" answered Drummond. "A mess over money doesn't make a fellow go in fear of his life; and most certainly a mess over money isn't going to cause them to murder him. No, Peter: it must be more than that. You may bet your bottom dollar that young Marton had served their purpose and had lost his nerve in so doing. They were afraid of his squealing, and wanted him out of the way. But what was the purpose? – that's the point."

He relapsed into silence and stared out of the window at the flying countryside. And though his most fervent admirer would never have called Hugh Drummond a second Newton, yet he possessed a great deal of sound common sense, which he could use to advantage on an occasion such as this. Essentially of a direct nature himself, he always sought to reduce a problem to fundamental facts. And here, it seemed to him, those facts were clear.

Marton had been murdered for some reason as yet unknown, and the murderers had got away with it as far as the police were concerned. But what the murderers did not know was how far they had got away with it where he and Ted and Peter were concerned.

He tried to put himself in the position of the opponents. Assuming his basic foundation was correct, what line of action would they take? Would they take the point of view that since they had bluffed the police the other thing didn't matter? Something big was on foot, since they had not hesitated to murder a man: would they merely carry on with their plans, and completely disregard him and the two sitting opposite him? They might reasonably assume that, since he had said nothing up to date, he proposed to let the matter drop altogether. They might even assume that their bluff had been successful all round. And it seemed to him that until they were certain one way or the other, their policy must be to wait and see. If they did anything else, if they gave the slightest hint that they were not sure if he believed the story, they gave themselves away at once. It was a question of the old chestnut – 'That's my story, and I'm going to stick to it.'

For the moment, therefore, it seemed to him that the other side would do nothing. In fact they would do nothing until their own next move proved that they had not been bluffed. Then the scrap would begin in earnest. But the difficulty lay in what the next move was going to be. Unless they could get some information out of Dick Newall, it looked as if they were up against a blank wall. And he realised that Jerningham's fears were not groundless: to ask a lawyer, however great a friend he might be, to reveal what were possibly office secrets was to ask a lot.

"When can we get in touch with your pal, Ted?" he asked.

"Almost certainly this evening, old boy. He's nearly always in the club before dinner. Hullo! here is Mr Peters."

The solicitor paused by their table on seeing Jerningham.

"Afternoon, Mr Peters. I didn't know you were on the train. Let me introduce Captain Drummond and Mr Darrell. Won't you take a seat at our table?"

"Thank you, thank you," cried the other. "With pleasure. I am really so worried and distracted over this shocking affair, coming so closely on top of the other, that I hardly know what I'm doing. I fear it will completely break up poor Mrs Marton. She idolised Bob."

"It's very sad indeed," agreed Drummond. Such shocking bad luck. By the way, Mr Peters, I didn't like to ask him personally, but perhaps you can tell me. My father knew a man called Hardcastle very well indeed a few years ago in South Africa. I was wondering if it was the same one."

"I really can't say," answered the lawyer. "He may have been in South Africa – in fact I should think it is more than likely he was. He seems to have travelled extensively. All I know about him is that he wanted to rent Glensham House. And as we have been the family solicitors for years, he naturally came to us about it. I was a little surprised, I must admit. It didn't strike me as at all the sort of place a man like him would want. But houses of that size are difficult things to let these days, especially so far away from London, and so I closed with his offer at once, though it was for a very short lease."

"So he is not proposing to make his home there?"

"Dear me, no! He has taken it for three months only."

"Then he certainly must be very wealthy," remarked Drummond. "He'll want a great deal of furniture to make it habitable."

"No: all the remainder is stored in Plymouth, so that he won't have to buy anything."

"I hear that he is inventing some cinema gadget," went on Drummond casually. "At least we gathered so from his daughter."

"I know he is interested in the films," said the lawyer. "In fact we did some business for him in that line. But I think he is a man with many irons in the fire."

"I suppose you don't happen to know anything about the legend of the house," put in Jerningham.

"My dear sir," said the other, "in my profession we deal with facts. Those give us quite enough trouble without going into suppositions. There is some legend, I believe – in fact, I think I once had it told me. But I pay no attention to that sort of thing at all, though from idle chatter I heard at the inquest today some idiot seems to have revived the story. And, of course, now I come to think of it, it was that that took you three young men over there in the first place."

He smiled tolerantly.

"Well, well, it's all very fine for people of your age. But when you come to mine you'll find that flesh and blood cause quite sufficient worry, without chasing round after spirits."

"Most old houses have some sort of legend attached to them, don't they?" said Drummond. "Especially when they have secret passages as well."

"Now that *is* a fact with regard to Glensham House," said the lawyer. "The place is honeycombed with them. And, funnily enough, that is a thing that particularly attracted Mr Hardcastle. As an American he seemed to consider that no old English house was worth ten cents – I think that was his phrase – unless it had a secret passage."

"Indeed," murmured Drummond. "Well, – he seems to have got his money's worth this time. Do you know the entrances to any of them?"

"I haven't an idea," answered the other. "And I can't say that I want to have one. Between ourselves, as I don't think I see a prospective tenant in any of you, the non-secret part of the house is sufficiently gloomy, to my mind, without worrying over anything else."

He called for his bill.

"Well, I must be getting back to my carriage," he continued. "I've got an hour's work in front of me before we reach London. Good day to you, gentlemen: good day."

"Interesting, that point about Hardcastle and the secret passages," said Drummond, as the lawyer disappeared. "May mean something: may not. What about the other half, chaps? And then I think I'll rejoin Pansy-face. I'd hate her to think my love for her had waned."

But the Comtessa was immersed in a novel when they returned to their compartment, and save for one swift smile and a hope that the tea had been good, nothing more was said till the train reached Paddington. And then in the general rising their shoulders touched.

"You won't forget the Custard Pot?" she murmured.

"I shall haunt the door," he answered, "till I get arrested as a street nuisance. Let me take your dressing-case and I'll see you into a taxi."

"The car should be here," she said leaning out of the window. "Yes: there's the chauffeur."

She beckoned to a man in livery who was standing on the platform.

"*Au revoir*, Captain Drummond. Don't forget, Mayfair 0218."

"The line will probably fuse," he murmured as he strolled at her side towards the car. "Is your husband – er – in London?"

"Not at present," she answered gravely. "He travels abroad a lot. Ah! *chérie*, let me introduce Captain Drummond – Madame Saumur."

And for a space there was utter silence. For Drummond and a woman already seated in the car were staring at one another speechlessly, while the Comtessa looked from one to the other in growing bewilderment.

"*Enchanté*, Madame," said Drummond at length. "It is a long time since we met, is it not? Saumur, did you say, Comtessa?"

"So you two know one another?" she cried.

"A rose by any other name, dear lady," remarked Drummond with a smile. "Does Madame also adorn the Custard Pot?"

He stood back as the chauffeur closed the door, and bowed.

"If so my cup of happiness will be complete."

"Posing as a statue, old lad," said Darrell a few moments later. "Or watching the last of the loved one?"

"Madame Saumur, Peter," answered Drummond dreamily. "Pansy-face's girl friend. She was in the car. Madame Saumur, Peter: think of it."

"I'm thinking," said the other. "What about it?"

"She was Irma, Peter: our long-lost Irma Peterson."

"Irma!" cried Darrell incredulously. "Rot, man!"

"Do you suppose I'd make a mistake over her?" said Drummond with a grin.

"Did she say anything?"

"Not a word. We were both so flabbergasted for a moment or two that we gaped at one another like a couple of codfish. Then I made some fatuous remark and they pushed off."

"What an amazing thing!" said Jerningham, as they got into a taxi. "How is it going to affect matters?"

"In this way, Ted. There's no earthly use now in our playing a canny game. We can still pretend, of course, that we agree with the verdict today, but we can't fool her into thinking we've dropped the matter. She knows us a great deal too well to believe it for an instant."

"And she didn't speak at all?"

Drummond shook his head.

"Not with her tongue. But just as the car drove off she gave me one look that said volumes. It was as clear as if she had shouted it through a megaphone. It's a fight to a finish this time."

CHAPTER 5

They drove to Ted Jerningham's club, and one of the first members they met in the smoking-room was the man they wanted. He was reading an evening paper, and the instant he saw them he gave a hail.

"Ted, old lad, come here. Of all the amazing things I've ever known this wins in a canter. Fancy you being mixed up in this performance."

"Evening, Dick," said Jerningham. "I want you to meet Drummond and Darrell."

"The three musketeers complete," grinned the other, and then grew serious again. "It's a pretty damnable business, isn't it? I suppose this account is accurate?"

Drummond, who had skimmed through the report, nodded.

"Yes," he said. "That just about gives the finding of twelve good men and true, and to that extent, therefore, it is accurate."

Newall stared at him.

"Are you implying that there is some inside information going around which is not mentioned in the report?"

"Is there any spot that we can go to, Ted," said Drummond, "where there will be no chance of our being overheard?"

"Sure bill," he answered. "The small card-room is bound to be empty."

He led the way to the lift, and the others followed with Newall, who was still carrying the paper in his hand. And, having ordered a round of the necessary, he closed the door.

"Now we shan't be disturbed," he said. "Get on with it, Hugh."

"Right oh!" answered Drummond. "Now then, Newall, we'll take the whole bally hurdle in one. That story as given in the paper you're holding is a lie from beginning to end."

"What on earth do you mean?" cried the other. "You aren't telling me that Bob Marton is still alive, are you?"

"No, not that. What I am telling you is that he was not murdered by Morris, the escaped convict."

"Then who the devil was he murdered by?"

"Before we go into that have I your word that what we're going to tell you won't go any further?"

"Yes," said Newall, "you have."

"Good! Then Marton was murdered by one of the trio Hardcastle, Slingsby and Penton – or by all of them."

"My dear sir," stuttered Newall after a pause, during which his eyes almost came out of his head, "you're pulling my leg. What under the sun should they want to murder Marton for?"

"That," said Drummond, with a faint smile, "is where we hope you'll be able to help us."

"I say, Ted," cried the other, "is he *really* being serious?"

"Absolutely, Dick. It's an extraordinary yarn, but you can take it from me that every word is gospel truth."

Briefly, but at the same time omitting nothing, Drummond gave him the story, and the lawyer listened with increasing amazement. But at the end he shook his head.

"Sorry," he said, "but I fear you haven't convinced my legal mind. It's quite clear that you believed the yarn this convict spun to you, but what I'm asking myself, in view of the well-nigh inconceivable alternative you suggest, is whether you weren't deceived by him yourselves."

"I expected you to say that," said Drummond quietly. "And it was the realisation that everybody would think that that made us say nothing about it. *Nevertheless, Morris did not deceive us: what he said was the truth.*"

"But, damn it, man," cried Newall, "what possible motive could there have been for such a thing? Hardcastle, a perfectly good American millionaire – why should he want to put Bob Marton out of the way? It's preposterous: it's – it's inconceivable, as I said before."

"There is no important document, or something of that sort, missing from the office, is there?"

"Nothing: nothing at all. Why, as far as I know, there isn't a document in the office that is worth a tanner to anyone else. Honestly, you fellows, I think you're after the wrong fox this time with a vengeance. And if you don't mind my giving you a word of professional advice, you'd better be damned careful. What you've said to me is safe – it won't go beyond me. But there's such a thing as libel, and a story like that renders you liable to thumping damages."

"You need have no fears on that score," said Drummond. "We aren't going to mention it. We didn't say a word about it even to old man Peters. One question, though, Newall. However much we imagined over what Morris said to us, there is no doubt over Marton's remarks to me. How do you account for those? Who are the 'they' he was terrified of?"

"I confess that defeats me," said the other slowly. "Of course he was in a rotten condition of nerves."

"Rotten enough to imagine some non-existent beings?"

Dick Newall lit a cigarette thoughtfully.

"It's a poser, I admit," he remarked. "You say he mentioned this woman Comtessa Bartelozzi by name?"

"Certainly," said Drummond. "He mentioned her in connection with his trouble, and she is Hardcastle's daughter."

"What is she like to look at?"

"Extraordinarily attractive. If you happen to frequent a night club called the Custard Pot, you may have seen her there."

"What's that?" cried the other. "The Custard Pot! Why, she must be the woman I saw there with Bob Marton one night. I pulled his leg about it next day, and he got quite shirty about it."

"Had Hardcastle been to your firm then?"

Newall stared at him.

"Yes, he had. Hardcastle came to us about two months ago, and this incident I'm talking about was last week."

"Seems strange that Marton didn't tell you who the lady was," said Drummond. "Look here, Newall," he went on quietly, "I know our story must seem a bit thin to you. For all that, it's the truth. Young Marton was foully murdered by Hardcastle and his bunch, and up to date they have got clean away with it. There is some big crime in contemplation: what it is I know no more than you. But Marton knew, and that's why they outed him."

A waiter entered, and came up to Newall.

"You're wanted on the telephone, sir," he announced.

"I'll come back at once," said the lawyer, rising. He followed the man from the room, and Drummond turned to the other two.

"I don't blame him in the slightest for being sceptical," he remarked. "So would we be in his place. And it only shows what the result would have been if we'd put it forward at the inquest."

"Would it be any use telling him about Irma?" suggested Darrell. "Birds of a feather and that sort of idea."

Drummond shrugged his shoulders.

"She would only be a name to him," he said. "He's had no first-hand experience of her little ways. Still, it's a possibility, Peter."

And at that moment Newall returned with a worried expression on his face.

"It's a very strange thing," he said, "in view of what we've been talking about, but my uncle has just rung me up. And quite obviously something is wrong. It's getting on for eight o'clock, and unless it was serious it could surely have kept till tomorrow.

I'm going round to see him at once. Will you fellows be dining here?"

"They can feed with me," said Jerningham.

"Right: I'll come back as soon as I've seen the old man. Of course it may be nothing at all, but it's the first time I've ever known him do such a thing."

He left the room, and Drummond rubbed his hands together.

"I wonder if that means we're on the track of something," he said. "Your pal seems a cheery sort of bloke, Ted: I hope he won't be as close as an oyster if he finds out anything."

"So do I, old boy," answered Jerningham. "On that point we'll just have to wait and see. But one can't expect him to tell us much if it's a secret concerning one of the firm's clients. Anyway, what about some food?"

There was no sign of Newall during dinner, and it was not until after ten that he came into the smoking-room and ordered some sandwiches. A glance at his face showed that something had happened, but he said nothing until the waiter had brought them. Then abruptly he turned to the other three.

"It is my turn now," he said, "to ask you to promise that you won't pass on what I'm going to tell you."

"You have it," answered Drummond.

"Whether I ought to say anything about it at all is doubtful," went on Newall, "because, as far as I can see, it has no connection with Bob Marton's death. I mean it doesn't in any way bear out your theory as to who murdered him. At the same time, since we have been discussing him confidentially, it may interest you to know that five thousand pounds' worth of bearer bonds, which were deposited with us a little while ago by a client, are missing. They should have been in his father's safe – a safe to which Bob had access, and their loss only became known to my uncle today when he was going through the contents. At first he thought old Marton might have taken them down to his house in Surbiton, though it would have been a very unusual proceeding. And so, though the funeral is not till tomorrow, he went down there himself this afternoon to see if he could find them. A particular reason for the haste is that the client who left them with us is now back in London, and she may want them at any moment. Well, they've gone: vanished completely. And since the bare idea of suspecting old Marton is simply laughable, I'm sorry to say that it looks as if it was proof of what you were saying about young Bob. There's no one else who can have taken the damned things. As you can appreciate, it's a most unpleasant thing for the firm, for though our client will suffer no financial loss – we shall naturally ante up the five thousand – yet she may cut up nasty. You know what women are in matters of that sort – especially foreigners."

Drummond leaned forward suddenly in his chair.

"Newall," he said quietly, "I'm going to ask you a question which you may think gross impertinence. What is the name of this client?"

"That I'm afraid I can't tell you," answered the other. "It can have no possible bearing on the matter, can it?"

"Then I will draw a bow at a venture," continued Drummond. "I can't help it: I've got a hunch. Is it by any chance Madame Saumur?"

The lawyer started and stared at him.

"I see that it is," said Drummond quietly. "Boys, this affair grows more mysterious every moment."

"But do you know her?" cried Newall.

"Do we know her?" Drummond laughed gently. "Yes, Newall, we do, though not under that name. Many times in the past have we enjoyed a merry roundelay with her, and you can take it from me that she is one of the most dangerous criminals alive today. And to complete the circle, so to speak, when the Comtessa Bartelozzi arrived at Paddington this afternoon, Madame Saumur was there to meet her. And it was that fact that made me ask you."

"Well, I'll be damned!" said Newall. "Confound it – are all our clients criminals?"

"You can take it from me that the Saumur–Hardcastle combination don't waste their time in a Sunday school," grinned Drummond.

"We must get the police on to them," cried the lawyer.

"And what are you going to say to the police?" demanded Drummond. "That some member of your firm, now dead, has embezzled five thousand quid! Guess again, boy: you've got nothing to go to the police about at present. This is a show in which we've got to act on our own. And at the moment we're simply blundering about blindly in the dark. What is the motive underlying the whole affair? That's what we've got to try and get at. What is all this leading up to?"

"But you surely don't mean to imply that there is any connection between Bob Marton's murder and the deposit of those bearer bonds," said Newall incredulously.

"It does sound a bit far-fetched, doesn't it?" admitted Drummond. "And yet they're all in the same bunch: don't forget that fact. What sort of reason did she give for leaving them with you?"

"I couldn't say," answered the other. "Her interview was with old Marton. I could find out, of course, quite easily, from his confidential clerk. But anyway, Drummond, you can't expect me to believe that she left them with us in order that they should be stolen."

"That is exactly what I do believe," said Drummond calmly. "For that reason and no other. Further, she intended that they should be stolen by young Marton and no one else."

"But it sounds fantastic," cried Newall. Surely it is a somewhat novel trait in a criminal to set about being robbed."

"She knew she would never lose her money," said Drummond. "What have you just said yourself? – the firm is going to make it up to her. She knew she was as safe as if the bonds were in a bank."

"Then what was the great idea?" said the other feebly. "My grey matter is failing me."

"The great idea was to get Marton in their power," answered Drummond. "Why – I haven't a notion, but that was the scheme. And it succeeded. He was in their power, and then, when he'd done what they told him to do, they got rid of him."

He lit a cigarette; then he leaned forward and tapped Newall on the knee.

"Look here, old lad," he said, "you've got to get one fact wedged in the legal brain. And you've got to readjust your ideas from a new standpoint. Leave out for the moment Hardcastle and his crowd: assume, if you will, that we are mistaken there. But with regard to Madame Saumur, as she now calls herself, you've *got* to believe us. She is a criminal of the first order – a woman without mercy or scruple. And so, as I say, get that into your head as a fact and not as surmise, and start from the beginning again."

"We can bear out every word of that, Dick," put in Jerningham.

"Right oh!" said the lawyer resignedly. "I'll take your word for it."

"Good!" cried Drummond. "Then let's start off by trying to get some sort of chronological order. First of all – do you know when young Marton first met this Bartelozzi woman?"

Newall shook his head.

"I'm afraid I don't," he said. "The only time I saw 'em together, as I told you, was last week." And then he paused suddenly. "By Jove! I wonder."

He closed his eyes as if trying to collect his thoughts.

"Wait a moment, you fellows," he said, "I'll get it shortly."

He pulled his notebook out of his pocket and studied it.

"Now, this is not proof: it's not even evidence, but it's a possibility. On April 15th, Bob Marton had a job of work given him to do in Liverpool, which entailed his being away for the night. He came to me the day before and asked me if I'd take it on for him, and when I asked him why, he told me that the most glorious woman he had ever seen in his life had got a date with him on the 15th. He said that if he didn't appear she'd get fed up, and, anyway, he was so darned serious about it that I said I would. Here's the entry in my diary – Liverpool, Baxter and Co. on the 15th: round at Hoylake in morning of the 16th. Furthermore – though on this point I've got to trust my memory – it was about then that he started talking about the Custard Pot. Well, you say this wench goes there a lot, so it is possible that that is when he met her."

"Which would make it about four months ago," said Drummond. "And Hardcastle came to you about two months after?"

Newall turned over the pages of his notebook.

"The first entry of him I have is on June 29th," he answered. "But old Marton did his business, and so it is quite on the cards he came earlier."

"When were the bonds deposited?"

"I couldn't say off-hand; but that, again, I can find out from Merridew, the confidential clerk tomorrow."

"But it was fairly recently?"

"If I had to guess, I should say it was some time in July."

"Therefore after Marton had met Comtessa Bartelozzi?"

"If our surmise about April 15th is correct – yes. But remember that is only surmise. The only proof we have there is that I saw 'em together a week ago."

"Were they pretty matey?"

"Taking it by and large – yes."

"So presumably it was not their first meeting?"

"If it was, rapidity must have been the order of the evening," said Newall, with a grin.

"Now look here, old boy," went on Drummond, "that's another point that strikes me. The poor devil is dead, so that's that; but frankly, what did you think of Marton? I only saw him for about ten minutes; but not to mince words, I didn't put him very high in the handicap."

"He wasn't a bad fellow," answered the other. "Why do you ask?"

"For this reason. The Bartelozzi woman, as far as looks are concerned at any rate, is a winner. Then why does she select Marton?"

"I get you," said Newall thoughtfully. "And there's a good deal in what you say. You mean it points definitely to an ulterior motive?"

"Of course it does. He may not have been a bad fellow, but, my dear old lad, if you were a damned pretty woman would you have selected him as your boy friend? Echo answers no, and I'll take a spot of ale."

"I suppose you're right," agreed Newall, beckoning to a waiter. "But the thing that stumps me is what that ulterior motive can possibly have been. We're back at the beginning again. Assuming that everything you say is true: assuming that the bonds were deposited with us and he was goaded into stealing 'em – what then? What earthly use can the junior member of a firm of respectable solicitors be to a bunch of crooks?"

"There you have me," said Drummond. "But I can't help thinking that when you go more carefully through the papers belonging to his father you'll find that something very important is missing. Our Bartelozzi, having fleeced him good and hearty, by some means or other lets him know that she is fully aware of the bond transaction. Possibly she pitched him some yarn about them having been stolen from her. Anyhow the poor sap pinches them. Then he's in the soup. The lady ceases to be kind, and puts the screw on. As the price of her silence, he's got to get the other thing."

"My dear fellow," cried Newall, "your theory would be admirable if I could even remotely begin to imagine what this other thing can be. That's where the snag comes."

"We'll find out in time," answered Drummond quietly. "You can put your shirt on that. But for the moment let's go to Hardcastle. What was the business that brought him to you in the first instance?"

"The lease of Glensham House, as far as I know. In fact, I'm sure that was it, because I remember the matter being discussed. And subsequently we put through some negotiations for him with regard to a studio down in Essex, which was empty. It belonged to a film company that went bust, and he wanted to carry out some experiments there."

"Where exactly is it?"

"About ten miles from Colchester on the main London road. Not far from the Tiptree jamworks. It's called the Blackwater studio." And then he began to laugh. "Do you anticipate villainy there?"

"I'd anticipate it in Canterbury Cathedral if that bunch was around," said Drummond grimly. "And so will you, old lad, by the time we've finished."

Newall rose with a smile.

"In which case I'd better fortify myself for it with some sleep. The old man wants me at the office at crack of dawn tomorrow, so I'll push off. And if you all want to make your wills, the firm might make a reduction for numbers."

With a cheery wave he was gone, and Drummond grinned.

"That lad is going to get an eye-opener before he's much older," he remarked. "Though I must admit he's got lots of excuse for being sceptical. The whole thing is damned obscure at the moment."

And the obscurity did not diminish during the next few days. It transpired that the bonds had been deposited on July 13th as cover for a deal in land which Madame Saumur was trying to put through. As she was going abroad for a few weeks, she wanted someone on the spot to act for her, and instead of giving them the money, she preferred to leave the bearer bonds, with instructions to sell should the transaction come to anything.

"All perfectly normal and in order," said Newall, when he met the three friends a few days later. "What was the good of selling out if the deal came to nothing? And since the agreement would have to be checked legally, it was necessary to do the business through a lawyer and not through a bank."

"Who put her on to your firm particularly?" demanded Drummond.

"Was there ever such a man?" laughed Newall. "If you must know, it was the Dean of Murchester's wife, whom she met at Mentone. You'll be telling me that she has got criminal instincts next."

Further, as the result of an exhaustive search, the only thing missing from the office was a sixpenny postal order for a football competition, on which dark matter the junior clerk and the office-boy had had words.

"Honestly, Drummond," said Newall, "I'm convinced you're barking up the wrong tree. Whatever the lady may have been in the past, there is nothing about this transaction which isn't absolutely straightforward. And it seems to me that there is a perfectly simple solution. Bob, the silly young ass, got tied up with the Bartelozzi woman, who, perhaps without meaning to, bled him. She is probably a fairy with expensive tastes who expects money to be poured out like water on her. And he, finding he couldn't stand the pace, stole the bonds. He had access to his father's safe: for all I know, he may have been present at the interview. There are a dozen ways in which he could have found out the bonds were there – quite normal ways. So why assume some dark conspiracy? And then, realising what he had done – presumably he sold 'em – his nerves went. He knew that sooner or later his father must find out. It wasn't as if it had been money, which conceivably he might have replaced: with bonds the position was hopeless. And that undoubtedly explains his remarks to you. He had always drunk a good deal more than was good for him, which didn't help matters, and that contributed to his condition of funk. By 'they,' he meant the police, and in the fog he must have thought the warders were policemen. And when he said it wasn't only a question of money, or that it was worse than that, he had in his mind that he had stolen bonds."

"You think, then," said Drummond, "that the verdict at the inquest was correct, and that Morris murdered him."

"Frankly, old boy, I do," answered Newall. "You were so in earnest about it, and so positive, that to start with you almost convinced me. But now that we find that nothing else has been stolen, the utter pointlessness of the crime is what I can't get over. Nobody out of a mad-house murders a man for no rhyme or reason whatever. And if you're going to tell me that by some method they found out he had stolen the bonds, and killed him as a punishment, well, frankly, I can't swallow it. No: now that we have a reasonable explanation for his agitation with you, which was the inexplicable thing before, I definitely accept the jury's verdict."

And for a while Hugh Drummond himself was shaken. It was the insuperable question of motive that defeated him. Of course it was possible that Marton had found out that they were plotting some crime, and had threatened to give them away. Then why the bearer bonds? How did they fit in? Could it be that he had made a howling blunder, and that everything was genuine from beginning to end? That the deal in land was a *bona fide* one: that it was merely a common or garden case of stealing money, and that Morris was the murderer after all? His reason answered yes: every instinct he possessed said no.

He had not yet heard from the Comtessa, nor had he rung her up, and the day following his last talk with Newall he came to a decision. He would ask her to go with him to the Custard Pot that night, and there he would settle things one way or the other. He would carry the war into the enemy's country by pretending he knew a great deal more than he did.

"If Dick Newall is right," he said, talking things over with Jerningham, "no harm is done. She will merely think I'm a bit loopy. If, on the contrary, I'm right, it may force their hand. And anything is preferable to sitting still and doing nothing, while they carry on and disregard us completely."

The Comtessa was at home when he rang up, and came to the telephone herself.

"I was afraid you'd quite forgotten me," she said. "I shall be delighted to come. I'm going to a play, so shall I meet you there at half-past eleven?"

"Excellent," he said. "Until then – *au revoir*."

He went back to the smoking-room, to find that Peter Darrell had arrived.

"I say, Hugh," he sang out, "it was Blackwater studio, wasn't it, that Hardcastle took?"

"That's right, Peter. Why?"

"Look at this advertisement in *Film Echoes*."

He held out the paper to Drummond.

"Blackwater Studio. Actor required for small but important character part. Must be young, clean shaven, fair, six feet tall, and between thirty-eight and forty inches round the chest. Previous experience desirable, but not essential. Applicants will be interviewed in person at the studio every day between ten and six."

"That looks as if the interest in the film business was genuine enough," said Drummond, handing the paper back. " 'Pon my soul, chaps, if it wasn't for our one and only Irma being mixed up in it, I'd almost be inclined to believe that the whole thing is a mare's nest."

"I thought I'd apply myself," said Darrell. "I comply with all the requirements, and it gives one an excuse for having a look round."

"Not a bad idea, Peter. Go down tomorrow I don't suppose for a moment they will take you, but you might spot something."

"I hear you're fixing a date with Pansy-face for tonight."

"Yes: we're meeting at the Custard Pot." Drummond shrugged his shoulders. "The Lord knows if it will lead anywhere, but one might be able to bluff her into saying something incriminating. Though it strikes me," he added with a grin, "that one would have to get up pretty early in the morning to trip that lady up, especially since she is being coached by Irma. So long, fellows: we might both come down with you tomorrow, Peter, to the studio."

He lounged out of the room, and hailing a taxi drove back to the service flat he was occupying during his wife's absence in America. Ever since he had met Irma at Paddington he had been conscious of a feeling of profound relief that Phyllis was out of harm's way: he had no wish for a repetition of that ghastly hunt which had so nearly terminated disastrously in the house on Salisbury Plain, and the mere remembrance of which could even now bring him out in a cold sweat. But this time, if Madame Saumur – to give her her present title – struck, she could not do it through Phyllis: it would have to be direct at him. And when, at eleven-thirty exactly, he passed through the swing doors of the Custard Pot, he was conscious of a feeling of exhilaration, of expectancy, like the hunter who hears hounds in the distance. Gone were all the doubts engendered by Dick Newall: he *knew* there was some game afoot. And it would not be for want of trying if he didn't play.

The club was typical of a score of others. After a small formality at the office, which cost him a pound, he duly became a member, and passing up a flight of stairs, he entered the dancing-room. The Comtessa, he had been told below, had not yet arrived, but on informing the head waiter he was expecting her, he was at once shown to a special table in the corner.

"Will M'sieur order now?" he was asked.

"Put a bottle of Clicquot on the ice," he answered, "and we'll leave the food till later."

The room was tastefully got up for a place of the type. It was small, but not too hot, and the lighting was soft and restful to the eyes. On a microscopic expanse of floor in the centre three couples were dancing to the music of a small band sitting in a balcony halfway up one wall.

The place was full: in fact, he had been shown to the last available table. And he realised the Comtessa must have telephoned through instructions that it was to be kept for her. The flowers, he noticed, were special ones: evidently the lady was something of a noise in the place.

His eyes travelled round the assembled company, but he saw no one whom he knew. The usual pairs; two or three parties of four – it might have been any of the smaller night clubs, save for one thing. There was about the whole atmosphere of the place a definite sense of smartness which as a rule is so conspicuously lacking from similar establishments. It might have been an overflow from the Embassy.

Suddenly there came a little buzz of interest, and Drummond glanced towards the door: the Comtessa had arrived. Escorted by an obsequious head waiter, she was crossing the room towards him, and he rose with a bow. The eyes of most people present followed her as she moved, and Drummond admitted to himself that an evening frock turned her into a ravishing beauty. She was wearing a clinging black chiffon dress, the long skirt of which floated gracefully out as she walked, and the low-cut back showed up the whiteness of her skin and her perfect figure.

"My dear Comtessa," he murmured, bending over her hand, "forgive my British bluntness, but you are superb."

"British bluntness, *mon ami*," she answered, with a dazzling smile, "is often preferable to Continental diplomacy."

"I left the question of food until you arrived," he said. "What about some caviare?"

"I adore it," she answered. "Just that, and nothing else."

He gave the necessary order; then he turned to his companion.

"Would you care to dance now, afterwards, or not at all?" he asked.

"Afterwards," she said. "For the moment I want to talk to you. I had no idea you knew Natalie so well."

"Natalie!" he murmured. "I presume you mean Madame Saumur?"

She nodded.

"She has talked a lot to me about you these last few days: in fact, I very nearly suggested that you should bring one of those nice friends of yours tonight and make a *parti carré*."

"That would have been most entertaining, Comtessa," he said, with a twinkle in his eyes. "I don't think I have ever had the pleasure of having supper with – er – Natalie. By the way, you must forgive me if I sometimes call her by the wrong name. In the past it has changed with such bewildering rapidity that it will be a little difficult to remember."

"It is about that past that I want to talk to you, Captain Drummond."

"That should certainly prove interesting, dear lady," he said grimly.

She laid her hand on his arm.

"No one regrets it more bitterly than she does – believe me. She came under the influence of that man Carl Peterson when she was little more than a child." The Comtessa broke off suddenly. "May I ask what you're laughing at?" she demanded.

"Forgive me, Comtessa," said Drummond, still shaking silently, "but this is richer than anything I ever dreamed of. You can't tell me that at this stage of history you're trying to kid me with the seduced girlhood stunt? Why, my dear soul, there were times when little Irma – I beg her pardon – Natalie left Carl Peterson at the post. If there was anything to it at all, I should say it was she who caught him young."

"Be that as it may, she's a changed woman now."

For a moment or two Drummond stared at her thoughtfully.

"What's the game, Comtessa?" he asked at length. "You are very far from being a fool: I also am conceited enough to regard myself as not quite an idiot. So once again I ask you – what's the game?"

"I find you somewhat *gauche*, Captain Drummond," she said coldly. "There is no game, as you call it. Natalie Saumur is a friend of mine, who admittedly in the past has been injudicious. She is sincerely sorry for that past, and wished me to tell you so. And I, believing that an Englishman generally accepted an apology in the spirit in which it was offered, undertook to give you her message."

"You used the word injudicious, Comtessa," he said quietly. "Is that how you would describe a cold-blooded attempt to murder my wife?"

She laughed merrily.

"My dear man," she cried, "you don't really imagine she ever intended to do it, do you? Why – she told me all about it: how you came in disguised as a nigger and all the rest of it."

"Shall we drop this fooling, Comtessa?" said Drummond, a little wearily. "If you are friends with her, you are friends with one of the most dangerous criminals in Europe. I know it, and all I'm wondering is whether you don't know it too."

"Are you aware what you're implying?" she cried angrily.

"Perfectly," he answered. "Come now, Comtessa, shall we put the cards on the table? Don't forget that that poor devil Marton and I did not sit in silence during the time he was at Merridale Hall."

Not a muscle of her face moved: her expression was one of bored indifference.

"Presumably not," she said. "What did you discuss: the weather?"

"Amongst other things," he answered. "And one of those other things was your charming self."

"Indeed! And why should he discuss me with a complete stranger?"

"You seemed to have a fascination for him which, now that I have met you, I can quite understand."

"You did not mention it at the inquest."

"There were several things I did not mention at the inquest," said Drummond calmly. "Muddy footmarks on the carpet for one."

"Really, Captain Drummond, you talk in riddles. What carpet are you alluding to?"

"The one in the smoking-room at Merridale Hall," he answered. "My dear Comtessa, there were more lies packed into that inquest than there are currants in a plum-pudding."

"You mean you perjured yourself?" she cried.

"In excellent company," he remarked. "Though my crime was more in the nature of suppressing the truth, rather than of inventing lies. By the way, how is your dear father, Mr Hardcastle?"

"Really, Captain Drummond, I find you perfectly intolerable," she exclaimed furiously. "First of all you are extremely rude to me personally, and then you imply that my father was telling lies. You know yourself that the only thing which it was agreed should not be mentioned was the appearance of the ghost."

He smiled faintly.

"Yes: that was the only thing which was *agreed*," he remarked.

"Captain Drummond," she said quietly, "I insist on your telling me what you are hinting at."

He looked at her steadily. What a superb actress she was! And for a moment he was tempted to tell her exactly what he was hinting at; then he decided to temporise.

"My dear Comtessa," he murmured, "aren't we becoming unduly serious? It was all most unpleasant, but it is over and done with. And the only thing that is worrying me is that perhaps I ought to have mentioned what Marton told me."

"What did he tell you?"

Was it his imagination, or was there a hint of anxiety in her voice?

He shook his head.

"I feel I must treat it as confidential even from you," he said gravely. "Let's talk of something else. You remember Peter Darrell, don't you? He is going down to your father's studio tomorrow to see if he is suitable for that vacancy that is being advertised."

And the next instant, to his unbounded amazement, he realised that he had scored a bull's-eye. Not by the quiver of an eyelid did he give away the fact; but he had noticed the knuckles of her right hand, which was loosely holding the edge of the table, suddenly gleam white. And the complete unexpectedness of it, for the moment, bewildered him. He had made the remark quite casually, for want of something better to say, and to extricate himself from a difficult position. Since Marton had said nothing to him, he couldn't very well tell the Comtessa what it was. And then to find that, by a sheer fluke, he had pierced her armour, was a most extraordinary thing – a thing, moreover, which required careful thought."

He drained his champagne and refilled both their glasses.

"He seems to fill the bill," he went on casually, "as far as physical requirements are concerned. You might put in a word for him, Comtessa."

"I'm afraid I have nothing to do with the running of the studio," she said. "By the way, how did you know it was my father's?"

Her voice was quite normal: save for that tell-tale tautening of her fingers, she had given no sign at all that he had got home.

"I think he mentioned it to me," he lied glibly. "And I was thinking of going down with Peter," he continued. "If Mr Hardcastle is there, he might perhaps allow me to look on for a bit."

She made some perfunctory reply, and then suggested they should dance, to which he at once agreed. He wanted time to think, and as the slow procession of packed sardines that now occupied the floor entailed no mental strain for steering, his brain could concentrate on this new development. Why had his casual remark upset her?

There could be no secret about the studio, since it was advertising publicly. What, then, had caused her agitation? And after puzzling it out through three fox-trots he decided that it could be only one thing – the fact that he had, quite accidentally, let his remark about Peter Darrell and the studio immediately follow the conversation about young Marton. In his mind there had been no connection whatever: in hers there had. And the thought at once opened up a new line of country.

Was it possible that the ordinary activities of the studio were a cloak for something criminal, and that Marton had found out about it? That that was why they had killed him, and that her agitation was due to the fear that he had been told about it by Marton on the afternoon of his death? The close juxtaposition of the two remarks might have made her think so – might have made her believe that he was playing a far deeper game than in reality he had been.

"I'm tired," she said suddenly, "and this crowd is insufferable. What were we talking about?" she continued as they sat down again. "Of course – I remember: your friend and the studio. Has he ever done any film work before?"

"Never," said Drummond. "But the advertisement says that previous experience is not essential. What film are they making?"

"I think it is called 'High Finance,'" she answered. "I know that part of it is going to be done down in Devonshire. That was why my father was so anxious to get hold of Glensham House. But perhaps Mr Marton told you that?"

"I don't think he actually mentioned that point," he said gravely.

He was conscious that she was watching him covertly, and he realised that it was going to be a battle of wits.

"But he talked about the film?"

"Vaguely," said Drummond. "In a general sort of way, you know."

"He was very keen to act himself, poor boy," she went on. "In fact, there was some talk of his having a small part in this very film."

"Indeed," he said. "A little difficult to fit in, I should think, with his other work."

"It was merely a walking-on part," she explained. "And, of course, he might not have been suitable."

"Quite," said Drummond politely, handing her his open cigarette case.

She took one, and as he held the match for her to light it he tried to puzzle out what was behind her apparently harmless remarks. What were they leading up to? Or was it just ordinary banal conversation?

"I'm surprised he didn't say that he might be acting, when he talked to you about the film," she said. "He was so very full of it, my father said, when he got to Glensham House."

"I think he was too nervy to talk about anything of that sort, Comtessa," remarked Drummond.

"I know – that money trouble. Captain Drummond, I rather blame myself over that. He used to take me out a good deal, and I suppose it must have cost more than he could afford. If only the poor boy had told me instead of posing as being very wealthy."

"The junior partner in a firm of solicitors is rarely very wealthy," he said curtly.

"If only I had realised that sooner," she sighed, glancing at her wrist-watch. "Will you think me very rude if I run away now? My father has a very important individual coming to lunch with him tomorrow, and I must appear at my best. I wonder if you know him by any chance – Sir Edward Greatorex?"

"Never heard of him in my life," he said. "Who is he?"

"A well-known business man," she answered. "But he spends most of his time abroad, so I'm not surprised that you don't know him."

He called the waiter and paid the bill; then he accompanied her to the door.

"I am calling for my father," she said, "so don't trouble to see me home. Good night. I wish I could persuade you about Natalie."

And ten minutes later she let herself into her maisonnette in South Audley Street. The sound of voices was coming from a downstair room, which ceased as she threw open the door. Hardcastle, Slingsby, and Penton were sitting round the table with a bottle of whisky between them, whilst curled up in an easy-chair was Natalie Saumur.

"How did the party go?" cried Hardcastle.

"Did you tell that guy, Tom, where your studio was?" she said as she flung off her cloak.

"I never even told him I had a studio," he answered. "What's happened, kid?"

"Just this. Captain Hugh Drummond has got to go."

"You mean he's wise to things?"

The three men sat motionless, staring at her.

"He's wise to a great deal too much. Especially about that young fool's death And when I tried the Christian repentance stunt about Natalie it didn't cut enough ice to keep a louse in cold storage."

"Damn all that," snarled Hardcastle. "What about the big thing?"

"I don't know, Tom: frankly, I don't know." She lit a cigarette and sat down. "He started talking about the studio: one of his friends is rolling up tomorrow in answer to the advertisement – that fair-haired man, Darrell. Drummond is going down too: wants to know if you'll let him look on. Now how did he know it was your studio? He said to me that you had told him."

"You mean Marton may have told him," said Penton softly.

"Exactly. And if he told him that, he may have told him other things as well."

"Then surely he would have informed the police," said Slingsby.

And then, for the first time, the woman in the chair spoke. Her voice was deep and musical: her English held no trace of any foreign accent.

"That is where you are wrong," she said. "Hugh Drummond does not tell the police unless it is absolutely essential. In all the years I have known him he has never once called them in: he prefers to keep the thing to himself."

"Then what do you suggest?" demanded Hardcastle.

She lit a fresh cigarette from the stump of the old one.

"Let us see where we stand," she answered. "The mere fact that you have not mentioned the studio to him proves nothing. There is no secret about the matter: there are several quite ordinary ways in which he could have found out that you had rented it. At the same time, I quite admit that Marton *may* have told him, and therefore we had better act on that assumption."

She paused suddenly, and a spasm of anger shook her.

"You damned fools – the lot of you – for letting that young cub know the whole truth. If it hadn't been for that this situation would never have arisen. However" – she controlled herself and continued calmly – "it is no good crying over that. The situation has arisen, and we've got to deal with it."

"Give me his address," said Penton harshly, "and leave him to me. I've dealt with his sort before."

The woman in the chair looked at him with a pitying smile.

"My poor friend," she murmured, "do not be more ridiculous than God intended you to be. You have no more chance of dealing single-handed with Hugh Drummond than a board-school child would have. He would simply play with you, as he has in the past with men of four times your ability. You can't handle him that way."

Penton, his face white with rage, started angrily to his feet.

"Sit down," she said curtly. "This is not the time for quarrelling: too much is at stake. After months of preparation, we are on the verge of pulling off the biggest *coup* of our lives, and once again – Drummond intervenes."

For a moment or two the others stared at her speechless; the expression on her face was almost that of a mad woman. And they realised that her mind was back in the past: she was thinking of those other encounters with this same large Englishman. Then abruptly the look faded: she was cool and collected once more.

"It is a pity," she went on thoughtfully, "that I met your train at Paddington, *chérie*. There was no harm in your trying to pretend about me tonight, but I knew it would be useless: he and I know one another too well. By the way, do you know where he is living now?"

"Queen Anne's Mansions, my dear one," came a genial voice from the door.

SAPPER

Drummond, his hat tilted on the back of his head, his hands in his pockets, was standing there, regarding them with a benevolent smile.

CHAPTER 6

For a moment or two there was dead silence in the room; then Hardcastle sprang to his feet.

"How the devil did you get in here, damn you!" he shouted.

Drummond held up a protesting hand.

"My dear sir, ladies are present. I will therefore remove my hat. Please take care of it: it isn't paid for yet. How did I get in? you asked. Through an open window in the basement. And I must beg of you, Comtessa, to remonstrate with your cook. A table on which I inadvertently sat was covered with old tea-leaves."

"How did you find this house, Captain Drummond?" said the Comtessa quietly.

"My heart smote me, dear lady, when you left the Custard Pot alone: there are so many rude men in London. So, waving my hand in sprightly fashion to that large beef-eater man at the door, I leaped into another taxi and told the driver to follow you. And he, scenting romance, and therefore a large tip, complied in masterly manner with my request."

A faint smile was playing round his lips: the looks passing between the three men had not escaped him.

"I think it is the grossest piece of impertinence I have ever heard of in my life," she said icily. "What is there to prevent me ringing up the police and giving you in charge for house-breaking?"

"Absolutely nothing," said Drummond brightly. "There is the telephone in the corner."

She bit her lip, and turned appealingly to Madame Saumur, who was staring thoughtfully at Drummond.

"Look here, young man," said Penton aggressively, "are you going to clear out of your own free will, or am I going to pitch you out on your ear?"

"Not on my ear, Harold, I beg of you," cried Drummond anxiously. "I shall probably have to consult an aurist anyhow tomorrow. The draught through that key-hole of yours is positively wicked."

"You mean that you've been listening?" said Hardcastle softly.

"Yes, dear Tom. My ear has been glued to the orifice for quite a time. I heard you all being ticked off by Irma – I beg your pardon, Madame, Natalie – you naughty things."

The three men began to crowd in on him, and Drummond's smile grew more pronounced.

"Apropos of ringing up the police, Comtessa," he remarked, "I wouldn't be surprised if there isn't one knocking about outside. There was when I got out of my taxi thirty or forty yards away. A charming young fellow: a credit to the Force. And the instant I saw him I felt impelled to give him my celebrated impersonation of a gentleman who has taken one over the eight. 'Ole friend of my youth,' I hiccupped at him, 'my name is Drummond, Captain Hugh Drummond. And I live at Queen Anne's Mansions. What, then, you ask me, am I doing up here? I will tell you. I am visiting a lady – a very beautiful lady – the Comtessa Bartelozzi. But, my dear old officer, like so many beautiful ladies, she has a jealous husband. If therefore my dead body is found lying about the streets you will know where to start inquiries.' Then I kissed him on both cheeks and we parted."

"I don't know what the devil to do with you," snarled Hardcastle.

"There would seem to be two alternatives," said Drummond affably. "Either get my young friend from outside, or else offer me a drink and we will chat on this and that. Of course, there is a third – we might have a rough house. But if we do, this furniture is going to look a bit tired tomorrow."

He strolled over to the fireplace and lit a cigarette.

"Do you know, Irma darling," he murmured, "I don't think that I like your new friends – always excepting this most delightful lady, of course – as much as I did Carl. You, if I may say so, are still your adorable self, but I don't know that I want any of them to tuck me up at night."

"So we meet again, Drummond, do we?" she said.

"My dear," he cried, "I protest. As a conversational effort after all these years, that remark is not worthy of you."

"How long have you been listening outside that door?"

"From the acute agony in my ear I should put it at a day or two," he answered. "But maybe it was worth it. Anyway, here we all are – a merry united party, brimming over with girlish secrets. Tell me – just to satisfy my vulgar curiosity – why did you murder young Marton?"

Once again dead silence settled on the room.

"He seemed to me," continued Drummond calmly, "a poor sort of specimen, but comparatively harmless withal."

"Are you mad?" said Hardcastle at length. "What possible reason could we have for killing him?"

"That's just what I'm asking you, Tom. It seems such a drastic method of dealing with the poor bloke."

"I presume you're trying to be funny, Captain Drummond," answered Hardcastle. "Or else your conversation with the policeman outside is indicative of your true condition. Why, if you suffered from this absurd delusion, did you say nothing about it at the inquest?"

"Middle stump gone west," said Drummond. "But I was forgetting that you know but little of our national game. I will tell you. I said nothing about it because, though I knew it, I was, and am, quite unable to prove it."

"Then how dare you make such a monstrous accusation?" shouted Slingsby. "Are you aware, you young cub, that we can sue you for libel?"

"Of course," agreed Drummond pleasantly. "Why not start proceedings tomorrow? My old friend Peanut of Peanut, Walnut and Chestnut has always acted for me in similar cases in the past. And in the meantime, may I help myself to a drink? In the past, Madame" – he turned to the woman in the chair, who was still watching him steadily – "I was a little chary of drinking at any of your parties, but I feel that, since you were not expecting me, this whisky will prove quite safe."

He splashed some soda into his glass and returned to the fireplace. It was a dangerous game that he was playing, and no one was more alive to it than Drummond himself. As a matter of fact he had heard very little outside the door; he had only got there a few seconds before he had heard the question as to where he lived. But he fully realised that whatever he might have heard would prove useless if they rang up the police. It was only his word against all of theirs, and they would simply deny his statements. Further, he had put himself outside the law by breaking into the house in the first place. In fact, they held every card except one: and, if they had only known it, they held that too. But because they did not know it, they dared not ring up the police station, for fear of what he might say, not with regard to the past, but with regard to the future. And the humour of the situation was that on that point they need not have feared at all.

"I don't think you're being at all matey," he remarked after a while. "I seem to be doing all the talking."

"As far as I can make out, Drummond," said Madame Saumur quietly, "your assertion is that young Marton was murdered by these three gentlemen."

"Exactly, Madame. You have put it in a nutshell."

"And, in view of the evidence, what makes you think so?"

"The conviction that he was not murdered by Morris."

She raised her eyebrows.

"Really. Your logic appears to me a little thin. Why because, for some obscure reason of your own, you consider Morris innocent, should you consider them guilty?"

"The reason is hardly obscure, but very simple. They were the only people who could have done it."

"My recollection of the evidence hardly bears that out. Who first found the body?"

And for the fraction of a second Drummond stiffened: all too clearly he saw the line she was going to take up. But his voice was perfectly calm as he answered – "My friends and I."

"Indeed," she murmured. "Then it seems to me that you also could have done it."

"Except for the trifling difficulty that the first thing that took us upstairs was the sight of the blood on the ceiling."

"So you say. I regret that I am unable to believe you. I have only your word for it."

"What possible reason could we have for murdering him?"

"What possible reason had they?"

Drummond began to laugh, though his brain was working at full pressure. A super bluff, of course; but a clever one. It was a bold attempt to force his hand one way or the other.

"Come, come, my dear lady," he answered, "you can't expect to catch an old stager like myself quite as easily as that. Marton when I saw him was in a state of pitiable agitation, far too pronounced to be accounted for by such comparative trifles as over-drinking and late hours. He was frightened out of his wits about something, and since I'd never seen the fellow before, it couldn't have been anything to do with me. A few hours later he is found battered to death at Glensham House. The connection seems obvious, doesn't it?"

"Once again we have only your word for all this," she said.

"And a pretty line in words it is, too," he remarked. "Irma, my pet, you have meant much to me in my young life, and I can assure you that any faint lingering doubts I possessed as to what happened that night at Glensham House were dispelled the moment I saw you at Paddington. And one other thing I propose to say," he continued grimly, swinging round on the three men. "Of all the damnable methods of killing the poor devil, yours won in a canter. I admit that it was quick to take advantage of Morris having blundered into the house, and act as you did on the spur of the moment. But it shows a cold-blooded ferocity that I have never heard equalled before. And I tell you here and now I'm going to get level with you over it."

The masks were off their faces now: in another moment the three of them would have been at him, and he crouched a little, waiting for the attack. And then Madame Saumur's quiet laugh broke the tension.

"The same old Drummond," she cried, "but this time with quite a hive of bees in his bonnet. Listen, *mon ami*, and we will see just where we stand. Evidently nothing that we can say will get this absurd delusion out of your head. And really, my dear Hugh, as far as we are concerned, it can remain there. I think I have shown you fairly clearly that, with your strange obsession to vindicate Morris, you and your friends have laid yourselves open – in the eyes of the police – to grave suspicion yourselves. In fact, were I in the police, I should regard your monstrous allegation as being due to a desire to cover your own crime by accusing someone else."

"Why not ring up the police now?" he said quietly.

"For a very good and simple reason," she answered. "My friends and I are engaged at the moment in a very important business deal. The last thing we desire is the publicity which would inevitably attend the investigation of your ridiculous charge. We really have not got the time for such folly. And it is for that reason, and that reason only, that we have tolerated your monstrous impertinence in breaking in here tonight."

"Splendid," laughed Drummond. "I congratulate you. And supposing I went to Scotland Yard, and told them one or two things. Emphasised, for instance, the strange fact that the weapon with which it was done has never been found: mentioned the footmarks on the carpet at Merridale Hall, and a few other points of that sort."

"You pain me, Drummond," she said: "positively pain me. In the past, my friend, you always had a rooted objection to the police, and this time it has recoiled on you. Their first remark to you would be to ask why these things were not mentioned at the inquest. You can't disregard them, you know, and then call them in. No, *mon ami*: somehow or other I don't quite see you going to Scotland Yard. You would get it – what is your English phrase? – most dreadfully in the neck if you did."

"Perhaps you're right," he agreed. "You were always quick on the uptake, weren't you, dear one? And so, that being that, I will reluctantly bid you *au revoir*, as I don't think we shall get very much further at the moment."

He crossed the room and picked up his hat.

"Doubtless we shall meet anon," he remarked from the door. "And please don't forget to tell your cook about the tea-leaves, Comtessa."

He let himself into the street, which was deserted, and began to stroll towards Piccadilly. And as he rounded the first corner, he almost ran into a man in evening clothes who was coming the other way.

"A thousand apologies, sir," remarked the stranger, taking off a soft black hat. "Could you tell me if I am anywhere near South Audley Street?"

He spoke with a strong foreign accent, and Drummond, glancing at his face by the light of a street lamp, put him down as an Italian.

"You are actually in South Audley Street," he answered. "I have just been walking along it."

"Thank you," said the other. "Sorry to have troubled you, but I am a stranger to London."

"Not at all," remarked Drummond politely. "Good night."

He walked on, and in a moment the incident had passed from his mind. Other somewhat disquieting thoughts occupied it, which, put in a nutshell, boiled down to the conviction that he had made a damned fool of himself. Useless to argue that he would do the same thing again: useless to say that the impulse to enter the room on hearing Irma's question had been so overwhelming that he could never have resisted it: the fact remained that he had acted like an ass.

Had he stopped outside the door, he might, and probably would, have heard something of value; as it was, he had learned nothing at all. And not only that, he had successfully put them on their guard. He had confirmation, which he did not require, that in spite of their indignant denials they had murdered Marton: no business, however important, would have prevented them ringing up the police had they been innocent. But with regard to the all-important point as to why they had done so, he was as much in the dark as ever.

Another thing, too, would be an inevitable result of his foolishness: he would not be received with a brass band and a red carpet at the studio. Having called the owner a murderer, he could scarcely expect to be greeted by him like a long-lost brother. Moreover, the same thing applied to Peter Darrell. It would be useless for him to turn up in the morning in answer to the advertisement. And the devil of it was that he felt instinctively that in the studio lay the solution to the whole problem.

One 't' had certainly been crossed as a result of the interview: the men were an ugly bunch of customers. His bluff concerning the policeman had worked all right this time, but he was under no delusions with regard to the future. Up to date they had not been sure as to what he knew: now that uncertainty was over. And he realised that if an opportunity arose they would have no scruples whatever in putting him out of the way if they could.

However, that aspect of the matter troubled him not at all: he had always preferred to have the gloves off. What did annoy him was that, as a result of his impetuosity in entering the room when he did, he was fighting in the dark. And as he let himself into his flat he was cursing himself wholeheartedly.

A light was shining under the sitting-room door: Darrell and Jerningham were inside waiting for him.

"Chaps," he remarked, "you here perceive the most triple-distilled damned fool in London."

They listened in silence while he told them what had happened, and then Ted Jerningham spoke.

"It's certainly not your brightest effort, old boy," he remarked. "In fact, it seems to me you've completely queered our pitch. We don't know where to begin."

"We begin in the studio, Ted, if only we can get inside the bally place."

"Look here," said Darrell, "Algy answers to that advertisement just as well as I do. And they don't know him."

"Irma does," said Drummond.

"We'll have to chance her not being there. I saw him this evening, as it happens, beetling round at Ciro's. It's a late night there: let's ring up and see if we can get hold of him."

"Right you are, Peter: it's worth trying. Tell him to come round here."

They caught him just as he was leaving, and a quarter of an hour later he arrived.

"I have met," he remarked on entering, "the only woman in the world. Her charm is as of an exotic orchid, her eyes are as mountain violets. And, straight from her arms, I come to you three horrible thugs. Give me rare wine, or I swoon at the contrast."

"Sit down, wart-face," said Drummond, "and cease talking such unmitigated bilge. You're going on the films tomorrow."

"I'm going on the what?" cried the other, a cigarette halfway to his lips.

"Listen, Algy," said Drummond, "the game is afoot. Who do you think we've butted into once more?"

Algy Longworth stared at him in amazement.

"Not Irma," he burst out at length. "Don't tell me that, old lad."

"Just her, and no one else," answered Drummond. "How much are you round the chest, Algy?"

"Look here," said the other feebly, "are you fellows tight, or am I?"

"Put your nose into that," cried Darrell, throwing the copy of *Film Echoes* at him. "It's the paragraph marked with a blue pencil."

"But what the deuce has this got to do with Irma?" he demanded after he had read it.

"Get outside some beer, Algy, and listen," said Drummond. "We've been having a bit of fun lately."

"I saw you were getting mixed up in something or other down in Devonshire," said the other. "In fact, I very nearly came down to see what was up. Tell me all about it."

Briefly Drummond ran over the events of the past few days, and when he had finished, Algy Longworth nodded thoughtfully.

"I get you," he said. "Rightly or wrongly, you believe that the key of the mystery lies in Blackwater studio, and you want me to see if I can spot anything."

"That's the notion, old lad. It's a forlorn hope, and if by chance Irma is there and sees you, you'll probably get bunged into the river. But that won't do you any harm: it's an awfully jolly sort of river."

"Oh! yeah – Cuthbert," grunted the other. "But, joking apart, old boy, it is, as you say, a mighty forlorn hope. I mean if there is any dirty work going on down there, it's not going to be where anyone walking in casual like is going to see it. The blokes will probably take one look at my face, burst into floods of tears, and that will end the interview."

"Can't help it, Algy: we've got to try it. It's the only hope. Why, dash it all, old boy, you might even get taken on, in which case you'd have the run of the studio."

"And get thrown daily into the Blackwater," said Longworth gloomily. "Damn it! I don't want to act in a film, Hugh. I am sick with love: every moment of my life is occupied."

"You haven't started to quote Ella Wheeler Wilcox at her, have you?" demanded Drummond suspiciously.

"Only one or two chosen fragments," said the other.

"Then it's high time, for the poor girl's sake, that you vanished from her sight. The last wretched woman you treated in that way had to go into a mental home. You're a menace, Algy, when you're in that condition. What is she like, this new wench of yours?"

With a howl of anguish, Darrell leaped from his seat.

"Are you mad, Hugh? You'll start him off."

"I find you rather offensive, Peter," said Longworth with dignity. "She is dark – "

"We'll take that for granted," cut in Drummond hurriedly. "What I want to know is whether she has a face at which an ordinary man can look without using smoked glasses. Yes or no."

"Most emphatically yes," spluttered Longworth indignantly.

"Right. Then take her down with you tomorrow," said Drummond. "When you're in love, your brain is more microscopic than usual, and she might very likely notice one or two things that you wouldn't. Tell her a certain amount, but not everything. Leave out all the Devonshire part of the show: just tell her to keep her eyes open and see if she can spot anything suspicious. She might even apply for a part herself. What is the matter with you, Algy? Are you in pain?"

"Listen, chaps," he said thoughtfully. "Two days ago, when I first met her at a cocktail party, and we talked awhile on the drama and bi-metallism, she said something about films."

He frowned horribly at the mental strain.

"Was it that she adored Charlie Chaplin, or was it that she herself had once played a part at Elstree?"

"There would seem to be a trifling difference," said Drummond mildly.

"At any rate, I think it's a deuced good idea," went on Longworth happily. "We will have a healthy day in Kent tomorrow."

"Essex, you damned fool! And no dallying on the road. If you want to quote Wilcox at her, you'll quote it in the studio. Now, push off: I want to go to bed."

But for a long time after the others had gone Hugh Drummond sat on smoking. And when at last he got up and switched off the light, there was a glint in his eyes which those who knew him well could have interpreted at once. He had evolved a plan, and the plan seemed to him to be good.

Moreover, it still seemed good to him when his servant Denny arrived the next morning with tea and the daily papers. Many an idea conceived overnight fails to stand the remorseless logic of the following day, but this one did. It was simple, and more or less foolproof, and for the space of two cigarettes he cogitated over it; then he opened *The Times*, more from habit than from any desire to see the news. And as he glanced down the Court Circular one item caught his eye.

"Sir Edward Greatorex arrived at the Ritz Carlton yesterday afternoon from Berlin. He expects to remain in London about a fortnight."

The name seemed vaguely familiar, and for a while he lay in bed trying to remember where he had heard it. And then suddenly it came to him: Greatorex was the man the Comtessa had mentioned overnight as lunching with Hardcastle that day. A well-known business man, was how she described him, in which case he presumably was quite capable of looking after himself. For his sake, at any rate, reflected Drummond as he went into the bathroom, he hoped so.

Breakfast over, he proceeded to ring up Algy Longworth.

"Look here, old boy," he said, "there's a point that occurred to me after you'd gone last night. If Irma is down at the studio you're stung anyway. But if she isn't it would be better for you not to give your real name. For if by any chance they do take you, she will certainly get to hear of it, and then the fat will be in the fire and you'll get the push."

"Right you are, Hugh," came the answer. "I've just rung up Laura, and she's all on for coming. And she has acted in a small part."

"You didn't say anything about what I told you last night over the 'phone, did you?"

"Not a word. I'm lunching with her, and we'll push down afterwards. Where shall I find you this evening to report the doings?"

"Come to the club, Algy, about nine."

He rang off, and lit a cigarette thoughtfully; then he shouted for Denny.

"We're on the warpath again, old warrior," he said as his servant came in. "And for the next few days I shall be here, and I shall not be here. Do you get me?"

"You mean, sir, that you wish to be thought within when in reality you are without."

"More or less, Denny. There will probably be a caller or two, and almost certainly some telephone messages. You will have to deal with them, and either I have just gone out or I am just coming in. If at luncheon-time, I am feeding at a private house – not an hotel: don't forget that. Dinner the same thing. In short, I want you to give the impression that I am leading my ordinary normal life in London. Do you get me?"

"Perfectly, sir. I am to be vague as to your actual movements, but definite that movement is taking place."

"You've hit it. I shall sleep here tonight: after that it's doubtful. Look up my small automatic some time today, and see that it is oiled and pulling light."

"Very good, sir. And in case of necessity where can I get hold of you?"

Drummond thought for a moment or two.

"Post Office, Colchester," he said. "Address me as Henry Johnson, and use a common envelope."

"Exactly, sir," said Denny, making a note on his cuff. "Is that all, sir?"

"Yes, Denny, it is. Give me my hat and stick: the club will find me for the next hour or so. Should anyone ring up, you can tell 'em so."

Refusing a taxi, he started to stroll across the Park. The birds were singing: the morning was perfect, and as he turned into his club, he felt at peace with the world.

Two men whom he knew slightly were in the smoking-room, and he nodded to them as he passed. And he was just going to sit down when a sentence from one of them caught his ear.

"I see that fellow Greatorex has arrived in London."

The speaker was a stockbroker, and, acting on a sudden impulse, Drummond crossed over to where they were sitting.

"I couldn't help over-hearing your remark, Blackton," he said. "Who is this man Greatorex? Somebody mentioned him last night, and seemed surprised I'd never heard of him. Business bird of sorts, isn't he?"

"I don't think he'd be particularly flattered at that description," answered the other, with a laugh. "Sir Edward Greatorex is a man before whom Governments tremble. He's an international financier with a finger in innumerable pies."

"Is he wealthy?"

"Wealthy! My dear fellow, he's one of the three richest men in the world. He *is* the richest, save for one or two Indian Maharajahs, outside America."

"What is he doing over here?"

"Ask me another: I'm not on dining terms with him. And he is one of the hardest men to get near there is. Making a few more millions, I suppose."

"I see," said Drummond. "No wonder people were surprised last night at my ignorance."

He lounged back to his own chair thoughtfully. What was a man like that doing in the Hardcastle galaxy? True, Hardcastle was reputed to be wealthy, but Greatorex seemed pretty high game for him to have a business lunch with. He glanced at his watch: a sudden idea had come to him. It was just half-past eleven: the bar at the Ritz Carlton would be open. Charlie, the barman, was an old friend: he would go round there and have a cocktail. With luck he might see the man himself: anyway, Charlie was a positive fountain of gossip.

The bar was empty when he got there, save for the barman polishing glasses, who hailed him delightedly.

"Good morning, sir," he cried. "It's a long while since you've been here."

" 'Morning, Charlie," said Drummond. "Your drinks are too damned expensive for anyone short of a millionaire to come here often. But since I am here, I'll gargle with a Bronx."

"How are you, sir?" continued the other. "You're looking as fit as ever."

"Just living from hour to hour. Anyone interesting stopping in the pub?"

Charlie shook his head.

"Business very slack, sir. We've had a good season on the whole, but it's pretty well over. Sir Edward Greatorex is here for a fortnight, but he's no help to me."

"Even he can't afford to pay your prices, I suppose?"

The barman grinned.

"Strict teetotaler, sir."

"What sort of a fellow is he, Charlie?"

"Well, sir," said the other confidentially, "the last time he was here he stayed for three weeks. He had the royal suite, and most of his meals were served in it. And when he left he tipped the floor waiter a quid in mistake for a ten-bob note, and then wanted change when he found out what he'd done."

"Mean as that, is he?"

"Mean, sir! Why, if people write him enclosing stamped envelopes for his reply, he first of all floats the stamps off, and then he borrows the hotel gum to stick 'em on his own letters."

"That's a good 'un, Charlie," laughed Drummond.

"I wouldn't be that poor bloke of a secretary of his – not if you paid me five thousand a year," went on the other. "Treats him like a dog, he does."

He gave a sudden cough, and, with a warning look at Drummond, turned to greet a man who had just entered the bar.

"Good morning, sir. The usual, I suppose?"

"Please, Charlie."

And Drummond, happening to glance at the newcomer, gave a little start of surprise. It was the man who had asked him the way to South Audley Street the previous night. He knew him immediately, though the other showed no sign of recognition. And then he remembered that during the few seconds they had talked his back had been to the street lamp, leaving his face in shadow.

For a moment or two he debated whether he should remind him of their meeting and ask him if he had found his destination all right: then he decided not to. He had no desire to drink with him, which the other would probably suggest if he spoke. So he picked up a midday paper and ran his eye down the racing news, until the man, having finished his drink, left the bar.

"Funny we should have been talking about him, sir, just as he came in," said Charlie.

Drummond stared at him in surprise.

"You mean that he is the secretary?" he said at length.

"Of course, sir. That's why I coughed."

"Well, I'm damned," said Drummond. "I thought you merely meant that someone was coming in and you wanted to change the conversation. So he is the secretary, is he? Charlie, give me another Bronx."

The barman looked at him curiously.

"Almost looks as if you knew him, sir."

"No, I don't know him; but I've seen him. He has the hell of a time, has he?"

"All of that, from what I hear, sir. And yet he seems to stick it all right. He was with Sir Edward the last time he was here, and that's eighteen months ago."

"Italian, I should imagine."

Charlie nodded.

"Gardini is his name – Benito Gardini. He generally comes in here in the morning for a quick one. Your Bronx, sir."

"Thank you, Charlie. Have one yourself. Look here, could you find out something for me? I want to know if Sir Edward is lunching in his suite today, or whether he's coming downstairs."

"Certainly, sir: nothing easier." He turned round. "Bert!" he called.

A youth in his shirt-sleeves popped his head out of an inner sanctum.

"Yes, Mr Green."

"Put on your coat and run upstairs to Number 40. Get hold of Leonard and find out whether lunch is being served in the room or not. And look slippy."

"I'm rather curious to see Sir Edward," said Drummond, as the boy departed. "I've heard so much about him, but to the best of my belief I've never even seen a picture of him."

"He doesn't look a bad sort at all, sir," said Charlie. "Tall, with a small fair beard. But handsome is as handsome does. Well, Bert?"

"Number 40 is going hout for lunch, Mr Green," said the boy. "Leonard don't know where, but 'e 'eard them talking abaht it this morning. There's a car coming for them at 'alf-past twelve."

"Well done, Bert," said Drummond, handing him a shilling. "Be sure and put it in the plate on Sunday."

He glanced at his watch: twenty minutes past twelve. He would take up a position in the lounge that commanded both exits, and since the secretary would almost certainly accompany him, at any rate as far as the car, there would be no difficulty in spotting him.

He found a suitable chair and lit a cigarette. The Comtessa's house was in South Audley Street: was that where the secretary had been going? He wished now that he had waited to see, but there had been nothing in the harmless request for direction which could possibly have aroused his suspicions. And so it was the purest guesswork that her house had been his destination, but if the guess was correct, it was a funny hour to make a call.

A sudden stir in the lounge roused him from his reverie. Two men were coming down the stairs, and one of them was Gardini. And for the second time that morning Drummond, as he studied the other, was conscious of a little shock of surprise. For somewhere, at some time or other, he had seen him before. The man's face was definitely familiar, and for a long time after they had passed through the lounge he sat on trying to puzzle out where they could have met. But try as he would, it eluded him, and when finally he left the hotel himself, he could only imagine that Sir Edward must have been pointed out to him on one of his previous visits to England, and that he had forgotten all about it. In any event, his hour at the Ritz Carlton had not been wasted.

For the rest of the afternoon he killed time: there was nothing to do now except wait for Algy Longworth. He turned up just after nine, and a glance at his face showed that something had happened.

"The most extraordinary thing, old boy," he cried. "They have engaged both of us."

"The devil they have," said Drummond. "Let's hear all about it."

"We rolled up to the studio at half-past three," began the other. "And the first thing that hit one was the army of blokes who had evidently come in answer to the advertisement. They were all over the place, scowling at one another, and it struck me that little Algy wasn't going to have much of a chance. However, I beetled up to a door-keeper warrior, and told him what I wanted.

" 'First left, second right,' he said wearily. 'There are only about sixty in front of you.'

"So we joined the glad throng, and after a while we noticed one thing. We might be sixtieth, but it wasn't going to take long. Each interview was the shortest thing on record: it was more like a procession passing by a judge. At last our turn came, and in I barged with Laura. A damned great fellow in shirt-sleeves with a cigar in his mouth was sitting at a table. He took one look at me and shook his head.

" 'No go,' he said. 'Next.'

"But I thought you said they'd taken you," cried Drummond.

"Wait a moment, old boy: I'm coming to that. Out we pushed again, wondering how we could get a closer look at the place. All we'd seen up to date were a couple of passages and a small room, and from what Laura had said on the way down I gathered it was about all we were likely to see. The door into the actual studio was shut, and when we started to go in the commissionaire fellow let out a shout.

" 'Not allowed in there,' he cried, 'without a permit.'

"And we were just on the point of pushing off when another man in shirt-sleeves came dodging through the crowd that still blocked the passage.

" 'Hi! you,' he called out to me, 'you're wanted. Come back to the office, and the young lady too.'

"So back we went, and found the big man still sitting there.

" 'Are you both wanting engagements?' he asked.

" 'That's the idea,' I said. 'Anything doing?'

" 'Not with regard to the advertisement,' he answered. 'You don't fill that bill. But it occurred to me after you'd gone that as there are two of you, we might be able to arrange something. Ever done any film work?'

"I told him that I hadn't, but that Laura had, and to cut a long story short, we were engaged at five pounds a week each. She gave her real name of Laura Mainwaring: I gave mine as Algy Wentworth.

" 'I don't quite know what we shall fix you with,' he said in conclusion, 'but there are one or two small parts that remain to be filled. Mr Slingsby' – he was the man who had come after us and fetched us back – 'will take you along into the studio and introduce you to our producer, Mr Haxton. You'd better just have a look round and get the atmosphere of the piece we are doing. Society picture, with strong human appeal.'

"So off we toddled to meet Mr Haxton, and to begin with Mr Haxton was not amused. He wanted to know what the adjectival hell he was expected to do with us, as he couldn't possibly begin shooting our bit for a week at least. However, Slingsby pacified him, and that was that. So the net result is that we have both been taken on, and if there's anything to find out we've got a reasonable chance of doing it."

"Did everything seem quite normal?" asked Drummond.

"Absolutely," said the other. "We watched 'em shoot an impassioned love-scene between the two principals; then we strolled about."

"What sort of place is it?"

"Pretty big. Laura says you could do three or four pictures there at the same time."

"Are you both going down tomorrow?"

"That's the notion. What are you going to do?"

"I shall totter about somewhere, Algy," he said vaguely. "I might even put my nose in at the studio: if I do, of course you don't know me."

"What happens if I find out anything?" demanded the other.

"If I'm in the club you can come and tell me about it; and if I'm not, drop me a line to the flat."

"Right you are, old boy. Laura and I are having a bite somewhere, so I'll push off."

The door swung to behind him, and Drummond ordered a whisky and soda. The big man had presumably been Penton: why had he changed his mind over engaging Algy Longworth? Was it that he genuinely did want to fill two minor parts; if so, there were scores of actors with experience from whom he could make a selection. So why Algy? It was possible that the two of them going in together had influenced him, but if that were so why didn't he think of it at once? And he was still cogitating over the problem when an hour later he switched off his bedroom light.

CHAPTER 7

Sir Edward Greatorex was enjoying himself. Stretched at ease in the most comfortable chair of his luxurious suite at the Ritz Carlton, he had permitted himself the extravagance of a cigar. On a small table at his side stood a shaded reading-lamp and a bottle of Vichy water, on his knees were some typewritten sheets of paper clipped together at one corner.

The title of the document he was reading was "High Finance," an eminently suitable one for the great financier, but one which, strangely enough, from time to time caused him to laugh, or at any rate give vent to a noise which was as close to laughter as he ever got. Occasionally, too, he frowned, making little clucking sounds indicative of displeasure.

But if any onlooker who had been privileged to intrude on Sir Edward's privacy had imagined that these manifestations were due to scorn or disapproval of the financial opinions expressed by the writer, he would have been sadly wrong. If, further, he had peeped over the reader's shoulder, he would have been hard put to it to reconcile the title with the script. What, for instance, had the following paragraph to do with the finer points of international exchanges?

"Paula enters the room, and believing for the moment that it is empty, allows her utter despair to show on her features. Ruin stares the man she loves in the face: foolishly, perhaps, but not fraudulently, he has been dabbling in interests which were too big for him, and now he has lost everything…"

"Serves the damned fool right," came a mutter from the chair.

" 'Is there nothing to be done?' she asks herself again. Must she stand by and see Jack go down and out? Distraught, she turns towards the window, and for the first time she sees that the man principally responsible for her lover's ruin is in the room watching her with an amused smile."

Once again Sir Edward laid the typescript on his knee: that, he reflected, was the stuff to give 'em. He fancied himself in that part, and with a cautious glance towards the next room, where his secretary was going through the evening mail, he got up and stood in front of the glass. Amused smile – slightly contemptuous, but slightly pitying. He rehearsed two or three effects, and Gardini, entering the room noiselessly, retreated badly shaken. Mercifully Sir Edward had not seen him, and after a quick drink to restore his nerves he gave a short cough and returned.

"Are you ready, sir, for your mail?" he asked deferentially.

Sir Edward reseated himself.

"In a minute or two," he said. "I like this stuff, Benito."

The secretary breathed more freely: 'Benito' evenings were all right: 'Gardini' ones were a toss up: 'you damned infernal idiot' ones distinctly trying.

"I think it's very good, Sir Edward," he agreed. "It's got punch in it, the action is rapid, and the love interest holds one."

Sir Edward snorted contemptuously.

"Far too much of it," he cried. "I shall speak to Hardcastle about that. Some of it might be cut, and the part in the office in

Paris where Sir John is making up his mind whether to crush Bessonia or not should, I think, be considerably strengthened."

"Perhaps so, sir," said the other tactfully. "Of course, one has to remember that the film-going public insist on having love, and you won't have a success unless you give it to them."

At which point the intelligent reader will guess that the document was not concerned with the flight of the dollar, but was a brief scenario of the film being made at the Blackwater studio. But what the intelligent reader will find a little difficult to understand is why the said scenario should have found its way into the hands, and the interested hands, of a man like Sir Edward Greatorex. And to make that clear it is necessary to reveal a secret, jealously guarded save from the very few, of Sir Edward's mentality.

Most male children have yearned passionately to drive a railway engine: to be a drum major: even perchance to draw a gun on sight and shoot apples flung in the air into a thousand pieces. And since most male children do none of these things in later life, presumably the yearning ceases with advancing years.

In Sir Edward's case, however, the yearning had been a different one and had not ceased. From the moment when he had first seen Douglas Fairbanks slaying thousands, and had watched Charlie Chaplin's magic feet twinkling over the screen, he had had but one real ambition, beside which a few odd millions more or less counted for nothing at all. And that ambition had been to play a leading part in a big film.

He had realised that he could hardly hope to compete against either of them in their own particular line: in fact, he had not wished to. A strong and silent role was what he passionately desired to play: a great statesman, calm and unruffled, steering the national ship through troubled waters; a great surgeon with life and death in his steady hand; a great financier with the destinies of hundreds in his control. A rugged and even ruthless type of part was what he saw himself in...

Now, beyond question, had he so wished he could have gratified his desire at any time. With a week's income he could have bought studios, camera men, authors, and even bribed the public to come and see the result. But two things prevented him. The first was a certain diffidence caused by the thought that it was just possible he might not be quite so successful as, say, John Barrymore; the second was the question of the money involved. It would cost a lot, and that was as gall and wormwood to the soul of Edward Greatorex. And so, but for a strange turn of the wheel, his secret ambition would in all probability have remained a secret till his death.

It had occurred six months previously, when he was taking the waters at Baden. Seated next to him one day in the lounge was an extremely pretty woman; and though he liked to pose as a misogynist, in reality he was far from being one. At heart he was a sensualist, and it was only the fact that women cost a lot of money that kept him in the straight and narrow path. However, there was no charge for a little mild conversation, and when she dropped her handkerchief he retrieved it for her.

It transpired that her name was Madame Saumur, who was staying there with a great friend, the Comtessa Bartelozzi, and for the next few days he was frequently with either one or the other. Indeed, so charming did he find them both, that his secretary was amazed at his expansiveness. Now it happened one evening that, in the course of the conversation, a film showing at one of the local cinemas was under discussion. And in criticising the performance Sir Edward delivered himself of some scathing comments on the actor playing the principal role.

"Had I been playing it," he remarked, "I should have given a totally different rendering. His conception of the part was all wrong."

Madame Saumur paused in the act of lighting a cigarette.

"Have you ever done any film-work, Sir Edward?" she asked.

"My dear lady," he answered, with a tolerant smile, "I'm afraid my life has been too busy for frivolities of that sort. At the same time, had it been cast along different lines, I feel moderately confident that my name would not have been entirely unknown to what I believe are called film fans."

"I'm sure of it," she said quietly. "Why don't you try in your spare time?"

He waved the suggestion away with an indulgent hand: not even to this lovely creature would he admit that her suggestion was one that had obsessed him for years. But as the days passed she returned to the subject more than once.

"I'm in earnest, Sir Edward," she said. "I have some knowledge of film requirements myself, and I have been studying your features. And I believe that for certain roles you possess a marvellous film face."

Again he waved a deprecating hand, but it was clear that he was not displeased at the idea.

"Now I am going to make a suggestion to you," she continued. "I have an American friend – a Mr Hardcastle – who is coming here in a day or two and staying a week. He is closely in touch with the film business, and, what is far more important, he could give you a candid and truthful opinion at once. Not that it would be of more than academic interest," she added. "Naturally, to a man like yourself such a matter is too trivial. But all the artist in me cries out in protest against features such as yours being wasted."

And Sir Edward was even less displeased: most certainly as a matter of academic interest he would be delighted to hear Mr Hardcastle's unbiased opinion. The trouble was that Mr Hardcastle's opinion would have been more unbiased but for an interview which took place before the meeting: an interview at which the financier was not present.

It occurred in Madame Saumur's sitting-room, and speech was frank.

"See here, Tom," she said. "I've got nothing worked out yet, but the details will come later. We've been in this hole a fortnight now sitting in that slob-eyed skate's pocket, and all we've got out of him is an orangeade he forgot to pay for. But he's got a hunch that he can act for the films. It doesn't matter that his face would empty any cinema in a minute, if it hadn't cracked the machine first: you've got to guy him good and hearty."

"Put me wise, honey, and I'll do what I can," said Hardcastle amiably.

"You're one of the big noises in the American film world," she explained. "A power behind the throne: a man with unrivalled experience in spotting winners for the screen. Goldwyns and Paramount never engage anyone without you giving him the once over."

"Sounds good to me," he said. "What comes next?"

"You've got to give an opinion on his face."

"Suffering Sam!" he cried "Have you got the necessary for a high ball?"

"You've got to tell him that his features fulfil every known requirement for a successful film career. Don't try any funny stuff: he knows he wouldn't beat Ronald Colman in a competition for looks, and he's no fool. Character parts – that's the line to take."

"I get you, honey," said Hardcastle. "Lead me to him."

"And don't forget you're a big noise in America."

"It would be easier to remember that bit if you could part with the equivalent of a ten-dollar bill. I'm broke."

"Here you are, Tom." She pressed some money into his hand. "You go down and take a walk. We'll join up with Sir Edward in the lounge. Then when you come in we'll meet for the first time. Don't rush things: he's a wary bird."

And twenty minutes later, Hardcastle, with a large cigar in the corner of his mouth, entered the hotel. For a few moments he stood looking round him; then, with a sudden start of recognition, he crossed to Madame Saumur.

"This is a real pleasure," he remarked, "though not unexpected. Lord Downingham told me you were here. And you, Comtessa. Well, well – this is bully."

"Mr Hardcastle, I don't know if you've ever met Sir Edward Greatorex?"

"Put it there, Sir Edward," he said cordially, holding out his hand. "I have not had that honour, though it would be idle to pretend that I don't know who you are. The penalty of fame, sir: the penalty of fame. Now may I offer you ladies a little light refreshment, or is it forbidden by the rules of the cure?"

"And what have you been doing since I last saw you?" asked Madame Saumur, as the waiter departed with an order.

"Trotting around," he said. "I was down in Hollywood for a couple of months."

He turned to Sir Edward.

"My line of business, sir, is a humble one compared to your great interests. I am in the film trade."

"Most interesting, Mr Hardcastle," said the financier. "And what particular branch of that business? Do you produce?"

"No, sir: at least not as a general rule. I have produced: two years ago I did one of the Metro super films for them. But my principal line is not that: it's something which very few people know exists."

He leaned forward confidentially.

"Now take this lounge at the present moment. Subconsciously I am taking in everyone's face from the point of view of screen work. There are many very good-looking people, Sir Edward, who are useless for film purposes: others, not so good looking, would be an instant success. Instinctively when I go into a room I find myself putting everyone I meet into one or other category. And because I don't make a mistake once in a hundred times, I have more or less specialised in that branch. Variety, sir: that's what the public wants. We're looking for new people all the time. Of course there will always be great popular favourites; but they've got to be supported by others. Ladies, your very good health. Sir Edward, I'm pleased to meet you."

"I find you most interesting, Mr Hardcastle," said the other. "Let us hear your criticisms on the people in this lounge."

Hardcastle shifted his chair slightly so as to get a better view.

"Wal," he said, "there are about forty one can dismiss at once. Ah! wait – here's a good example. You see that pretty girl who has just come in. Good figure: good mover: exactly the type which throngs round studio doors believing they are second Mary Pickfords. Whereas I can see in a moment that that girl would be useless on the screen. It's a gift, Sir Edward, which I happen to possess. Once again – take that rather big ugly guy over by the door: in certain roles that man would be bully."

"What about me, Mr Hardcastle?" asked Madame Saumur, with a smile.

"I'll answer you seriously, Madame," he said. "And as a matter of fact here is a very interesting example, Sir Edward, of my job. Take these two ladies: both equally beautiful in their different ways. And yet I say, without a shadow of doubt, that whereas Madame Saumur would be a success on the screen, the Comtessa would not."

"That's one for me," laughed the Comtessa. "Now we'll put Sir Edward through it: what about him?"

"Sir Edward! Why, he was sorted out in my mind as soon as I saw him." He tapped the table with his finger impressively. "If Sir Edward had not been who he is, and I had happened to meet him nine months ago, it would have saved me weeks of frenzied search. And when I think of what I finally managed to get hold of…"

He lifted despairing hands to heaven.

"No, sir," he continued quietly, "if you weren't who you are, I should be tempted to make you an offer on the spot. At the most you could only turn it down. You are one of the finest examples of a type that is in great demand, but which for some reason or other is the hardest to find. Film face! Gee whizz! If ever you lose your money, Sir Edward" – and he laughed heartily at the bare idea – "you just cable Tom Hardcastle, Hollywood. He'll find you your weekly pocket money."

"You really mean that you think I'm suitable, Mr Hardcastle," said the financier.

"Believe me, Sir Edward, in my profession we get out of the habit of wasting time. And paying compliments to a woman, or telling lies to a man *is* waste of time. In jest the Comtessa asked me what I thought of you: I've told you. If the necessity arose in your case, you could earn big money – very big money. Wal! I guess I must be getting along; and I hope I may see something of you during the time I'm here."

He bowed to them all and sauntered out of the hotel – a typical, prosperous American businessman.

"What did I tell you, Sir Edward?" said Madame Saumur, with a smile. "The question of academic interest has been answered in the way I knew it would be."

"Undoubtedly a most interesting and intelligent man," he remarked. "I should like to have another talk with him on the subject."

A wish, had he known it, that there was every promise of being fulfilled. The only trouble was that it was a little difficult to decide what the next move was going to be. And at a council of war held that afternoon in Madame Saumur's sitting-room not much progress was made.

"I reckon I played my part pretty well, girls," said Hardcastle. "But for the life of me I don't see what good it's going to do us. We've made that guy believe that his dial bears some resemblance to a face, but where's it lead to? If he went incognito to any studio and asked for a job they'd set the dog on him."

"Doesn't matter, Tom," said Madame Saumur: "we've taken the first step. He's interested in you, and if we can't find some method of making him part, we must have lost our cunning. Keep him going: we'll think of something."

"All right, honey," he answered. "I'll do my best. By the way, as I came in there was a man asking for Sir Edward's letters – a foreign-looking chap. Who is he?"

"Gardini – the private secretary. Why?"

Hardcastle shifted his cigar to the other corner of his mouth.

"Watch him," he said tersely. "I didn't like the look he gave me. Yours truly may know nothing about film faces, but he knows the hell of a lot about ordinary ones. So watch him."

For the next three or four days nothing happened, if the inconceivable fact that Sir Edward invited Hardcastle to dinner can be regarded as nothing. But as far as coming to any decision as to how to relieve the financier of any dough, the situation remained unchanged. It became increasingly obvious that the trout had swallowed the fly – time after time he brought the conversation back to films in general and himself in particular – but at that it stuck, and at that it would have stuck, in all probability, for good, but for a very unexpected development.

They were all sitting despondently in Madame Saumur's room one morning when there came a knock at the door and the secretary entered.

"Come right in, Mr Gardini," said Hardcastle heartily, but with shrewd eyes fixed intently on the other's face. "Take a seat."

The Italian bowed and sat down.

"I do not propose," he began, "to waste time by beating about the bush. To do so would be an insult to all our mentalities. Let us therefore come to the point. In the first place, it was no matter of health that brought any of you here, was it?"

It was not a question: it was a statement, and no one bothered to reply.

"I admit," he continued, "that when Mr Hardcastle first came on the scene I was deceived. You ladies, if I may be forgiven for saying so, were comparatively easy: there was nothing original about you. But Mr Hardcastle was different. However, being of an inquiring turn of mind, I cabled a man I know very well in Los Angeles, who is one of the big people in the Metro firm. Here is his answer."

He produced it from his pocket.

" 'Never heard of the man in my life.' Once again," he continued with a smile, "I will not insult your intelligence by asking you to what question that is an answer. All I want to know is what you are hoping to get out of it."

And suddenly Hardcastle lay back in his chair and roared with laughter. Nothing criminal had been done; he could afford to laugh. And the humour of the situation struck him.

"That's all *we* want to know, Mr Gardini," he said.

"Then you have no plan?" said the other, puzzled.

"Devil a one," cried Hardcastle. "It was just a chance shot, and it doesn't really matter that you're wise to it, because, as far as I can see, nothing could ever have come of it."

"Then, my dear Mr Hardcastle," said the Italian softly, "you are not as clever a man as I thought you to be."

An instant silence settled on the room, and the three of them stared at the secretary. What was he driving at?

"I don't quite get you, Mr Gardini," said Hardcastle quietly. "You are presumably acting in Sir Edward's interests."

And the answer came before the Italian spoke a word. For there flashed over his face a look of such diabolical hatred as only a Southerner can give. There was murder in it – murder by torture – and the American whistled under his breath.

"In his interests?" hissed the other. "If I could see him lying dead at my feet, knowing that I had killed him, I would dance on his body."

"Is that so?" remarked Hardcastle genially. "Have a drink, and tell us all about it."

"For months he has treated me like a dog," snarled the other, "generally in front of other people. And I, because I have no money, must put up with it."

"Quite so," said the American soothingly. "But shall we get to the point? The thought of you dancing on his dead body, though a charming picture, is not going to help us much. Now are we to understand that you have some scheme in your head which is likely to part Sir Edward from a considerable wad of money?"

"I have," answered the other quietly. "And if you listen to me I will tell it to you."

"Fire ahead," said Hardcastle. "We'll do the listening all right."

And when, ten minutes later, the Italian had finished, the eyes of his audience were gleaming with excitement.

"It's genius," cried the American: "sheer genius. Gardini, you're wasted."

"There are many details still to be thought out," said the secretary, "but we have plenty of time. I would suggest that you approach him as soon as possible, but wait for a sign from me that he is in a good temper. For on this first step rests everything. And then, my friends, if that is successful, we shall know what to do. You working at your end, and I at mine, will between us get that devil where he has put so many others – in the dust."

And with a gloating look of anticipation in his eyes Benito Gardini left the room.

"You're right, Tom," said the Comtessa, as the door closed, "it's sheer genius. But can we pull it off?"

"We can have a damned good shot at it, my dear," he answered. "You'd better let me put it up to him first as a business proposition; then if he havers about it you two might be able to turn the scales. But you'll know nothing about it till I tip you the wink."

It was after dinner that same night that the secretary gave Hardcastle a meaning glance which told him that the moment was propitious. The millionaire was in the lounge enjoying a cup of coffee, and as the American halted by his table he smiled at him.

"Come and join me, Mr Hardcastle," he said affably. "Where are the two charming ladies?"

"Playing bridge, I think."

He pulled up a chair and sat down: he had already decided that direct methods would be the most likely to succeed.

"And I am rather glad they are, Sir Edward," he continued, "because I should like the pleasure of a few minutes' private conversation with you. For the last two or three days I have been turning over in my mind a certain idea, and with your permission I would like to put it before you. I may say at once that it is connected with film work."

The slight frown that had been gathering on the financier's forehead disappeared.

"Now we are both men who are accustomed to come to the point at once, so I will do so now. Does the thought of playing a big part in a story I have in mind appeal to you at all? Wait a moment, Sir Edward, before you reply. My reason for asking a man of your great wealth and position is a simple one. It is solely a question of art. You fulfil my conception of this part, in a way that no one else can – at least no one else that I have yet met. And it occurred to me that it might amuse you, in the same way that amateur theatricals amuse some people, to act this role. It would be an experience, if nothing else, and the whole thing could be arranged to suit your convenience as far as time is concerned."

"It is a matter that requires careful thought, Mr Hardcastle," said the other. "You will readily appreciate that a man in my position has to be very careful what he does."

Not a muscle in Hardcastle's face moved, but he knew the fish was rising.

"Naturally, Sir Edward," he remarked. "And those points would all have to be considered. But before wasting time over that, the thing I would like to know is whether – always provided they can be settled satisfactorily – you would be prepared to act the part."

"I think I may say," said the millionaire, after a pause, "that, subject to my other manifold interests not being interfered with, I would be prepared to do so."

Hardcastle lit a cigar: the fish was hooked.

"Good," he said quietly. "Then from now on we can talk business. That main vital point being settled, we can come to the details. And the details will not be uninteresting, I venture to think, for there is going to be money in this, and big money. To begin at the beginning, however. Until I met you I had proposed to hand this story over to one of the American firms, take my fee as author, and wash my hands of the business. Now I have a very much larger scheme in my mind. And it is nothing less than this, Sir Edward: that you and I should go into partnership over it with the predominating interest yours. That we should acquire a studio – I know of one going for a mere song in England – get our own cameramen, scenario writers and all the usual paraphernalia of the film trade. I will obtain a first-class cast to support you, and then we will stage the thing ourselves, with you in the principal role."

"Why should the predominating interest be mine?" said the financier shrewdly.

"Because, Sir Edward, you are the predominating draw," answered the other candidly. "I realise, of course, that it will be impossible officially to state that Sir Edward Greatorex, the great financier, is acting on the films. But," he smiled meaningly, "there are methods of letting these things be known unofficially. You will be billed as Mr X – the unknown man. That in itself will prove an attraction. But when, after a while, whispers get about as to who Mr X really is, we'll have the biggest winner of modern times."

He smacked the palm of his hand with his fist enthusiastically.

"And what sort of a part are you proposing for me?" asked Sir Edward.

"That, sir, is where the cream of the idea comes. I want you to play the role of a world-famous financier: in other words, you will be yourself. Can you beat it? It would be indiscreet of me to mention the name of the very exalted person who was approached with the idea of playing the part of royalty in a recent production. But you can take it from me that so keen was the firm on getting royalty to play royalty that the terms they offered would have made the country solvent. And this is the same idea. To play the part of an international financier we get the greatest of them all."

His enthusiasm was contagious, and the millionaire's eyes began to glisten.

"It really seems a very sound proposition," he remarked.

"Sound, sir!" snorted the other. "Two or three more of the same sort and Tom Hardcastle can retire. I'll be candid with you, Sir Edward. I'm not in my business for the good of my health: I want money. And when I see a lump of it lying about waiting to be picked up, I don't look the other way."

The financier nodded approvingly: such sentiments always commanded his warmest admiration.

"Now I've worked out this thing pretty carefully," continued Hardcastle, "and if I'm any judge at all you may take it from me that we'll each of us handle six figures in pounds – not dollars – by the time we're through. Of course," he added, with a deprecating smile, "I know that such a sum as that is nothing to you. Still, you will have had the satisfaction of playing a big part for which you are entirely suited, and of showing the world that it is possible to combine intellectual and artistic genius."

He paused for a moment: was he laying it on a bit too thick? Apparently not: Sir Edward's face registered nothing but pleasure.

"Have you the story with you, Mr Hardcastle?" he asked.

"Yes, sir. But it's only in here at the moment." The American tapped his forehead. "And it's only roughed out. Until I get it cut and dried I would sooner not run the risk of giving you a false impression about it."

"Quite: quite. And one other thing. What about the original costs: the renting of the studio and other preliminaries?"

For the fraction of a second Hardcastle paused: should he chance it? In view of the millionaire's extreme affability, was it worthwhile trying to touch him for that? And then he remembered that there is always a tomorrow morning, and even if Greatorex agreed that night, it might just be sufficient to make him change his mind later.

"Leave all that to me, Sir Edward," he said, with a wave of his hand, "I will give you a full account of all expenses, and shall naturally deduct that sum from our total profits before we share the residue."

"And the basis of the sharing?"

Hardcastle considered the point.

"Sixty–forty?" he said tentatively. "The sixty to you."

"Very fair," answered the other. "Then I take it you will keep me posted in all details?"

"Most certainly. But don't expect results too soon. To hurry anything when we have such a marvellous winner as this would be a crime. And one other thing, Sir Edward, which is most important. Say nothing about it to anyone. Half the punch will be gone if the secret leaks out too soon."

"I quite agree," said the financier, rising. "Well, Mr Hardcastle, I am more than ever pleased that I met you."

"Mutual, sir: mutual. And between us we will show 'em what can be done."

He watched the millionaire cross the lounge and enter the lift; then he beckoned a waiter.

"Bring me a bottle of Bollinger, boy," he said. "I haven't the capacity for a magnum."

Which brief account of how certain people drank the waters at Baden may serve to explain to the intelligent reader the reason of the scenario in Sir Edward's hands as he sat in his suite at the Ritz Carlton. And if it has also revealed the fact that Benito Gardini was not the model secretary he appeared to be on the surface, I can only retort that since his first introduction was when wearing a soft black hat, the intelligent reader should have been wise to his character long ago.

"They would like you at the studio as soon after ten-thirty as possible, sir," remarked Gardini. "The car will be here at half-past nine."

"I can manage that," said Sir Edward, putting down the scenario with obvious reluctance. "Anything important tonight?"

"The question of Peruvian Eagles is still in abeyance."

"What did they close at tonight?"

"They gave way to $5^1/_4$."

The millionaire grinned sardonically.

"Did they indeed? Snap up every share you can tomorrow at that price and up to $5^1/_2$."

The secretary made a note.

"The report is here from Upper Burma," he continued.

"Good or bad?"

"I have not had time to read it very carefully, sir, but from a brief glance I should call it indifferent."

"I'll look at it later. What else?"

One by one Gardini ran through the items, receiving curt and concise instructions on each: Sir Edward prided himself on his brevity. Not once was an alteration necessary: he never spoke till his mind was made up, and then he went straight to the root of the matter. He had the gift of sloughing off irrelevant details and seeing in an instant the real point: in a complicated problem, while other men followed elusive will-o'-the-wisps, he found the vital issue, and never left it. And as Gardini stood there, motionless and deferential, pencil in hand, waiting for each decision, he was conscious, not for the first time, of an unwilling admiration for the brain that could control such vast destinies with so little apparent effort. And not for the first time also, did he marvel at the amazing mixture which, at one moment, dealt calmly with millions and the next haggled over sixpence in a bill.

The last letter finished with, Gardini returned to his own room, and Sir Edward threw himself back in his chair. For a while he did not pick up the script of the film: his frame of mind lay, at the moment, more in an abstract survey of his position rather than in the concrete study of the scenario. It amused him to think that the very scene he had just enacted with his secretary was going to be seen by millions of people all over the world. Would they realise, he wondered, that it was the actual truth? That that was how big finance was carried through? Just two men: a few quiet words, and later the repercussions felt in every corner of the globe. Or would they imagine enormous offices with typewriters clicking, and excited men dashing in and out all day? That had been his idea, he remembered, when he was a boy: he had pictured himself sitting in an inner holy of holies, with dozens of telephones on his desk and different coloured lights that flashed on according to who it was who wanted an interview. But then he had been earning a pound a week: now – what was he worth?

A sudden gleam came into his eyes as the realisation of the power he wielded crossed his mind. Done on his own, too – from nothing. Every penny he possessed had been made by his own brain: he was indebted to no one. And if a few thousand people had crashed by the wayside to mark his victorious progress, the more fools they. That was more or less the theme of the film, and he picked up the scenario again.

But he still did not open it: another train of thought had started. Could it really be possible that he, a man of machine-like habits and customs, whose life was run on timetable methods, was actually going to act in a film next day? Now that the moment had come so near, he almost wished he had never consented. Supposing he made a mess of it: supposing Hardcastle for once had made a mistake, and he was not suitable for the part. He had been amazingly enthusiastic at lunch, but there was always the possibility that he was wrong. What was it he had said? "The most stupendous winner of the last ten years."

Good fellow – Hardcastle, and a capable business man. He seemed to have kept down expenses wonderfully, and from what Gardini said there was no sign of cheeseparing at the studio. However, that he would see for himself next day: no one could spot more quickly than he any wasteful extravagances. Must be a man with a certain amount of money, too, since he ran a yacht. Some idea of using it for one or two of the scenes, and at that a sudden fear struck him.

"Gardini," he called, and the Italian entered. "That yacht of Hardcastle's: is it his own or has he hired it?"

"I really couldn't say, Sir Edward," answered the other.

"There's no question of that being added to the expenses, is there, if he uses her for making some of the film?"

"I will inquire into the matter," said the secretary, turning away lest his employer should see the look of utter contempt in his eyes. "By the way, sir," he resumed a moment later, "I don't know if you have seen this paragraph in the evening paper."

He handed a copy to Sir Edward and indicated the place.

"It is rumoured that a most sensational disclosure may take place in the near future with regard to one of the principal actors in the film 'High Finance,' which is now being made at Blackwater studio. Inquiries there failed to elicit anything more than that his identity is cloaked under the pseudonym Mr X."

"Excellent!" said Sir Edward. "He's doing it well, Benito: very well."

"Strict orders have been given, sir, at the studio, that your name is not to be mentioned. It is bound to leak out in time, of course, but he is very anxious that the air of mystery should be maintained as long as possible. So we have arranged that you should always drive up to a special private entrance, and just come on the stage for your own scenes."

The other nodded.

"Very wise. What is the exact programme for tomorrow?"

"He is first of all going to run through what has been done already. You will realise, sir, that that will be quite disjointed. I mean we shall dodge from scene to scene, as no film is ever taken consecutively. Then he wants to do your three scenes in the room in Paris."

"I know them: I've been reading them tonight."

"Then, if there is time for any more, he proposes to tackle the ones in the London office."

"I must get on to them. Do you think, Benito" – and for the first time in their association his voice was almost diffident – "that I shall do all right?"

"Of course, Sir Edward," cried the other. "Who could possibly doubt it? You may feel a little nervous to start with, but that will soon pass off."

"It's a damned good story," said the financier. "The more I read it, the more I like it."

"And it might have been written specially for you," remarked the secretary suavely.

"It shows rare insight into the world of finance," said Sir Edward. "By the way, have you seen my understudy?"

"No, sir. But I gather they found a suitable man today."

"Do you really think it is essential to have one?"

"I don't, as things have turned out," answered Gardini. "But it was a wise precaution, I think. Anything might have occurred. Even now, sir, you may find yourself unable to go down some morning, in which case he can double you in certain of your smaller scenes where you do not figure prominently, thus saving everyone standing about idle. You see, sir, it is practically only your scenes now that are left to take, certainly as far as interiors are concerned."

"Anyway, he's there if he's wanted," said Sir Edward. "Well, good night, Benito: I shall be ready by half-past nine tomorrow."

And as the secretary bowed and retired, the millionaire again picked up the scenario and started to study his own scenes.

CHAPTER 8

"You know, old soul, I think Hugh is on a stumer this time. The whole show here seems to me to be perfectly genuine."

Algy Longworth was seated beside Laura Mainwaring on a pile of old planks in a corner of the studio. In the centre the scene was set for the morning's work, but no one had yet started. The producer Haxton was talking earnestly to Jake Slingsby: the cameramen, in their shirt-sleeves, lounged about aimlessly.

"What are they waiting for anyway?" demanded the girl.

"Haven't you heard?" he cried. "The loud noise is performing: they are going to shoot Sir John Harborough's scenes this morning."

"Who is he?" she said indifferently.

"That's where the hush-hush part comes in," he explained. "If you ask me, they've got a pretty cute boost across. It was in the evening papers yesterday. Mysterious individual known as Mr X."

"I never saw it," she cried. "Algy – how exciting! Do you know who it is?"

"I haven't an earthly," he answered. "But he's somebody who is pretty well known."

"Excuse me, miss, but a couple of these 'ere planks are wanted."

A hefty-looking stage-hand came up, and they both rose.

"When are we beginning?" asked Longworth.

"Dunno, sir. They've got 'is nibs in the theatre showing 'im wot's been done up to date."

"Who is it? D'you know?"

The man lowered his voice confidentially.

"Sir Hedward Greatorex," he said. "But nobody hain't supposed to let on. I only know through over'earing Mr 'Axton."

"And who the hell is Sir Edward Greatorex?" demanded Longworth blankly.

"Hask me another, sir. If it was 'Obbs, now, or 'Ammond, I could 'ave hunderstood it. But this 'ere bloke beats me. Financier, they calls 'im."

He went off with his planks, and they sat down again as Haxton strolled up.

" 'Morning, Miss Mainwaring," he said affably. "We'll probably be shooting one of your scenes later on."

"Who is Sir Edward Greatorex, Mr Haxton?" she asked.

"So you've heard, have you? I told Slingsby it was hopeless trying to keep it dark. He's a multi-millionaire, and he's got a hunch he can act for the films."

"Can he?"

"God knows! I've never seen him. But he's so keen on trying that he's put up the necessary dough for the whole of this outfit."

"What happens if he's a complete frost?" demanded Longworth.

"You remember that advertisement that brought you here in the first instance? That was to try and get somebody who could be made up sufficiently to double him. Well, we got a fellow yesterday afternoon. And if the worst comes to the worst, we'll have to shoot all Sir John Harborough's scenes twice."

"But he's bound to spot it when he sees 'em being run through."

Mr Haxton winked.

"He'll see his own in the run through. Then later, when he's out of it, we'll substitute the others. And if he gets angry when he sees the final result we'll have to spin him some yarn about his length of film having got spoiled. But don't forget," he continued, "we've all got to play the game. Whatever he's like we've got to pretend that he's the goods. And another thing too: don't go shouting it all round London that he's playing this part. We want to keep it dark as long as we can for the sake of the ad."

He wandered away, and Algy Longworth lit a cigarette.

"So that's the scheme, is it?" he said. "But I'm blowed if I see what's the object of all this mystery. Hullo! there he is, presumably. Come on, old bean: let's go and inspect the blighter from a close up."

They sauntered over towards a small group that had just emerged from the theatre. It consisted of Hardcastle and Penton, who were deferentially talking to a man with a fair beard accompanied by a dark-skinned, foreign-looking individual.

"So you approve of it up to date, Sir Edward," Hardcastle was saying.

"Very much indeed," answered the bearded man.

"Good! Then I should like you to meet our producer – Mr Haxton. And this is Miss Gayford – our leading lady: Mr Montrevor – our junior lead."

"I must congratulate you," said Sir Edward. "The scenes I have just been looking at are admirable."

"And now, Sir Edward, I will show you to your dressing-room," went on Hardcastle. "There is someone there to make you up."

The group passed on, and Mr Montrevor contemplated Miss Gayford thoughtfully.

"Lettice, darling," he remarked, "that bloke is going to act us off the stage – I do not think. Paul, old warrior, what's the great idea?"

Paul Haxton grinned.

"Just this, my boy. D'you know whose pocket your hundred a week is coming out of? His. He's paying for the whole outfit, and that being so, he considers he's entitled to play a part."

Jack Montrevor shrugged a pair of exquisitely tailored shoulders.

"He can play forty, old boy, so long as his cheques ain't stumers."

"Not much fear of that," laughed Haxton. "His passbooks have to be specially printed with seven spaces in the pounds column. Now then, boys: set it alight. Scene 84. Let's get the set dressed before he comes. Lettice – you're here, darling: Wentworth – just sit there where Sir John is going to be. Jack, you're up left by the window."

He examined the grouping for a moment or two; then he nodded.

"OK. All right, Wentworth, thank you. I'll probably take yours and Miss Mainwaring's next. 93, isn't it? Ah! here comes Sir Edward. Lights, please."

The arcs hissed and sizzled, then held steady as the financier stepped on to the stage.

"Now, Sir Edward," he went on, "we're taking Scene 84. It's the sitting-room in your hotel in Paris. Switch off some of those lights for the present, while we try it through. Jack and Lettice are here waiting for you, having come to plead for mercy. He is ruined as the result of having speculated foolishly in schemes controlled by you, and as a forlorn hope they have come to beg you to stay your hand. Their marriage cannot take place: their whole future is finished unless, perchance, you will relent. After all, you have countless millions: what are a few beggarly thousands? Everything to them: nothing to you. That is their reaction: what is yours? Amused contempt. If you did it for them, you'd have to do it for everybody in like position. And do they really imagine that you've got nothing better to do than to trot round after a bunch of damned fools, returning them money they ought never to have lost? That all clear? Good: let's start. You come in through that door, Sir Edward, holding in your hand some document. They are both here, but for a moment or two you do not see them: you are engrossed in what you are reading – something that evidently pleases you. Then some little sound makes you look up, and you realise you are not alone. You frown indignantly: who are these people who have forced their way into your private sitting-room? Then you realise that Lettice is an extraordinarily pretty girl, and the frown disappears: you like pretty girls. You close the door, and standing with your back to it you say, 'May I ask what you are doing in my private sitting-room?' Then, without waiting for an answer, you cross to the desk, sit down, and, still looking at Lettice, you say, 'Well, I am waiting for an answer.' Let's try as far as that. You go off, Sir Edward, and try your entrance."

Haxton stepped off the stage and joined Hardcastle, who, with Penton, was watching in silence.

"All right, Sir Edward, you can begin. Take it slowly: that's right. Now you're reading. Register pleasure, Sir Edward – pleasure. My sainted aunt!" he muttered under his breath, "the man looks as if he'd eaten a dead rat. Now look up. Frown: that's right. Close the door, and turn round. Now you see Lettice is a pretty girl. Yes, you can moderate that a little, Sir Edward: I mean – er – you don't usually look at pretty girls like that, I'm sure. Now your sentence, sarcastic and coldly polite. Now over to your desk: slowly, Sir Edward, don't run. Sit down. Second remark, still addressed to Lettice. Thank you: that will do for the moment."

He turned to Hardcastle, and lowered his voice.

"Well, now we know," he remarked. "It may be stage fright, which will wear off: let's hope to Heaven it does. But he moves like a king penguin suffering from an acute attack of locomotorataxy; when he registered pleasure he looked like a deaf mute at a funeral who had fallen into the grave instead of the corpse; and the look he gave Lettice would have turned the butter rancid."

"Doesn't matter," said Hardcastle. "It can't be helped. Thank God! we've got the understudy. Shoot the scenes as quickly as you can, and don't let him see what you think."

"All right, old boy," answered the other. "But if one of the cameramen falls off the ladders from laughing and breaks his neck, don't blame me."

"But, Laura, my angel, he's simply dreadful," said Algy Longworth, as the scene proceeded. "Come with me into some remote corner, and make love to me: I need bucking up."

"He's pretty grim, Algy, isn't he? Still, I suppose, as he's paying for it, it's his worry if he wastes everybody's time and his own money."

"Do you really suppose it's being wasted?"

They both swung round: standing just behind them was a youngish man. He was smiling cynically, and they recognised him as one of the office staff, by the name of Tredgold.

"Well, the scenes will all have to be retaken," said the girl.

"My dear Miss Mainwaring," he replied, "that's no answer to my question. I don't mind telling you that there's something deuced fishy going on here."

"What do you mean?" cried Longworth quickly.

"There aren't many flies on yours truly," remarked the other. "I've been mixed up in this business for a good few years, and I tell you there's the hell of a lot more in this affair than meets the eye."

"What exactly are you driving at?"

"Never you mind," said Tredgold, with a knowing grin. "I'm keeping my eyes open, and if I don't find out something soon, my name ain't Henry Tredgold."

"Well, I haven't seen anything," remarked Longworth.

"Nor have I – yet," said the other. "But you're not in the office, and I am. And though I haven't seen, I've heard. And you

can take it from me this isn't a *bona-fide* film studio. At least, it's
a film studio all right, but it's not only that. Don't say I said so,
and keep it to yourself. But if I don't spot what it is in the next
two or three days I'll eat my hat."

"Now what the dickens is that bird getting at?" said
Longworth, as the other moved off.

"If he's right, Algy, it seems to show that your friend Captain
Drummond is not mistaken after all," answered the girl.

He lit a cigarette thoughtfully.

"That's so," he agreed. "But the only thing that beats me is
what particular form of fun and laughter they can be up to. They
might soak that man Greatorex in for a few odd thousands over
expenses, but it seems a very elaborate scheme for such a small
result, especially as I should think he's the type of man that it's
mighty difficult to swindle."

And at that moment their friend the stage-hand came up
again.

"More planks," he said. "Gaw lumme, Miss, 'ave you ever
seen hanything to equal that there bloke? Why, I'd do it better
myself."

A sentiment which, as the morning proceeded, was cordially
shared by everyone in the studio. There was no question of stage
fright about it: the man could not act to save his life; he could not
even walk naturally across the stage and sit down; he couldn't
make the most ordinary movement or remark without appearing
self-conscious. In short, he completely wrecked every scene he
came on in. And when he returned to London after lunch – it
having been decided, for his benefit, not to take any scenes in the
afternoon – a council of war was immediately held.

"It's out of the question," said Haxton firmly, "to use one foot
of what was taken this morning. It is absolutely useless – the
whole lot of it. I quite understand that we've got to keep up
the pretence in front of him, and that we'll have to waste every
morning same as we've done this. But in the afternoons we

must shoot the morning scenes over again with the understudy. Where is he?"

"Here I am, Mr Haxton."

He appeared on the stage, and as he did so there came a loud crash. For the stage-hand, whose perpetual job seemed to be carrying planks, had selected that moment to drop them.

"Confound you!" shouted Haxton, "must you drop tons of wood on my feet?"

Then he resumed his inspection of the understudy.

"Have you got the beard ready?" he asked. "You have. Good! Then go and get made up. What's his name, Mr Hardcastle?"

"Travers. And with the beard he's the living spit of Sir Edward."

"Well, let's hope to Heaven he can act. That damned man this morning nearly sent me loopy. Set for Scene 84 again, boys. I know you're faint for food, Lettice, darling, but you'll be a good grown-up girl for your Paul's sake. By Jove!"

He broke off abruptly: Travers had returned made up.

"Well, I'm damned!" he remarked. "It's extraordinary. At this distance it might be Sir Edward himself. We'll still be able to keep the ad., Mr Hardcastle. I'll defy the public ever to know the difference. Now then, let's get on with it. Were you watching this morning, Travers?"

The others nodded.

"Yes, I remember the scene."

"Right. Then walk through it now. Good," he cried, after watching for a bit, "that's OK! Lettice, you'll get your tea quite soon after all. Do it once more, and then we'll shoot."

And for the next four days the same programme was repeated. Every morning Sir Edward Greatorex solemnly waded through his scenes: every afternoon they were retaken with Travers in his place. But as far as Mr Henry Tredgold was concerned, there seemed to be an imminent danger of his having to consume his headgear. His investigations had evidently not progressed according to Cocker.

In fact, Algy Longworth had almost forgotten their conversation, when, one day after lunch, Tredgold strolled up with his hands in his pockets and a general air of mystery about him.

"You remember what I told you the other day, Mr Wentworth," he remarked, "about there being more in this show than meets the eye?"

"I do," said Longworth. "Found out anything more?"

"You bet I have," announced the other complacently. "Trust yours truly for that. I'm on the trail, as they say. And do you know where the trail leads to?"

"Not an earthly," answered Longworth.

"I don't know if you've ever been round these studios properly," continued the other. "I hadn't – not till yesterday afternoon. And then, having nothing to do, I started on a tour of inspection. I wandered all over the place, and suddenly over in that corner, behind a pile of rubbish, I came on a door. Quite in innocence, I opened it and walked through, wondering where it led to. A passage with stone walls lay in front of me, but I hadn't taken two steps when I heard someone coming towards me. And the next instant that man Penton came in sight. You know what a great, big, hulking fellow he is, and one glance at his face showed that he was in the hell of a rage."

" 'What the something, something,' he shouted, 'are you doing here?'

" 'Keep it clean, girlie,' I said. 'I'm not doing anything particular. Just taking a little walking exercise, that's all.'

" 'Then in future you can damned well take your walking exercise elsewhere,' he snarled. 'This is private in here.'

" 'Then why don't you put up a notice to that effect on the door?' I cried.

"He didn't answer: just hustled me out of the place. Then he shut and locked the door, and went back to the office. What do you make of that, Mr Wentworth?"

"I can't say that I make very much," answered Algy. "Why shouldn't there be some private place through that door? I don't see that there is anything particularly suspicious about it."

"I had a dekko outside," went on Tredgold, "and that part beyond the door is where the stone cellars are."

"Well, what of it?"

"Do you think they can be hiding anything in them?" said the other mysteriously.

Algy Longworth began to laugh.

"What the dickens should they want to hide things for? And what sort of things, anyway?"

But Tredgold was in no way perturbed by his laughter.

"I'm not going to say what I think, yet, Mr Wentworth," he answered quietly. "But you mark my words: there's going to be some fun here before we've finished."

"Well, they'll have to hurry up, then," said Algy. "There is only about another week to go before we're through."

"Just so," agreed Tredgold. "And within that week we shall see what we shall see, if we keep our eyes open." Once again he lowered his voice mysteriously. "What was a motorcar doing at the entrance round at the back there at eleven o'clock last night?"

"If it comes to that," said Longworth, "what were you doing there?"

"Watching," said the other, in no way abashed. "I've got digs in the village, and after supper yesterday I took a walk up here. The whole place was in darkness, but as I rounded a corner I heard voices in front of me. I was wearing rubber shoes, so I made no noise. And as I crept nearer I recognised who they were, though they were talking low. Hardcastle was one of them, and Penton and Slingsby were with him. They'd got the door open –

the one that leads from the outside to the cellars, and it seemed to me they were taking stuff out of the car and carrying it inside."

In spite of himself, Algy Longworth began to feel impressed. After all, Drummond had specifically stated that he thought something was going on: was it possible that this foxy little man had ferreted it out?

"You can't tell me," continued Tredgold, "that it's the normal thing for the three boss men of a show like this to be creeping about at eleven o'clock at night in the back premises of the place. No lights, mark you: not even a torch."

"You're quite right," agreed Algy. "It does seem a bit fishy."

"Fishy!" snorted the other. "It smells to me like Billingsgate Market."

"But I still can't think what they can be hiding, and why they should bother to hide it here."

Tredgold lit a cigarette.

"I don't know if you've studied psychology at all, Mr Wentworth," he remarked – "crime psychology in particular. I have; and one of the first principles is that the more obvious a thing is the more likely a man is to get away with it. Within limits, of course. Put a valuable paper in the middle of your desk, and the betting is that a thief will overlook it and spend his time forcing the safe. Now in a different respect it's the same here. Everything on the face of it is straight and above-board: the making of the film has been advertised; the public know all about it; visitors are admitted to the studio; a well-known millionaire is actually acting. No one would dream of suspecting anything: why should they? In short, you have here the ideal atmosphere for carrying out a big coup right under everybody's nose."

Algy was listening intently: more and more was he getting impressed.

"Now," continued the other, "let's take the practical side of the show. Greatorex is putting up the money for this film. All right. But what does that amount to? What are the Hardcastle bunch going to get out of it? Even if this film is a howling success – which it won't be – they're not going to get enough by the time it's split up amongst 'em to pay for cigars. It isn't as if this was a regular company, making films all the year round, of which this was one. This is the first they've done, and so far as I know it's going to be the last. At any rate they've taken no steps to renew their lease. Of course Greatorex may be paying 'em a big fee. Even so, there's not going to be a vast amount in it. And my humble opinion is that they are using this film as a cloak for something else: something from which they really will handle big money."

"But how were they to know that Greatorex would put up the money?" said Algy. "If he hadn't, they'd never have been here."

"That's no objection, Mr Wentworth. It was only *after* he had said he'd ante up, and presumably had commissioned them to go ahead, that this other scheme suggested itself to them."

"And have you any idea in your mind as to what this other scheme is?"

Tredgold glanced round cautiously.

"What is it, Mr Wentworth, that there is always a demand for? What is it that for its bulk is the most paying proposition in the world to unscrupulous men?"

"You mean dope?" cried Algy.

"Sh!" said the other warningly. "Yes: that's what I mean. Mark you, I've got no proof. It's only suspicion on my part. But I believe those beauties have taken advantage of having this studio to smuggle drugs on a large scale. You can take it from me that some pretty queer fish come floating around that office: men who have got nothing to do with the film business."

"How are we going to find out?"

Tredgold winked mysteriously.

"You leave that to me," he said. "Mr Blooming Penton isn't quite as clever as he thinks he is. And I know where he keeps the key of the door. It's in a drawer in his desk, and sometimes he forgets to lock it if he goes out for a few minutes. Now the next chance I get I'll take a wax impression; then we can have a key made. And once that is done it will be just a question of waiting for a suitable opportunity. Not a word to a soul, don't forget: I'll keep you posted as to how things go."

He sauntered off, leaving Algy Longworth thinking deeply. Not a particularly pleasant little man, Mr Tredgold, but he knew the breed: as sharp as they make them, and a regular nosey-Parker to boot. And the more he thought over their conversation, the more did it seem to him that there might be a lot in it. As far as he could see, there was no flaw in the reasoning: not only was it logically sound, but in addition, bearing in mind what he knew of the characters of the three men, it was inherently likely. And though he had purposely refrained from saying anything about that to Tredgold, he realised that his inside knowledge was strong confirmation of the little man's theory. It supplied at once a plausible motive for the murder of young Marton. Somehow or other he must have found out what was going on behind the scenes, and had threatened to split on them. The whole sequence of events fitted together perfectly, and the first thing to be done now was to get in touch with Drummond.

He wished Laura had been there, but she had not been wanted that afternoon. He would like to have had her opinion on it: she might have spotted some flaw. But try as he would, he couldn't: the thing seemed not only plausible, but probable. The fact of the three men having been there in the middle of the night, secretly, without lights, was in itself almost damning in its suspiciousness.

He strolled over to the corner indicated by Tredgold: there was the door. He tried the handle: it was locked. And then, since his scene was not due for another half-hour, he decided to have a little tour of inspection outside. He found that it was just as Tredgold had said – that end of the building was evidently the older, and constructed entirely of stone. A few small, cobwebby windows covered with iron bars occurred at intervals: the whole exterior gave the impression of decay and neglect.

Halfway round he came to the door, which was clearly the one at which Tredgold had seen the car. And he was on the point of trying that handle too when it suddenly opened and Hardcastle stepped out.

"Good afternoon, Mr Wentworth," he said quietly. "Not acting for the moment?"

"No," answered Algy. "Not for the next half-hour."

"I see. And so you're taking a little constitutional?"

"That's the notion. Quaint old studio, isn't it?"

Hardcastle locked the door before replying.

"Very quaint," he remarked. "But this end of the place is *not* the studio, Mr Wentworth. Don't let me detain you from your walk."

Algy Longworth strolled on, feeling more convinced than ever that Tredgold was right. Something fishy was going on in that part of the building, and the instant he got back to London he went round to Drummond's club. But there was no sign of him, and the hall porter said he had not been in for several days. There was nothing for it but to write him, which he did, at length: a letter which in due course found its way to the Post Office, Colchester, addressed to Mr Henry Johnson, a gentleman who bore a striking resemblance to the hefty-looking stage-hand whose hobby was carrying planks.

To Drummond it came as a ray of light in the most impenetrable darkness. Quite frankly, he had admitted himself defeated; the fact, unknown of course to Algy, which had caused him to drop the planks in his surprise had seemed to lead nowhere on further thought. For as Travers had come on the stage he had spotted suddenly a thing that had eluded him till then. When he had first seen Sir Edward Greatorex in the Ritz Carlton, he had felt vaguely that he had met him before. But in that moment at the studio he realised the truth. For Travers might well have been Marton's brother, and it was Marton he had been reminded of when he saw the financier in the lounge of the hotel.

The difference in their ages had deceived him, but the instant he saw another young man who was like Marton the thing was obvious. Marton was to have been the understudy for the millionaire, and when he was killed it became necessary to find someone else. Hence the advertisement.

So far, so good; but it was after that that he had stuck. The motive for Marton's murder was still as obscure as ever. Why kill a perfectly good double when it might prove to be a matter of very considerable difficulty to replace him? That was what had been defeating him, and Longworth's letter seemed to supply the answer. In fact, it looked as if the whole plot could be reconstructed.

Sir Edward Greatorex had commissioned the Hardcastle crowd to stage a film for him, in which he proposed to play a part. They, realising the possibility of his being no use, had looked around for an understudy. By chance the Comtessa had met young Marton, and had instantly seen that there was the very man for their purpose owing to his amazing likeness to the millionaire. In some way or other he had discovered that other things beside making a film were intended, and had threatened to split on them.

There were difficulties, of course; not the least being the theft of the bearer bonds. Drummond had believed that that had been a deliberate plant, designed to get Marton more completely in their power; now, in view of this new development, he began to wonder. Because the thing which had been so obscure before was now as clear as daylight – namely, why Marton in particular should have been selected. The point that had stumped Newall and all of them as to why a junior partner in a solicitor's office should have come into the picture at all was explained. Indeed, it seemed to Drummond that they had been starting from the wrong end. It was young Marton who had led Hardcastle and Co. to the firm, not the firm to young Marton. By chance they had found that the man they wanted was a lawyer, and so, to save trouble, they used his firm for their business. In short, had the murdered man been anything but what he was, Messrs Marton, Peters and Newall would never have come into the show at all.

It certainly simplified things enormously, because it permitted a much easier solution of the theft of the bonds. In the past Carl Peterson and Irma had combined legitimate business with their life of crime – there was no reason why the new combination should not do the same. It was more than possible that Newall was right: that Madame Saumur's transaction had been a perfectly genuine one, and that the theft was a simple case of embezzlement without any ulterior motive on the other side.

He re-read Longworth's letter, and another point struck him. It accounted for a further difficulty which had puzzled him up to date – why Glensham House in particular had been taken. If his reconstruction was right, it all fitted in perfectly. From the foundation stone of young Marton's likeness to the millionaire, which was the beginning of the whole thing, they were led to Marton, Peters and Newall. From Marton, Peters and Newall they were led to a suitable house for taking exteriors, and it proved to be Glensham House. In fact, all the mystery which had appeared to surround the events of the last few days turned out to be no mystery at all. Every single thing was the logical outcome of the fact that a young man, who bore a striking resemblance to a millionaire, happened to belong to a certain firm of lawyers.

He called for a pint of ale gloomily: a sorry end to what had seemed a more promising beginning. He didn't see himself getting any kick out of finding cocaine in a draughty cellar. It would be amusing to sting them good and hearty, but he had hoped for better things than that. He regretted now that he had ever bothered to go to the studio: it looked as if it was going to prove sheer waste of time. And what was still more galling was that he could take no credit to himself for anything: it was this man Tredgold who had done the unearthing of the whole plot. And a damned uninteresting plot it was at that; the next time he saw Irma he would tell her she must do better in future – she seemed to have lost her form.

For a while he pondered over things: should he chuck the whole show up and go back to London? He could always get down at once if Algy wanted him, and he was getting rather bored with carting scenery about. But after a second pint had gone the way of its predecessor he decided to stick it out. There were only a few days more to go, and something amusing might happen. And so the following morning found Mr Henry Johnson once again at the studio.

Up to date, somewhat to his relief, there had been no sign of Irma. With the others, and even with Algy, he knew he could escape recognition, so perfectly had he disguised himself: with her he was not so sure. He remembered of old her uncanny powers of detection. And though it would not matter very much now if he was spotted, he would have preferred to see it through to the end.

As a matter of fact he was becoming genuinely interested in the actual film. There was no denying that it was good stuff, and since a lot of the scenes now being taken were consecutive ones in the script, it was easy to follow. Every day, religiously at half-past nine, Sir Edward Greatorex appeared; every day his scenes were retaken with Travers in the part during the afternoon. Presumably the secretary had concocted some satisfactory explanation as to why he was only required in the mornings: at any rate he showed no signs of suspecting anything. And with everybody pulling together to keep him in ignorance of the truth, the work ran smoothly.

It was on the third day after he had got Longworth's letter that Henry Johnson arrived at the studio to find a conference in progress. Sir Edward had not yet come, and a pow-wow was being held on the stage.

"We'll have to alter things a little today, boys," Haxton was saying, "because this night scene has got to be shot. Now Sir Edward will smell a rat if he doesn't play it, and that means he'll have to stop here the whole afternoon. And that further means that Travers will have to do all the repeats tomorrow: today will be entirely Sir Edward."

"I think Travers had better double him in the rough-house scene," said Hardcastle.

Haxton consulted his script.

"That's tonight. Well, I suggest that Sir Edward plays it up to the actual knock-out, and then Travers can do the bit in the lorry. We may as well let him do as much as he can, since we've got to waste the day anyhow. Then we'll tell him that he's not wanted at all tomorrow. Hullo! here he is. Good morning, sir: can you manage the whole day today? We want to do your night scene this evening."

"Certainly, Mr Haxton," said the millionaire. "I have no engagement, have I, Gardini?"

"No, sir: you're quite free," answered the secretary.

For a while Drummond hung about; then, seeing that he would not be wanted, he wandered outside. It was boring watching the same thing twice, and he preferred to see it when done by Travers.

The amusement of watching the financier performing had long worn off, and he was strolling along aimlessly when he saw on the path in front of him the butt end of a cigarette. It was still smoking, and the red marks of lipstick could be seen on the purple tip. He glanced up: above his head was an open window. Evidently it had come from there, and almost as evidently it meant that the Comtessa was honouring the studio with a visit.

He began to stuff his pipe as an excuse for remaining where he was in case anyone looked out. And almost immediately he heard Penton's voice.

"It's risky: damned risky. Why bring him here at all?"

"It's Natalie's idea," the Comtessa answered.

There came some grumbling remark from Penton which Drummond could not catch; then a door opened and shut, and he heard Hardcastle speaking.

"Everything is fixed, but I can't say I like it. However, since she insists on it... Here, what the devil are you doing hanging about there?"

He had come to the window, and Drummond looked up.

"Just lighting me pipe, guv'nor," he said. "Got to get 'old of a bit o' four by three for that there wing."

He walked on towards a dump of timber, and busied himself turning over the wood. Who were they alluding to that it was risky to bring to the studio? He was conscious that Hardcastle was still watching him, but when, having found a suitable strut, he sauntered back again, the American had gone. And on re-entering the studio he saw him watching the work.

"Now, Sir Edward, get a good hold of the situation."

Haxton was speaking, and, in accordance with his invariable custom, he was giving the millionaire as full instructions as if he intended to use the result. It saved time in the afternoon with Travers, and helped to foster the illusion for Sir Edward.

"You're putting up your proposal to the girl. If she will dispense with the trifling formality of a wedding ring, you will be prepared to see that the letters are returned to her fiancé. He need never know: for her sake you will pretend to him that pity has softened your heart. But there has got to be no mistake about her side of the bargain. Now you have sent for her to come to you at your hotel: you are waiting for her to arrive. You pace up and down the room, gloating anticipation in your expression. Try that."

"Hell's bells," he muttered under his breath, "he looks as if he had a fish-bone stuck in his false teeth."

"Now then, Lettice, darling," he continued, "in you come. Register dawning hope: after all, he's not as hard as you thought him. Then you see his face: you realise the truth: you stand aghast."

"That shouldn't be difficult," he whispered to Hardcastle, "unless it sends her into hysterics."

For a while Drummond watched; then at the other end of the studio he saw Algy Longworth and Tredgold in earnest conversation. And as unobtrusively as possible he edged his way towards them. But before he reached them their talk had ended, and Algy had joined Laura Mainwaring.

He touched his forehead with his forefinger.

" 'Morning, Miss," he said. "A fair bit of orl rite, Sir Hedward, ain't 'e, in that scene?"

"Good morning, Mr Johnson," cried the girl with a smile.

" 'Morning, Johnson," said Algy. "Look here, my dear," he went on urgently, "I must get hold of Hugh somehow." He lowered his voice. "It's tonight, according to what Tredgold says."

For a moment or two Drummond hesitated: should he reveal his identity to them or not?

"I can't make out where the old blighter has disappeared to." Algy was speaking again. "Three times have I tried to get him and failed. Damn it! here's our scene. Come on."

They both went off, and Drummond made up his mind. It was better not to give his disguise away: it was possible it would come in useful later on. And so, having sought out the foreman, and developed an agonising and quite imaginary toothache, he obtained leave of absence for the rest of the day.

Three hours later, having done certain things to his appearance in an old second-hand clothes shop in Whitechapel, he entered his flat in Queen Anne's Mansions.

"Yes, sir: quite a number of people have rung up," said Denny, in answer to his question. "Mr Longworth some three or four times, and two ladies who would not give their names. I answered them as you told me."

"Good! And now I want you to ring up Blackwater studio and ask for Mr Wentworth, which is the name Mr Longworth is acting under. Don't say who you are, above all don't say I want him; but as soon as you hear his voice at the other end I'll take the receiver."

He waited, and five minutes later his servant beckoned to him.

"Don't mention my name, Algy," he said. "It's Hugh speaking. I'm very anxious to see you."

"Same here, old boy," answered Algy eagerly. "In fact, it's imperative that I should talk to you today, and I can't over the 'phone."

"Meet me at the Plough at Witham tonight at seven-thirty," said Drummond.

"Right," said Algy. "Did you get my letter?"

"I did."

"What I said in it has been confirmed today. Bring" – came a pause, and Drummond realised he was looking round for fear of being overheard – "bring a gun."

"Right oh, Algy!" he cried. "Seven-thirty – sharp."

He rang off, and told Denny to mix him a cocktail. Then he lit a cigarette, and once more turned his mind to the problem that had worried him ever since he had overheard Penton's remark that morning. Who was the 'him' he had alluded to? Natalie – Irma – had insisted on it, whatever 'it' was, so could it be that the person referred to was himself? And if so, what did it mean? So far as he knew, no effort had been made to get him to the studio.

"Denny," he called. "Those ladies that rang up – did they seem to want anything in particular?"

"No, sir," said his servant. "They wanted to know when you were likely to be in, and I simply said I couldn't tell them."

Drummond lit another cigarette: the thing was beyond him at the moment. And he was still feeling just as much in the dark when he met Algy Longworth at the Plough that evening.

CHAPTER 9

Laura Mainwaring was with him, and Drummond was formally introduced.

"She insisted on coming, old bean," said Algy, "and we've both got to be back at the studio in an hour."

"Right," cried Drummond. "Heaven knows if the dinner here will poison us, but let's get down to it."

"I've ordered some gin and vermouth," said the other. "We might have 'em here. Hugh, unless I'm much mistaken, we're on a big thing."

"Fire ahead, old boy," remarked Drummond. "I'm all at sea myself."

"It's as I told you over the 'phone – confirmation of my letter."

"You mean you've found out for certain that they're using one end of the building as a distributing centre for dope?"

"I can't think what else it can be. There's certainly something damned mysterious going on there. Moreover, according to Tredgold it's coming to a head very shortly. I'll just give you the story as briefly as I can. We're doing scenes tonight, and consequently there will be a lot of activity going on round the studio. The centre of it will be at the genuine end of the place, and his theory is that that is the sort of occasion when it is safest for them to carry on at the other."

"Sound on the face of it," agreed Drummond.

"Now you remember I told you that he was going to get a wax impression of the key of the inside door. Well, he's done better than that. He's got one of the outside door, and here" – he produced a large key from his pocket – "is the result. Now Laura and I are acting tonight, and he will have to be on hand too. And his suggestion is that you should take this key – "

"Hold hard, Algy," cried Drummond quickly. "How does this man Tredgold know anything about me?"

"He doesn't. He merely said to me this morning, 'Do you know anyone on whom you can absolutely rely who could explore the place while the main scene is being taken?' I told him I did, though I didn't tell him your name."

"You didn't? Good! Go on."

"Well, his suggestion is this. When that scene is being taken tonight – it's a scene where a small lorry is used – Sir Edward will be watching it. I told you in my letter about the understudy, didn't I? And Travers – that's the bloke's name – will be doubling him in the lorry scene with his full knowledge and consent. Of course he has no idea at all that it's been done all the way through: it's the one thing that he's not been allowed to find out. But, because this is a rough-house bit, he has been persuaded not to do it himself for fear of getting hurt. And so, as I said before, he will be watching it. Now when he's around, Hardcastle and Co. simply sit in his pocket, and Tredgold's idea is that that is the most favourable moment for the place to be explored. They will all be out of the way, almost for certain, and he can think of no other time when the same thing is likely to occur. Tomorrow night, for instance, when all the scenes except the lorry one will be taken again, Sir Edward won't be there: Travers will be playing. So there will be nothing to keep them at the other end of the building. In fact, I agree with him, Hugh, that it's a gorgeous opportunity, and one that is much too good to be missed. And Laura thinks so too."

"I do, Captain Drummond," said the girl. "It does seem to me that it's the best chance we're ever likely to get of finding out what really is going on there."

"Well, chaps, you seem to have settled my evening for me," said Drummond, with a grin. "I have no objection to having a look round. One point, though, Algy, you haven't made clear. What is the additional evidence that has come to light since you wrote me that letter?"

"Principally what Tredgold has overheard," said the other. "He's a foxy little blighter, with ears a yard long, and he keeps 'em open. And up to date it has really been more the cumulative effect of a lot of small things than anything specific. But this morning, just as he was going into the office, he heard Penton say to Hardcastle, 'The stuff is all there: we shan't have time for more.' And he was convinced by the way they both shut up on seeing him that they were not talking film business."

"Right oh!" cried Drummond. "I'll have a dart at it. Though what the deuce one does when one finds oneself completely surrounded by cocaine is at the moment a little beyond me."

"Get in touch with the police," said the girl.

"My dear soul, what a ghastly conclusion to the performance! Things going to the bow-wows, Algy, when the old firm have to rope in the minions of the law. However, I'd like to do that bunch down, I must say: that murder was a bit too cold-blooded to be funny."

He turned to the waitress.

"Sweet maiden, bring mugs of port, I pray thee. Because I take it, Algy, that you will shortly have to be getting back?"

"That's so, old boy. Do you know the way to the studio?"

"I do," said Drummond, with a faint smile.

"Well, we thought that nine o'clock would be a good sort of hour for you to get there. There's a track that leads up to it from behind, and there's a turning about a quarter of a mile away where you can leave your car. Hullo! here's Tredgold himself: I told him I was dining here."

"Good evening, Miss Mainwaring," said Tredgold, coming up to the table. "Is it all right, Mr Wentworth? Is your friend on?"

"Absolutely. Let me introduce you to Captain Drummond. Hugh – this is Mr Tredgold, who I've been telling you about."

"Draw up and put your nose inside a beaker of port," cried Drummond. "Anything new from the seat of war?"

"Quite a lot, Captain Drummond," said the other knowingly. "And it's most favourable. Penton and Slingsby left in a car for London about half an hour ago, which means that only Hardcastle will be there when they start work. Which further means that you're bound to have a free run. If the three of them had been there they might not all have remained with Sir Edward, but with only one of them it's a cinch Hardcastle won't leave his side till he goes back to London."

"And when is that likely to be?"

"Let me think," said Tredgold. "The drugging scene is being taken at nine-fifteen; the lorry one, which Sir Edward will be watching, comes after it. I should think you can rely on being undisturbed from nine-thirty to ten."

"That should give me plenty of time," said Drummond.

"More than enough," cried the other. "But they're cunning, don't forget. Just look and see what there is to be seen, but don't disturb anything. They may spot it, and if they did they'd have the stuff away in an instant. And we want tomorrow: we don't propose to ring up Scotland Yard tonight. And pretty fools we should look if the police arrived and found nothing at all."

"Admirable advice," murmured Drummond. "Well, you people had better push off: I'll come on later."

Gloomily he ordered himself some more port. What a ghastly fiasco the whole thing had turned out! He felt bored stiff, and though he tried to assure himself that he was acting as a worthy and God-fearing citizen in unmasking such villainy, his boredom only increased. There was no sport in it. No humour of any sort whatever. He was simply doing a common or garden spying job for a nasty-looking specimen of humanity who wanted the notoriety without incurring the risk.

At last he rose: the sooner he got down to it, the sooner he could get back to London. And having paid his bill, he drove off towards the studio. It was nearly dusk, and as he passed by it on the main road he could just see that activity outside was beginning. Cameras were being wheeled into position, lights put into their proper places; and he wondered cynically if they were missing Henry Johnson.

He reached the turning and parked his car; then, pulling out his cigarette case, he sat and waited. It was a little early yet to approach the studio, even though everyone was at the other end. Some parties of villagers attracted by the novelty went past him towards the fun, but nobody took any notice of the big man moodily smoking by the side of the track.

At last he decided it was safe to start, though he would have to wait till the sightseers were out of the way before entering. And the spot he was making for was a small clump of bushes where he could remain under cover till the road was clear. From his hiding-place he could see them acting in the distance, and Haxton's voice came distinctly through the air. Standing by one of the flares was Sir Edward Greatorex, talking to Hardcastle and Gardini; in the centre of the beam Algy and Jack Montrevor were waiting to run through their scene.

Suddenly he saw Sir Edward's two companions both turn to him solicitously, and the next moment Gardini hurried away to return with an overcoat. Evidently the great man was feeling chilly, and it instantly occurred to Drummond that it might precipitate his return to London, in which case Hardcastle would be free. And so, though he would have preferred to give it another ten minutes, he decided to act at once. With a quick glance round, he left his cover, and skirting cautiously out of sight of the acting, he reached the door.

The bolt slipped back smoothly, and he stepped inside, closing and locking the door behind him. The darkness was intense, but he could feel the rough walls on each side of him as he cautiously moved forward along the passage. He did not want to use his torch until he was further into the building for fear of the gleam being seen from the outside, and so his progress was slow. Every now and then he paused and listened, but he could hear nothing save an occasional faint shout from outside. And after a while even that ceased.

The passage was sloping downwards, and at length he decided it was safe to have some light. He flashed his torch on cautiously: in front of him a flight of steps led down to a very solid-looking door – a door which, somewhat to his surprise, proved to be unlocked. He found himself in a fair-sized room. The walls were of stone, and high up in one of them was a small barred window encrusted in dirt. A few old sacks lay about the floor: otherwise it was empty. And opposite him was another door similar to the one he had come in by, which also, on inspection, proved to be open. A further flight of steps led down to yet a third door, beyond which was a much smaller room. And as the light of his torch travelled round it, he realised with a sudden thrill that his quest was over. Neatly arranged around the walls were scores of small brown-paper parcels, and he was on the point of picking up one of them to examine it, when from behind him there came a metallic click. He swung round, gun in hand: the door had shut.

For a moment he stared at it in bewilderment; then his mouth set grimly. For there was no handle on this side of it – only a keyhole. And he had no key. The door was evidently fitted with an automatic shutting device, and he was trapped.

He became conscious of a faint ticking noise coming from somewhere – a clock, presumably, which meant the room was used fairly constantly. But that did not alter the predicament he found himself in. Sooner or later he was bound to be discovered unless he could find some method of escape.

He flashed his torch around the walls: there was no trace of any window. He was in a central strong room well below ground level – caught as securely as a rat in a trap. And so, having satisfied himself by an inspection of the door that there was no fear of suffocation, he lit a cigarette and proceeded to size up the situation.

Algy was the first hope. He would almost certainly go to the place where the car had been left, and, finding it there, he would know that Drummond was still in the building. But he would not be able to get in, as he had no key to the outside door. All he could do would be to hang about outside.

The next possibility was Hardcastle. Was he likely to come? If so, it was easy money: Hardcastle wouldn't have an earthly. If the other two were with him it would be different: Penton was a singularly powerful individual. And he couldn't hope to lay out the three of them. So clearly his best chance lay in Hardcastle coming alone.

He went to the door and listened intently, but everything was silent except for the monotonous ticking of the clock. And he was idly flashing his torch round in an endeavour to locate it when a sudden rasping noise started in one corner, and the next instant, to his utter amazement, he heard Irma speaking.

"Good evening, *mon ami.*"

Completely dumbfounded, he turned his torch in the direction of the voice, and the mystery was solved. Partially hidden behind some of the packages was a gramophone which had just been turned on.

"I am more than sorry," continued the voice, "that I was not there personally to receive you. And before I go any further I will say at once that I quite realise you may now smash the record and terminate the entertainment. I hope you won't, for two reasons. First, I took a lot of trouble over making it; second, there is a very important message for you that comes right at the end. In that hope, therefore, I will proceed.

"I don't think, Hugh, that you've been very clever this time. In fact, dear friend, I am terribly disappointed in you. That you should walk straight into one of the most palpable traps imaginable is a sign of deplorably weakening intellect. Did you really believe that anyone in their senses would take on that unmitigated buffoon Longworth to do anything except scare crows? But happening to be behind the scenes when he arrived that day, I realised he might be of assistance to me. And so I told Penton to engage him.

"That little man Tredgold is a good actor, isn't he? Quite good enough, anyway, to deceive poor Algy. And I must say he has played his part very well. A few mysterious references to dope, and your idiot friend rose like a fish. And so did you didn't you, Hugh?

"However, to proceed. You will have guessed by now that your present unpleasant predicament is very largely due to a system of electrical wiring. Your progress along the passage was marked by lights in the office upstairs. As you came to each door in turn a bulb went out: as you shut the door it went on again. And so your arrival in the room where you now find yourself was timed by us to a second. It would have been a pity to turn on the electric gramophone too soon.

"And now, because a record does not go on for ever, I must come to the point. Can you guess why I have taken the trouble to do all this? I think you can, Drummond, damn you! For years now I have had at the bottom of my mind one idea only. At times I have been occupied with other things, but ever and always has that main object of my life been with me – revenge on you. And now it is coming. Like the fly, you have walked straight into my parlour, and this time there is no escape. I could weep that I shall not be there actually to see it, but I am in the building,

Drummond, alone with my imagination. And shortly I shall visualise you sweating with fear as you claw vainly for a way out.

"Did you hear that ticking noise when you first came in? What did you think it was, you fool – a clock? Guess again, Drummond, guess again. Go and look in the right-hand corner opposite the door. The only hour that that clock will ever mark is the second that sends you to eternity. It's a bomb, Drummond, and what are you going to do with it? Throw it out of the window? There is no window? Throw it through the door? You cannot open the door. You're alone with it, locked up, in that room.

"The others don't know that I've put it there, Drummond: they only think that you've been lured into your prison as a punishment for your unwarranted interference. They might have been frightened of the consequences of murdering you, but I'm not. As you hear these words I am sitting in an ecstasy of anticipation knowing that the aim of my life is about to be accomplished. I don't care if the building is blown sky high; I don't care if the things around you are scattered to the four winds of Heaven; I don't care who is killed so long as you die screaming for mercy. I may be mad, Drummond: perhaps I am. But that isn't going to help you much, is it? You've got ten minutes to live, and during those ten minutes you can ask yourself who has won in the long run, you or I."

The voice ceased, though the scraping of the machine still continued, and Hugh Drummond, putting his hand to his forehead, found that it was wet with perspiration. And then abruptly the gramophone itself stopped: the only sound was the monotonous ticking in the right-hand corner opposite the door.

He switched his torch in that direction, and cursed himself savagely when he found the beam was shaking. There it was – a harmless-looking brown box, and for a while he stared at it, his mind a blank. What was he going to do? Was there anything to do?

He was under no delusions, though the whole thing seemed like some monstrous nightmare. He knew, none better, that she was capable of anything where he was concerned, that to kill him she would willingly run the risk of being tried for murder herself.

With a tremendous effort he pulled himself together: he was not going under without some sort of fight. Feverishly he tore off his coat and trousers, and wrapped them as tightly as he could round the bomb: working like a maniac, he piled packages of dope against it to try and minimise the force of the explosion. Then, seizing more packages, he hurled them in a heap near the opposite corner with the idea of taking what cover he could behind them. And then, with nothing further to do to occupy his mind, the full horror of the situation came over him.

He glanced at his wrist-watch: two minutes of life left. God! what a fool he had been. He ought to have spotted that it was a trap all along. And yet as he looked back he could think of nothing definite which should have given it away. Tredgold – curse the little swine! – was a good actor: when he laid his hands on him next time…

His jaw set grimly: he'd forgotten. There wasn't going to be a next time. It was the end. In the bottom of his heart he knew that his feeble precautions were utterly useless: he knew that he had a minute left to live. And for a few seconds his nerve broke, and he raved like a madman. Then, with iron control, he got himself in hand again. Even if he was going out alone – like a rat in a trap, with no one to see – he'd go out decently.

He craved for a cigarette, but his case was in the pocket of his coat now wrapped round the bomb. There was no time to get it: even that solace was denied him. And suddenly, such can be the reactions of the human mind, he began to laugh. That the show which a little while before he had regarded as the most boring of his career should have turned out to be the one when he was to meet his death struck him as humorous. But the laughter soon died, and with another glance at his watch he lay down behind the heap of packages.

He waited tensely, muscles braced for the shock. Now that the end had come, he felt strangely calm: anyway, it would be quick. One second – two – three, and then from the corner opposite came a little pouf, followed by a strong smell of burning cloth.

Cautiously he raised his head: smoke was issuing from the pile surrounding the bomb. And at first his brain refused to function. What had happened? He stared at it foolishly, and then, with a sudden mad revulsion of feeling, he understood. The bomb had failed to explode.

With a shout of triumph he jumped up and dashed across the room. He hurled the packages away, and was just unwrapping his coat and trousers when roars of laughter came from behind him. He straightened up and swung round: Hardcastle and Slingsby were standing in the open doorway.

"Wal," said Hardcastle, "if that don't beat cockfighting! Natalie, darling," he called over his shoulder, "I don't think you can come in. Captain Drummond is hardly dressed to receive ladies."

"So I see you believed it, my friend," she said quietly, as she joined the others. "I think your last ten minutes has equalised our score a little."

A cold, overmastering rage took hold of Drummond, though he said no word. Never in the course of his life had he found himself in such an utterly ignominious position. He realised it all now: the whole thing had been a leg-pull from beginning to end. There never had been a bomb – merely a box with a clock ticking inside it and some inflammable powder of sorts. And, to add insult to injury, the only things that had caught fire and were still smouldering were his trousers.

"A much-needed lesson, Drummond," she continued, still in the same quiet voice. "But I must confess that in my wildest dreams I never anticipated seeing you look such a complete fool as you do at the present moment."

She turned away, and he scrambled into his clothes. Damn the woman! She was right: never had he felt such a complete fool. But his voice as he answered her was quite normal.

"I quite admit you've scored this time," he remarked. "But you seem to have overlooked one small point. What do you propose to do about these?"

He picked up one of the packages, and again the two men began to laugh.

"Say, Captain," said Hardcastle, "you surely are the colour of the green, green grass. Why, you poor sap, you don't suppose, do you, that if that was really dope we were going to lead you to it? Open it and see. It's castor sugar: I guess the grocery department at Harrods thought we were starting a wholesale store. But we had to get something that would get you into the room and away from the door. Even you might have thought it funny at finding nothing but a gramophone and a bomb on the floor."

The muscles of Drummond's face tightened: fooled again. Fooled all along the line from the word "Go."

"As I said before, you're certainly one up on this evening's entertainment," he said quietly. "However, there will doubtless be other rounds in the game."

Hardcastle's expression grew ugly.

"Look here, young man," he said, "we've had enough of you. If you give us any further trouble by butting in, you won't get off so easily next time. You keep clear of us, or it will be the worse for you."

Drummond smiled genially.

"I have an affection for you, Tom," he remarked, "that borders on madness. And you may rest assured that whilst you honour our shores with your presence I shall never be far from your side. You see, I've got to get back the price of this pair of trousers somehow. By the way, is the door at the other end open? Because if so I will now leave you."

"It's open," said Hardcastle. "And if you take my advice, Drummond, you'll say goodbye and not *au revoir*. We've been kind to you this time, and let you off with making the most unholy fool of yourself. Next time, should you be so foolish as to let there be a next time, the bomb may be real."

"A thousand thanks, Tom, for your remarks. But, as Irma knows, I'm one of those people who just can't take advice."

Filming was over when he got outside, and one of the first people he saw was Algy Longworth, who was hanging about near the door.

"Careful, Hugh," he said warningly. "Sir Edward has gone back to London, so Hardcastle may be anywhere."

"As you say, he may," answered Drummond grimly. "You don't happen to know where Mr Tredgold is, do you?"

"As a matter of fact I haven't seen him for the last half-hour. Why?"

"I want a few words with Mr Tredgold. And when I do have a few words with him Mr Tredgold's mother won't know her baby boy for a week."

"Good Lord! old man, what's happened?"

"We've been stung, Algy: stung as we've never been stung before. And I'm sore as hell about it. The whole thing, my dear boy, was a plant from beginning to end. Irma was here the day you came, and it was because of her that you were engaged. Then, at her instigation, Tredgold fooled you with the sole object of getting me into the most ignominious position I've ever been in in my life. And, by Gad! they succeeded."

They were strolling towards Drumrnond's car, and he briefly told Algy what had occurred.

"Just think of it," he concluded. "Me standing there in my shirt and pants, while they split their sides with laughter. Gosh! Algy, I could kick myself."

"I'm awfully sorry, old boy," said the other contritely. "It is more my fault than yours. But it never dawned on me that Tredgold was lying. I thought he was a foul little reptile, but I could have sworn he was speaking the truth."

Drummond laughed shortly.

"Don't worry: it doesn't matter. But you may take it from me, old lad, that I have known a pleasanter quarter of an hour than the one I spent down in that damned room."

He stopped suddenly and whistled under his breath.

"Great Scott!" he cried, "I hadn't thought of that. This show has driven everything else out of my head."

"What's stung you?" said Algy.

"Marton – young Marton. We thought we'd got the reason why they killed him, and we haven't."

They stared at one another in silence: it was only too true. Since there never had been any question of drugs, and the whole thing had proved a ramp, obviously they would have to look elsewhere for the solution of that mystery. But the point was – where?

"Is your girl still here, Algy?" said Drummond.

"No, she's taken the bus back to Town."

"Then let's get a move on in mine, and we'll try and think things out on the way up. Because I'm damned if this bunch is going to get away with it as easily as this. Confound my trousers: there's the dickens of a draught coming through the seat."

He swung the car round, and headed for London. He drove slowly, engrossed in thought, and Algy Longworth, after a glance at his profile, was silent too.

"There are a lot of little points, Algy," he said at length, "which, now that I look back in the light of this new development, seem to me to stand out."

"Such as?" demanded his companion.

"To start with, I overheard Penton and the Comtessa talking at the studio this morning."

"What's that? How the devil did you overhear them?"

Drummond laughed.

"I forgot I hadn't told you. Henry Johnson, at your service."

"Well, I'm blowed!" cried the other. "You old devil!"

"In the course of their conversation a remark occurred which I now know applied to me: at the time I wasn't sure. Penton said, 'It's risky: damned risky. Why bring him here at all?' Now what was there risky in their performance of tonight?"

"They might have thought you'd give someone a thick ear."

"Weak, old boy: very weak. Let's go a bit further. The work here finishes tomorrow, doesn't it? after which exteriors are going to be taken down at Glensham House. Now you have to act tomorrow; after that you're not wanted. Well, it's going to be a little awkward for them if you don't turn up."

"Granted. And I certainly shan't."

"That we'll see about: let's stick to the point. Why should they make it awkward for themselves unnecessarily? They could have soaked me tomorrow just as easily as tonight."

"It was the fact that Sir Edward was here that made 'em choose this evening."

"A perfectly sound reason if Tredgold had been speaking the truth. But he wasn't: he was in the plot. And so it would have been just as simple for him to cough up some other yarn which would have made tomorrow night the most suitable one."

"I don't quite get what you're driving at, Hugh."

"Just this. Was the whole of this elaborate hoax perpetrated merely to give me ten minutes' hell? If so, why choose tonight, when tomorrow would have been better?"

The other stared at him curiously: it seemed to him such an unimportant point. But he knew of old that Drummond did not harp on unimportant points.

"What else can it have been designed for?" he demanded.

"If I knew that I'd have solved the problem, Algy. Can it be that they wanted to be sure I should be out of the way tonight?"

"Why should they? Nothing happened of the smallest interest. We took a couple of scenes, which Sir Edward watched. Then apparently he felt chilly and went back to London with that secretary fellow. Travers did the lorry scene, and then came back, and that concluded the entertainment. Frankly, old boy, I think you're making a mystery where no mystery exists. Don't forget that Tredgold's bluff all the way through has been very good, and his reason for choosing tonight was a very convincing one. He might not have been able to get anything like such a good excuse for tomorrow."

"Perhaps you're right, Algy," said Drummond at length. "And yet every instinct I possess tells me you're wrong."

"Am I to go there tomorrow?"

"Certainly. And Henry Johnson will be there too. My debt to Mr Tredgold will have to wait."

But if he thought he was going to discover anything more, he was doomed to disappointment. Once again the same scenes were re-enacted, with Travers playing the millionaire's part, and since he had not seen them the previous day, he watched them for something better to do. Only Haxton was there: none of the Hardcastle gang put in an appearance. And after a while he again began to ask himself whether the whole thing wasn't a mare's nest.

For the film was a good one, especially this bit in the country house, where, having failed to move the financier to pity, the hero and a friend drug the glass of sherry which, according to invariable custom, he always drinks at half-past seven. He falls unconscious on the floor, and from behind the curtains the two men emerge. They bind him and gag him, and then, as they are on the point of removing him, steps are heard outside. There is just time to bundle the body into a large cupboard and dart back behind the curtains, when the door opens and his wife comes in. The room is empty: it is her chance to recover the letters.

He watched part of the walk through; then, wandering round behind one of the wings, he came on Travers, being freed from his bonds. Haxton's approving remarks could be heard, but it struck him that the actor was nervous and irritable, and after chancing a facetious remark which was met with a snarl, he moved away.

"Once more, boys," came Haxton's voice, "and then we'll shoot. Well done, old man," as Travers appeared, "you were fine. It's the last scene: we won't bother about the lorry bit again. I've seen the run through, and last night's was bully."

He strolled across the studio to where Algy and the girl were sitting, and after a cautious look round he spoke in his natural voice.

"I believe you're right, Algy," he said. "We're on a dud."

"What a marvellous disguise, Captain Drummond!" cried the girl. "I wouldn't believe Algy when he told me."

"All wasted," he grunted despondently. "I suppose he's told you about last night's little show."

She nodded.

"It must have been a ghastly experience. I haven't seen that little brute Tredgold here today."

"Nor have I," said Drummond grimly. "Something heavy would have connected with him if I had. Hullo! They've finished. I say, I'm awfully sorry that you two should have wasted your time like this."

"Not a bit," she cried. "The person I'm sorry for is you. But I really think Algy is right, and that this film is perfectly genuine. After all, Sir Edward is a multi-millionaire, and he can afford to pay for his hobbies."

"That's true," agreed Drummond. "Well, so long: we'll meet again in the old village. At any rate I propose to touch these blighters for my pay."

With a grin, Henry Johnson moved off and joined a group of stage-hands.

" 'Ullo, mate!" said one of them, " 'ow's yer toothache?"

"Orl right. 'Ad the perisher out."

"Dodged a job o' work yesterday, you did."

" 'Ow's that?"

" 'Is nib's best girl come along. And may you hor I look at 'er? Ho no. So we 'as to rig hup a partition be'ind which 'er royal 'ighness may sit hunobserved. Not 'arf a peach she wasn't: could 'ave done with a bit like 'er meself."

For a moment or two Drummond stared at the speaker; then he remembered his role.

"Where did you put the partition?" he asked.

"Cross there. So as hevery time 'e went off 'e could walk right hinto 'er lovely harms. And when they bunged 'im hinto the cupboard, she could massage 'is bruises hunseen."

"Wot did she look like?"

"Dark: furriner, I should say. Natalie – or some name like that – 'e called 'er."

Drummond turned away. So Irma had been watching. There seemed no reason why she shouldn't, but why the secrecy? Was it merely to prevent the risk of Algy seeing her? And with yet another unexplained riddle to puzzle him, Henry Johnson finished his work, drew his pay, and ceased to exist.

He found a wire from Ted Jerningham, who had returned to Merridale Hall, awaiting him at his flat.

"Penton arrived Glensham. Any further developments?"

He rolled it into a ball and flung it savagely into the paper basket. No, confound it! there were no further developments. Nor did he see the slightest chance of there ever being any further developments. The whole thing was a frost of the worst order. And yet, strive as he would, the thought kept coming back to his mind that there was something he had missed – some clue that had eluded him.

It was the following morning that a paragraph in the society page of one of the illustrated dailies caught his eye.

"Sir Edward Greatorex, the well-known financier, has left the Ritz Carlton for a cruise in the steam yacht *Firefly*. The *Firefly*, which belongs to Lord Derringham, has been hired for two months by Mr Hardcastle, a well-known American, and it is as his guest that Sir Edward is travelling. Though the secret has been well kept, it is now more or less common property that the millionaire has recently added yet a further activity to his many others, and that he has been playing the principal part in a film entitled 'High Finance.' The idea of getting Sir Edward to play the same role on the screen as he habitually plays in real life is ingenious, and should assist in making the film, which I am told is very good already, a still greater success. It is understood that some further scenes will be taken on board the yacht."

So that was where Hardcastle had got the yacht from. He knew Sandy Derringham quite well – one of those cheery individuals with an enormous income who, in spite of it, still managed to be permanently semi-broke. Not that it mattered much: once again on the face of it the whole thing seemed perfectly genuine. And he had almost succeeded in dismissing the affair from his mind when yet another announcement in the morning papers some four days later brought it all back again. For this time it was not in the society columns, but in the financial.

"SENSATION IN THE CITY.

"Extraordinary scenes occurred on the Stock Exchange yesterday in connection with Peruvian Eagles. This concern is largely under the control of Sir Edward Greatorex, the well-known financier, who is at present on a yachting trip. A complete panic set in, which resulted in the shares dropping to the unprecedentedly low price of

$2^1/_4$. It will be recalled that ten days ago they were standing at over 7. It is understood that Sir Edward is in close touch with the situation by wireless."

He read on, but the details soon became technical, and he threw the paper aside. His knowledge of stocks and shares was microscopic: on the rare occasions that he had any money to invest he rang up his broker and resigned himself to fate. But the first part of the paragraph required no expert knowledge to understand. An upheaval had taken place in the City which was closely connected with Sir Edward, and that was quite enough to make Drummond desire to know more. And so, having finished his breakfast, he chartered a taxi and drove off to see his stockbroker, one Bill Templeton.

"Great Scott! old lad," cried that worthy as he entered the office, "what brings you down these parts at this ungodly hour? Are you selling the war-saving certificate?"

"I would hold converse with you, Bill," he remarked, depositing himself in a chair. "Being what you are, you presumably know something about stocks and shares."

"You flatter me, dear boy. Do you want to invest some money?"

"God forbid! Whenever I do so the only sum that isn't irretrievably lost in a week is your commission. No, Bill: I want you to tell me all that is in your heart concerning Peruvian Eagles."

The other stared at him.

"You don't hold any, do you?"

"Not so far as I know. But what I want to get at is the cause of the excitement amongst your brother robbers concerning them. For God's sake don't talk to me about bulls and bears or selling short, because I shan't have an idea what you mean. Just plain simple language."

Templeton lit a cigarette and pushed the box over the table.

"I can tell you in a few sentences, Hugh," he said. "Peruvian Eagles are a big oil concern. Up to a few days ago they were regarded in the City as being one of the finest investments – a little speculative, of course – obtainable. Then rumours began to circulate that all was not too well with the child. At first it was nothing more than that; then suddenly it began to come out that Sir Edward Greatorex, a man you may have heard of, and who holds far more than fifty per cent of the shares, was selling them as fast as he could. That started the rot."

A clerk entered the office.

"What are Perus at now?" asked Templeton.

"$1^1/_8$ to $1^1/_4$, sir."

"You see, Hugh: they've dropped another point this morning."

"And is that all there is to it?" demanded Drummond.

"All!" echoed the other. "A good many people are going to be ruined over it. And incidentally Sir Edward must have dropped a packet himself."

"Why did he sell?"

"He must have got inside information that something is very wrong," explained the other, "so he's cutting his losses. Up to a week ago he was buying the whole time: now he sells. It can only mean that. I should say it's the first time for many years that that gentleman has burnt his fingers," he added, with a short laugh. "Hullo! Jerry, you seem excited. What's stung you?"

A man, his top hat on the back of his head, had dashed into the office.

"Bill," he shouted, "have you heard the latest about Perus? Rawlings has just got the report, and it exceeds anything that one could have hoped for in one's wildest dreams. Buy, man, buy, and go on buying."

Templeton leapt to his feet.

"Good God! Has Greatorex gone mad?"

He gave some orders down the telephone, and reached for his hat.

"Come and lunch with me at Sherry's, Hugh. I must dash. I'll get a thousand for you if you like."

"Right oh! old boy. I can't pay, but that doesn't matter, does it?"

He strolled out, and even to his eye, unused though he was to the City, he could see that the activity was unusual. Men, some bareheaded, some in toppers, were either running hard or else were standing about in little groups talking excitedly. And Perus was the one word he heard on everyone's lips.

It was the same at Sherry's, where Bill Templeton joined him at one o'clock.

"Gosh! boy," he cried, mopping his forehead, "what a morning! I've bought you a thousand."

"Splendid, old lad! you shall have the postal order in due course. But what I'm even more interested in is what all the song and dance is about."

"It's this way," explained the other, spearing an oyster. "As I told you this morning, when Sir Edward started to sell, we all assumed that there was something wrong. Then out came the report, and, far from there being anything wrong, it's righter than anyone could have possibly hoped for. In short, either Greatorex is playing some astoundingly deep game – so deep, in fact, that none of us can understand it – or he's gone mad. In either case he's dropped about half a million. I gather he's been acting in a film called 'High Finance': better for him if he'd stuck to the genuine thing in real life."

"When did he start selling?" asked Drummond thoughtfully.

"Can't tell you exactly. But it was after he started on a yachting cruise."

"So instructions came by wireless?"

"They must have. Wait a moment" – he lowered his voice – "that's one of his brokers who has just come in. He's coming over here: I'll see if I can draw him. Morning, Lionel."

"Morning," snapped the other, and Templeton nudged Drummond. "Does every man who acts in a film go off his rocker?" he added savagely.

"You see, Hugh," said Templeton, as the other moved away," he has been let down: they all have. I don't wonder: it's the most amazing thing of modern times. I mean, Greatorex may be a swine, but he's a genius. And for him to make such a colossal mistake as this is simply unbelievable."

And for a space Drummond was silent: an idea was beginning to dawn in his mind which almost staggered him with its possibilities.

"Listen, Bill," he said at length. "How do you know the instructions to sell came from Greatorex?"

"Because he uses a secret code, old boy, which only he knows. And it varies with each broker he deals with."

"But his secretary knows it."

"Naturally his secretary would know it also. What of it?"

Once again Drummond fell silent: a glimpse of light was there, but the rest was still in darkness.

"Tell me, Bill," he said at length, "am I right in supposing that because he has lost this money somebody else has made it?"

"Not quite, old boy," answered the broker. "But you would be perfectly right in supposing that anyone who bought shares yesterday or early this morning is going to net a very handsome profit. What's worrying you, Hugh? You're going to make a nice little packet yourself, you know."

But the other was too intent on his line of reasoning to think about that.

"You're sure that no one but Greatorex or his secretary could have sent those instructions?"

"Certain. And you may take it from me that with a man like Greatorex such a thing is not left to his secretary. Have you got some suspicion of dark villainy in your mind?" Templeton added, with a laugh. "It might do for the film he was making, but it doesn't wash in real life."

"Perhaps you're right, Bill. Well, so long: we might have a round at Walton Heath one day."

He left the restaurant still deep in thought. Was it possible that Hardcastle and his crowd were holding the millionaire a prisoner on board the yacht, and issuing false instructions which purported to come from him? That would presuppose that the secretary Gardini was in league with them – an assumption which was quite feasible when he recalled their first meeting in South Audley Street.

He hailed a taxi and told the driver to take him to the Junior Sports Club. Sandy Derringham was usually to be found there round about that hour, and there were one or two things over which he might prove helpful. He found him at lunch, and came to the point at once.

"This is for your ears only, Sandy," he said. "You hired your yacht to one Hardcastle, didn't you?"

"That's the bally fellow's name, old boy."

"Is your own crew on board?"

"Yes, every one of them."

"And your own skipper?"

"Sure thing. Why?"

Briefly Drummond told him his suspicions, and Lord Derringham's eyes grew rounder and rounder as he listened.

"Impossible, Hugh," he said. "Old man Wilkinson, the skipper, would never allow it for an instant. He's the most reliable man I know, and the hell of a martinet. And you can't keep a man a prisoner in a small yacht without the Captain finding out."

"Perhaps he's ill, Sandy: or they've doped him."

The other shook his head.

"If he was so ill that he couldn't attend to business," he said shrewdly, "they'd put back to port. And if he can attend to business your idea goes bust."

"Never mind," persisted Drummond. "I want you to do something for me. Send a private marconigram to Wilkinson, couched more or less like this – 'Is passenger with fair beard well?' and sign it with your name."

The other shrugged his shoulders.

"All right, old lad, I will if you like: though it seems pretty fair bilge to me. I'll send it at once. Let's go and have a spot of coffee and I'll get a form. Now then," he said, as they went into the smoking-room, "what is it you want me to say? 'Is Greatorex well?'

"No, don't mention him by name. Marconigrams can be read by other people, and I may be up the pole. Say what I told you, and then put – 'Do not mention this cable to anyone.'"

"Right oh!" said Derringham resignedly. "Old Wilkinson will probably think I've gone bughouse, but it can't be helped."

He signed the message, and gave it to a waiter to send.

"Do you want to wait for the answer?" he asked. "If so, we can probably get a rubber."

And it was perhaps as well that they were not in the middle of a hand when the reply came – a reply which caused Drummond to scratch his head in hopeless bewilderment. For it ran as follows.

"Cannot understand question. Only passenger on board clean-shaven dark man who is quite well. Wilkinson."

Where, then, was Sir Edward Greatorex? Clearly Gardini was manipulating the market from the yacht, but what had happened to the millionaire? Was he in London doing some super-cunning financial wangle?

"Don't say anything about it, Sandy," said Drummond, as he left the club. "There's something deuced rum somewhere, but at the moment it's beyond me."

He decided to walk across the Park, and it was as he was passing the Ritz Carlton that, acting on a sudden impulse, he stopped and spoke to the commissionaire at the door.

"You didn't happen to be here the day Sir Edward Greatorex left, did you?"

The man, who knew him well, grinned.

"As a matter of fact, I was, sir," he said, "though Sir Edward didn't seem to notice it. He very rarely does notice people when he's leaving. Why, if I may ask, sir, do you want to know?"

"He's on a cruise now, isn't he?"

"That's right, sir. He was going straight to Plymouth when he left. Seemed to have a bit of a chill: he was all muffled up."

Drummond nodded and walked on. What had happened between leaving the hotel and reaching Plymouth to make him change his mind? Or had he never intended to go? He could well understand that for a man in his position it might frequently be an advantage if people believed he was somewhere when in reality he was nothing of the sort. But in this case, if what Bill Templeton had said was correct, it was a little difficult to see where the advantage came in. And yet, why had he even gone to the extent of having it advertised in the morning papers unless he had some very good reason for doing so?

"Hugh! Wait a moment."

He swung round: Algy Longworth and Peter Darrell were behind him.

"Hullo! chaps," he said. "How goes it?"

"Extraordinary thing, this Peruvian Eagle business," said Longworth. "I've just been talking to Peter about it. It might be the film in real life."

"How do you mean?" demanded Drummond.

"It's exactly the same story, only this time it's actually happened."

"I don't get you, Algy. To be candid, I'm not very clear as to what the end of the film was."

"Don't you remember they abducted the millionaire in a lorry, and kidnapped him on board a yacht. Then, by rigging the market in his absence, they nearly ruined him, and made a pot of money themselves."

"The only difference is," said Drummond, "that in this case he doesn't happen to be on board the yacht."

He told them about Derringham's marconigram and the captain's answer.

"So the analogy fails a bit, old boy," he concluded. "What his game is I can't guess, but I gather he's lost money all right."

"I saw Ted yesterday," said Darrell. "They're hard at work filming down at Glensham House."

"I suppose Sir Edward isn't there by any chance?"

"No," said Longworth. "I beetled down to have a look see the other day. Travers is doing it. Well, we must push on, Peter. So long, Hugh. It sure has been a frost this show."

Drummond continued his walk gloomily: Algy was right. And not the least frozen part of the performance was that the only person who had really been in the ice-chest was he himself. To give it up and try and forget about it seemed the only thing, but it was easier said than done. And even after he had turned in that night he still found his thoughts running on it ceaselessly. Surely there must be a clue somewhere that he'd missed.

Suddenly he sat up in bed and switched on the light: a thought had struck him for the first time. All the way through, the one endeavour of everybody at the studio had been to prevent Sir Edward realising that Travers was re-doing his scenes. How, then, did it come about that now, quite openly, the whole thing was being done by the understudy, a fact which was bound sooner or later to be found out by Sir Edward? Had he really been in the yacht, and safely out of the way, it was understandable: they could take the genuine shots first, and then go through the farce again with Sir Edward when he returned. But he wasn't in the yacht: at any moment he might turn up at Glensham House, when the fat would be in the fire.

He lit a cigarette: the more he thought of it, the stranger it seemed. It was so utterly illogical to take elaborate precautions to prevent him finding out the truth during part of the film, and then relax them entirely. Unless they *knew* that he wouldn't turn up. And how could they *know* that, unless...

He sprang out of bed and began pacing up and down the room. They couldn't *know* that unless he was a prisoner. But how could they have made him a prisoner? Prominent men cannot be abducted from a Great Western Railway express, or in the broad light of day in London. And the commissionaire had seen him leaving the Ritz Carlton. Muffled up, true; but...

He halted abruptly, his mouth open. Then he made one wild bound for the telephone, and twiddled the dial feverishly.

"Who the hell is that?" came a sleepy voice from the other end.

"Algy," he cried, "come round here at once. I've had a brain-storm."

"Damn it, old boy, it's two o'clock," came a plaintive voice from the other end: "the hour before dawn, when people die."

"Put a coat over your pyjamas, Algy, and get a move on."

A quarter of an hour later Longworth appeared.

"You're the ruddy limit, Hugh," he protested. "It could surely have waited till the morning."

"Dry up, Algy, and get the grey matter working. I want you to tell me exactly what took place as far as the taking of the film was concerned that night that they decoyed me into the cellar. Begin with the scene in the study."

"You mean where they drugged the financier? He drank the sherry, and a few moments later pitched forward unconscious.

210

Then Montrevor and that other bloke whose name I can't remember came out from behind the curtains, bound and gagged him, and were just going to carry him through the window when they were interrupted by the wife's arrival. So they hid him in the big cupboard. Then the wife…"

"Doesn't matter about her. How was Sir Edward gagged?"

"With a handkerchief round his mouth and nose."

Drummond rubbed his hands.

"Did you see him again after that?"

"Not until later, when he was watching the lorry scene with Hardcastle."

"He didn't come back on the stage?"

"No. I gathered from a remark of Hardcastle's that he was having dinner."

"All right: carry on with the lorry scene."

"That was two hours after. Travers, bound and gagged just as Sir Edward had been, was in the cupboard. Montrevor and the other fellow carried him out, threw him into the lorry, which then drove off."

"Did Montrevor go in the lorry?"

"No: the driver was supposed to be in league with them."

"Who was the driver?"

Algy Longworth stared at him.

"Funny you should ask that. As a matter of fact it struck me as a bit odd at the time. It was Penton."

"Think carefully, Algy. Did that lorry come back after the scene was shot?"

"No, I don't think it did. I'm sure it didn't."

"Why didn't it?" Drummond's eyes were gleaming with excitement. "We're getting on to it, Algy. Go back a bit. What was Sir Edward doing?"

"Talking to Hardcastle and Gardini."

"And my recollection is that he was standing in the shadow of one of the arcs."

"Yes, he was. Then he drove off in his car to London."

"Before or after the lorry had gone?"

"Before. I gathered he had got a chill."

"And then?"

"That's the lot, old boy. Travers returned and we shut up shop."

"How long was it before Travers returned?"

"About a quarter of an hour, I should say. What's the great idea, Hugh?"

Drummond took two or three turns up and down the room before replying, whilst the other watched him curiously.

"The great idea," he said at length, "is that my brain during the last few days would have disgraced an aboriginal lunatic."

CHAPTER 10

"A most interesting and instructive day, Mr Hardcastle. I am not a great film fan myself, I admit, though I go now and then. But this is the first occasion on which I have ever seen one in the making."

Mr Joseph Hetterbury stretched out his legs under the dining-table and gently twisted the stem of his port-glass between a podgy finger and thumb. The big windows were open, the moor, turning slowly from purple to black, lay in front of him. He had just finished an excellent dinner, and felt at peace with the world. Glensham House was a welcome change after London.

"I thought it might amuse you," remarked his host, pushing the decanter towards him. "It is, as you say, most interesting to see the way the different scenes are taken, and then compare them with the finished article."

"It should be a great success. I suppose it is the first time that such an idea has been carried out?"

"You mean getting a well-known man to play himself, so to speak, in a film? I think it is. And when Sir Edward suggested it to me, the possibilities struck me at once."

"Ah! he was the originator of the idea?"

Hardcastle nodded.

"Yes. He has always been keen on acting, and I could see what a valuable box-office draw he would prove. So between us we evolved a story round his central idea. You will hardly believe it, Mr Hetterbury, but it had never occurred to me until then how far-reaching might be the results if a financier of his standing was kidnapped. To you, moving as you do in the City, doubtless it would have been obvious. But to me, though I am not exactly a poor man, it came quite as a revelation."

"That is the plot of the film, is it?"

"In brief, it is. I was talking to him one day concerning high finance – which is what we have called the film, as you know – and I asked him whether he ever took a holiday. He said to me, 'A man in my position can never afford one. I must always be in touch with the market.' And realising that if a man like him said so it must be true, the idea grew on me that it would make a wonderful peg on which to hang the story. Let him be kidnapped, and held prisoner on board a yacht, from which by wireless false information is sent to his brokers in London."

"And why particularly a yacht?" asked Hetterbury.

"For two reasons. The first and less important one is that sea scenes are always popular in a film. But the second was what made it imperative. As he pointed out, big operations such as his abductors intended would be bound to cause an upheaval in the City. Now if the instructions which were supposed to emanate from him came from anywhere on land, his brokers would descend on him like a hive of bees. If they then found they couldn't see him, they would at once smell a rat. In parentheses I may tell you, Mr Hetterbury, that every year the public grows more insistent on details in a film being correct. And when he explained that aspect of the case to me, I at once saw the force of it. We therefore had to think of some place from which his supposed instructions could come, and where he could not be reached by his brokers. And a yacht suggested itself immediately."

"He is actually on board your yacht now, I believe?"

"That is so," said Hardcastle, with a genial smile. "But not, I assure you, in durance vile."

The other laughed heartily and filled his glass.

"He developed a slight chill down at the studio, and I gather there is a certain tendency to bronchial weakness. At any rate, both his secretary and I agreed that it would be much better for him to have a complete rest before completing the rather arduous part of the film which has to be taken on board."

"Quite," remarked Hetterbury. "A very wise precaution. But reverting to the film for a moment – because I really am very interested in it – there is one point that strikes me, Mr Hardcastle. What is there to prevent the brokers getting in touch with the yacht by marconigram, and asking for confirmation of the instructions?"

"We had to take a little licence there," explained the other. "Admittedly it is a thing which would be difficult to arrange in real life, but I don't think it matters in a film. We imagine that the entire yacht's crew, captain and everyone on board, are all in the pay of the abductors, so that the financier is a virtual prisoner. Messages do reach him, but they are answered by his secretary in his name. You see, no question of signature comes in where a telegram is concerned, and, since a secret code is used, the brokers have no alternative but to treat the communications as coming from him, and act on them. And I have no doubt that when we come to shooting the scenes, Lord Derringham's admirable Scotch skipper will play his part with gusto, even to the extent of putting Sir Edward in irons!"

"In view of the story, it certainly is a most amazing coincidence over Peruvian Eagles."

"Peruvian Eagles! I think I hold a few. What has happened?"

"My dear sir!" Hetterbury stared at him in amazement. "You don't mean to say that you don't know?"

"To tell you the truth, Mr Hetterbury," said Hardcastle, "I have been so engrossed down here with the film for the last few days that I have hardly seen a paper. I trust that nothing has gone wrong with them, for, though my holding is small, in these hard days one doesn't want to lose the little one has."

"It has been the talk of the City for the last ten days. Sir Edward, as you may know, is, or rather was, the largest shareholder, and up till recently he has been buying all the time. A fortnight ago the shares were standing at 7, when it suddenly came out that he was selling as fast as he could. Down came the price with a rush, until at one period they actually dropped below par. The Stock Exchange was humming with excitement, naturally, and then, to everyone's amazement, it transpired that, far from anything being wrong with the company, its condition was even sounder than had been thought. And now the shares are back again to 6."

"What an extraordinary thing! Do you think Sir Edward really sold, or was it just a rumour started in his absence?"

"He sold all right, towards the end naturally at a dead loss. And what his game was no one can make out."

"Has he lost much money?"

"A packet, though he can well afford that. But what is defeating everybody is how a man of his uncanny astuteness can have made such a mistake."

Hardcastle lit a cigar thoughtfully; then, leaning over the table towards his guest, he lowered his voice.

"Mr Hetterbury," he said confidentially, "this is all news to me – as I told you, I have hardly glanced at the papers lately – but I wonder if I can supply a possible reason to account for it."

"It will interest me profoundly if you can," remarked the other.

"I have, of course, been seeing a lot of Sir Edward recently. In fact, until he went off in my yacht I met him every day for some hours at a stretch. And it struck me – I don't want to exaggerate – that he was, shall I say, a little queer at times."

"In what way do you mean, Mr Hardcastle?"

"It is difficult to answer your question in so many words," said the other. "There was nothing specific on which one could lay hold and say that it was peculiar. But I think my daughter summed it up best one day when she said that he seemed to her to be on the verge of a nervous breakdown. Things take different people in different ways, and it is just conceivable that the unusual experience of acting in a film, coming at a time when perhaps he was not too fit, may have been too much for him."

"To the extent of selling Perus for no rhyme or reason!" cried Hetterbury. "In any event, surely his secretary would have prevented him."

Hardcastle pursed his lips.

"From what I saw of the relations between those two," he remarked dryly, "it would have been useless for the secretary to say anything if Sir Edward had announced his intention of walking down Piccadilly in his birthday suit. Mind you, Mr Hetterbury, it is only an idea of mine, put forward to try to account for what seems an amazing action on Sir Edward's part. Or again, there may be some deep underlying motive which only he knows."

"Of the two suggestions the first is the more likely," said the other. "In fact, it does supply a possible explanation for what has occurred, and one that I shall mention when I get back to London."

Hardcastle held up a warning hand.

"I beg of you to be discreet in what you say," he cried. "I would not like it to come to Sir Edward's ears that I had been spreading statements of that sort about him."

"My dear sir," protested the other, "you may rely on my discretion. Your name will not come into it at all. But everyone is asking the same question, and it is certainly a feasible answer. By the way, how much longer is he remaining at sea?"

"I couldn't tell you. Not very much longer, presumably, because the yacht will have to refuel. My honey! what is the matter?"

He swung round in his chair as the door burst open and the Comtessa came running in. She was in a state of great agitation, though she endeavoured to control herself on seeing Hetterbury, who had risen to his feet.

"The ghost, Tom," she cried, forgetting her role completely. "I've just seen the ghost."

"Come, come," laughed Hardcastle, though he gave her a warning frown. "We've all seen it, my love, and she's quite harmless. Come and drink a glass of port with your old Dad, and forget about it."

"I seem to remember reading something about a ghost in that dreadful murder case you had here," said Hetterbury.

"There was a little about it in the papers," answered Hardcastle. "Three young fools came over here ghost-hunting the very night it took place, though, to do them justice, we all saw it afterwards."

"What form did it take?"

"An elderly woman of the caretaker class. We saw her as clearly as I see you now, standing at the top of the stairs; then she vanished through the door of my daughter's bedroom."

"How terrible for you, Comtessa! What did you do?"

"I'm sorry to say I was stupid enough to faint," she answered. "She was so close to me, and then she put out her hand and touched me. It was awful."

"And you have just seen her again in your bedroom?"

"It was in the passage this time," she said. "It's stupid of me, I know, but I dread anything of that sort."

"Very natural," remarked Hetterbury sympathetically. "Well, Mr Hardcastle, I am sure the Comtessa would like to be quiet, so I will take my departure. Perhaps you could ring for my car."

"Certainly," said his host, with an alacrity that apparently his guest failed to notice. "I think it would be as well for my girl to rest."

Hetterbury bowed over the Comtessa's hand.

"I trust your visitor will not trouble you again tonight," he murmured, giving it a gentle squeeze. "Being a lady, it should confine its attention to our sex. And I must thank you for a most enjoyable afternoon."

He followed Hardcastle into the hall, and a few moments later his car drove off.

"For the love of Mike, what stung you, kid?" cried Hardcastle, coming back into the room. "What's all this bologney about a ghost? The only one we've ever had in the house was yourself, and darned well you did it."

"I haven't told you about it, Tom," she said: "in fact, until tonight I'd forgotten about it. You remember that I went up in the train with that man Drummond and his two friends. Well, it was the one called Jerningham who owns Merridale Hall who told me on the way up to London. This house *is* haunted."

"Bologney," repeated Hardcastle incredulously. "We worked a ramp then, but there's nothing to it."

"You listen to me, Tom Hardcastle," she said angrily, "and quit talking out of your turn. Haven't I told you I'd forgotten all about it till tonight? I'd gone down to see that he had got something to eat – incidentally he's getting weaker and weaker, and unless we watch it he'll die on us before we're ready. Anyway, he was moaning and groaning as usual, when suddenly I noticed a most peculiar smell, just the same as you get sometimes from that foul bog outside. I looked around, trying to locate it, when just beyond the range of the candle I saw something move. It didn't walk: it didn't seem to do anything except just give a sort of heave. Then it vanished without a sound."

"But what was it?" cried the man.

"A great black, shapeless sort of mass," she said, with a violent shudder. "And it stank."

"There, there, my dear," he said soothingly. "It was a trick of the light."

"I tell you it wasn't," she stormed. "It's an elemental – that's what that man Jerningham said. It's called the Horror of Glensham House, and people who see it either go mad or die."

"Well, honey, you haven't done either," he said quietly, though his eyes were fixed on her searchingly. She was in an acute state of nerves; obviously the shock had been very great. Now that Hetterbury had gone and there was no longer any necessity for her to control herself, her quivering lips and shaking fingers told their own tale.

He poured her out another glass of port.

"Take it easy, kid," he said, "and try and forget it. It's not much longer now."

"Nothing would induce me to go down there again, Tom," she cried.

"There's no reason why you should, honey," he assured her. "And if it was an elemental, or whatever you said, which sends people mad, it might save us a lot of trouble. I did a bit of good work at dinner tonight, after you'd left us."

"I never quite got who the man was," she said, pulling herself together with an effort.

"A guy from the City who has been doing some fishing near by. He was motoring back to London when he saw us working outside and stopped to look."

"And you asked him to dinner on that! You must be plumb crazy."

"Easy, honey: easy. Where's the harm in asking him to dinner? Where's the harm in asking the whole world to dinner? Ain't we all straight and above-board in this outfit? There's nothing we mind anybody seeing."

"I'm getting nervy, Tom," she said. "I wish to God it was all over."

"It's this darned ghost has got you, dearie: don't you think about it. But listen here, kid: I'm telling you about dinner. This Hetterbury guy suddenly starts talking about Peruvian Eagles.

Of course I know nothing about them: buried down here in my work and all that sort of bunk. So he tells me the whole story, and says that nobody in London can make out what Sir Edward is up to. That gives me my cue, and I flatter myself I took it well. Brought you into it: said that you had mentioned to me one day that you thought he was on the verge of a nervous breakdown. It's the thin end of the wedge: you mark my words. I told him to be sure he didn't mention my name as having said so, but it will be all over London to-morrow. What are you staring at, honey?"

"I thought I saw something move in those bushes out there, Tom," she cried.

The man went to the window and stared out. The light had almost gone, and for a moment it seemed to him also as if some dark object flitted through the undergrowth. Then all was still again.

"Tom – is it absolutely necessary? Must it be done?"

He swung round angrily: she was still sitting at the table.

"Of course it must be done," he said harshly. "You don't want to spend the next few years of your life in prison, do you? To say nothing of losing every dime we've made. You're crazy – there's no risk. Haven't we planned out every detail? Let 'em suspect what they like: they can't prove anything. There, there, honey," he went on soothingly, laying his hand on her shoulder, "you're rattled tonight. This ghost business has upset you. We've just got the other big *coup* to pull off, and then we'll beat it."

"You got the radio from Gardini?"

"Sure. The boys were getting busy in London today. Now you get off to bed: I'm just going along to see that his nibs is all right."

Obediently she left the room, and for a while he sat on smoking. There were times when the amazing success of their plan up to date almost staggered him. Everything had worked literally without a hitch, and the results had exceeded their wildest expectations. And now two more days would see the whole thing through, with another enormous sum of money to their credit.

He ran over every detail in his mind since the commencement of the plot in Baden, and as a connoisseur he found no flaw save one – the butting in of those three damned young Englishmen on the night they had murdered Marton. And yet even that did not really spoil his appreciation of their scheme, because it had been in the nature of a fluke. The expert card-player whose plan is temporarily endangered by some card, led for no reason at all by a fourth-rate performer, does not feel that his reputation has suffered. And the steps they had at once taken to euchre this man Drummond had proved amply sufficient. In fact, he was sadly disappointed in him after all that Natalie had said. A large bovine type of great strength undoubtedly, but an unworthy opponent for a man of brains.

He refilled his glass, sipping the wine appreciatively, as became a man who in future would be able to afford a good cellar. Then his thoughts returned to the past few weeks, and this time to the film itself. How amusing it would be later on to go and see it with his inside knowledge of what it had served to cover. To be able to say to himself at the psychological moment, "There under your noses, my dear audience, is one of the master crimes of the century being carried out and you don't know it."

Again he lifted the decanter: it seemed a pity not to finish it. There was no hurry, and the port was undoubtedly good. So good, in fact, that, having discovered another bottle in the sideboard, it was a full hour before he finally rose from the table. And had anyone been present to see his exit from the room he would have had to admit that Mr Hardcastle's progress to the door did not exactly conform to Euclid's definition of a straight line.

Not that he was drunk: it took him only two attempts to find the nobs in the woodwork which operated the secret panel in the hall. But there was no denying that he was in a condition which is variously known as "slightly oiled" or "one over the eight."

The passage was narrow, and he took each side impartially as he walked along it, his torch throwing a beam of light in front of him. And at length he came to some steps leading off it, at the top of which he paused for a moment with an evil smile on his face. The wine had brought out all the bully in his nature, and he was proposing to enjoy himself.

He went down the steps and opened the door at the bottom. Then, swaying slightly, he gave a drunken chuckle as he contemplated the man lying bound and gagged on the bed with his back towards him.

"Are you awake, Sir Edward?" he said thickly, and a slight movement showed that he was.

"All right: don't answer. I don't care. All the same to me. But I'm going to have a little chat with you. That's what I came for, you damned old fool."

He lit a cigarette and sat down on the only chair.

"Had a gentleman asking about you this evening. Hetter... Hetter...forgotten his name. Doesn't matter. Big noise in the City. He couldn't understand about Peruvian Eagles: nobody in London can understand. Why should you lose so much money? Course I didn't tell him it was so that we could make it: he might have thought that a little peculiar. So I told him what I thought: that you'd suddenly gone loopy. Nervous breakdown. Sending orders from yachts to sell when you meant to buy! Shocking error of judgment, my boy: quite shocking. And this next one is worse. What the poor old stockbrokers in London will say when they get your instructions over Robitos I shudder to think."

No reply came from the man on the bed, and Hardcastle gave an ugly laugh.

"Still struck dumb, are you? I'll give you something to make you think, you fool. What d'you suppose is going to be the end of this? You've got the plot up to date – haven't you? – but you don't know what's to come. Well, I'll tell you. When we've skinned you over Robitos the yacht will come in to Plymouth again. I shall meet her there, and to my amazement I shall find out that you are not on board. Pretty good that bit, isn't it? You can think of me registering amazement, with Gardini doing the same thing. He thought, you see, that there was some deep motive behind your orders to him. By the way, have I ever told you what your orders were? You told Gardini to go for a cruise, and to let it be understood if anyone sent a radio that you were with him on board. You also gave him instructions as to what to do about Perus and Robitos, which was devilish considerate of you, my dear fellow. He thought they were a bit rum at the time, but, being a model secretary, he dutifully carried them out. All right so far, isn't it? But now, though, comes the point – where are you? Where is the great Sir Edward Greatorex? Not on board the yacht: not anywhere. Tremendous hue and cry started by me. And what do you think is the answer? You've been suffering from loss of memory, brought on by a nervous breakdown. You've been wandering, and one night you unexpectedly turn up here, still in a strange condition. Doctors, specialists, bone-setters, dentists – I'll get the whole outfit – are wired for: the great Sir Edward has reappeared. And then a terrible thing takes place. Unknown to us, you go out for a walk before going to bed. Suddenly from Grimstone Mire there comes a scream of mortal terror. We rush horrified to the scene: a slight tremor in that treacherous bog is all that remains of the great financier. The doctors, specialists, bone-setters, dentists are all too late. Pretty good, don't you think?"

Still no word came from the other, and with a snarl of rage Hardcastle leaned forward.

"You're going to die, damn you: do you understand that?"

And then suddenly he became conscious of something else – something that brought the sweat out on his forehead. A strange, fetid smell was filling the room. He had forgotten about the ghost, and now it came back with a rush to his mind. He tried to turn round and could not: he *knew* that some appalling thing was in the room just behind him. And at last, with a croak of terror, he looked over his shoulder.

A monstrous black object was between him and the door, and Hardcastle, screaming with fear, backed against the wall. It slithered nearer him, and he clawed at the brickwork with his fingers in a frantic endeavour to escape. Nearer – still nearer it came, till the stench was overpowering. And then it sprang: seemed completely to envelop him. He was conscious of a vice-like grip round his throat, there came a roaring in his ears: then – oblivion.

When he came to himself he was lying huddled up on the floor. His torch was beginning to grow dim, but of the ghostly visitor there was no trace, save a faint smell which lingered in the air. On the bed Sir Edward still lay motionless, and once again the same overmastering terror gripped him. Suppose it returned.

He scrambled to his feet, and seizing the torch, rushed blindly along the passage. Not until he was in the main part of the house would he feel safe, and as he fumbled with the secret door he kept glancing behind him in an agony of fear. At last he stumbled into the hall, and slammed the panel behind him.

The time was four o'clock: dawn had come. For five hours he had been lying unconscious. He walked shakily to the dining-room, and with a trembling hand poured himself out a glass of neat whisky. He gulped it down, and felt a little better.

Five hours! But what had it been – that ghastly foul-smelling black horror? He rubbed his neck gingerly: there had been nothing ghostly about the grip round his throat.

The window was still open, and he stepped through it on to the lawn. Bed was out of the question, and after a while, as he paced up and down in the cool morning air, he began to feel calmer. When all was said and done, save for a stiff neck he was none the worse for his terrible experience.

Suddenly he paused, staring over the moor. There was a column of dust in the distance, and even as he watched it a motorcar breasted a rise. It was moving fast from the direction of London, and he wondered idly who could be out at such an hour. And then, to his surprise, it swung off the road, and came up the drive towards him. He walked round to the front door, and to his amazement found that Penton and Slingsby were the occupants. Their faces were haggard, and with a queer feeling of foreboding he greeted them.

"Hullo! boys," he cried. "What brings you here?"

"There's something up," said Penton. "Something damned queer. Or else Gardini has double-crossed us."

"What do you mean?" snarled Hardcastle. "How could he?"

"The markets are all going crazy: just exactly the opposite to his instructions."

"Over Robitos?"

The other nodded, and walked into the house.

"Where's the whisky? we need one."

"You haven't lost?"

"Every penny we made over Perus, and a wad more besides."

"When did it happen?"

"Yesterday. Something started the rot in the afternoon. It's all up, Tom, as far as the boodle is concerned."

"But what can have started it?"

"Search me," cried Penton. "Jake and I have been trying to get at it the whole way down. Anyway, we've got to clear."

"Clear out?" shouted Hardcastle. "Why?"

"Because we can't go near meeting our liabilities," answered the other. "And that means an investigation, which I guess we daren't risk. The point is – what are we going to do with him?"

He pointed with his thumb over his shoulder towards the secret passage.

"Do with him," said Hardcastle grimly. "There's only one thing we can do with him, unless we want prison. And that's what we intended."

The other two nodded.

"There's no time to be lost," grunted Penton. "I'll get him now. We'll steer him down through the trees. There's no one about."

He left the room, whilst the other two helped themselves again to whisky.

"I don't like it," muttered Slingsby uneasily.

"What I don't like," cried Hardcastle, "is losing the dough. All this damned business for nothing. You must have been crazy, you two. Suffering Pete! what's that?"

From the hall had come a bellow of rage, and the next instant Penton burst into the room. He was almost inarticulate, and the veins were standing out on his forehead as he made for Hardcastle.

"You blasted crook," he said thickly, "what's your game?"

The other stared at him in amazement.

"What are you getting at?" he cried.

"Come and look in the hall."

The three of them crowded through the door. Lying on the floor was the bound-and-gagged body of a man. But it was not Sir Edward Greatorex: it was the understudy Travers.

For a while Hardcastle stared at him foolishly.

"What under the sun does it mean?" he muttered. "Where's Sir Edward?"

"Where indeed?" came an amiable voice from the front door, and they all swung round. Drummond, with a cheerful grin on his face, was standing there, with Darrell and Jerningham behind him.

"Strong liquor at this hour!" he said reprovingly. "Terrible, polluting the dawn like this. And have we had a nice run from London?"

"Get out, damn you!" snarled Hardcastle, "or I'll have you gaoled for trespassing."

"The English law of trespass is a very intricate one, my dear sir," answered Drummond. "Dear me," he continued commiseratingly, "I fear your neck is hurting you. Try some arnica. No! Well, it's your neck. However, to return to what you were discussing when I arrived – where is Sir Edward?"

The three men stared at him, with dawning fear in their eyes.

"I don't know what you're talking about," said Hardcastle at length.

"You pain me, Tom: positively pain me. Here am I taking a walk in the coolth of the morning, and your conversation descends to that level. But tell me – why is this poor fellow on the floor all bound up? More film work? Ah, good morning, Comtessa. We're having an awfully jolly little party."

With a wrap over her pyjamas, the Comtessa was coming down the stairs. She gave a start of surprise as she saw Travers on the floor: then, with an air of calmness that did her credit, she turned to Hardcastle:

"What's it all mean, Tom?"

"It means, Comtessa," said Drummond quietly, "that the game is up. Sir Edward Greatorex arrived in London early yesterday afternoon – a fact which may help Mr Penton and Mr Slingsby to understand the failure of their financial operations."

"Have we got you to thank for this?" said Hardcastle thickly.

"You have, Tom," answered Drummond affably. "I owed you something for that little episode at the studio, didn't I? And as far as I am concerned my debt is paid. But I fear you will not find the same happy state of affairs with regard to Sir Edward, who is just about as wild as I have ever seen a man in my life. Still, I believe our prisons are very comfortable, even if the diet is a little monotonous. Well, I will say *au revoir*: we shall doubtless meet again at the trial. And, by the way, if you should find a large black cloak, smelling strongly of that stinking bog, lying about anywhere, you may keep it: it has served its purpose. I think we may say that the second ghost was quite as successful as the first."

CHAPTER 11

"So they've got the lot except Irma. I never thought they'd catch her."

Hugh Drummond threw down the evening paper and lit a cigarette. It was after dinner the same day, and they were all in the smoking-room at Merridale Hall, with Mr Joseph Hetterbury an interested listener.

" 'Pon my soul," he continued, "if it hadn't been for that brutal murder of young Marton I wish they'd got away with it: it was a deuced clever idea – carrying out a real crime under the cover of the same crime on the film."

"I'm still very much in the dark," said Hetterbury.

Drummond grinned.

"So was I for a long while, though I ought to have tumbled to it when I spotted Marton's extraordinary resemblance to Sir Edward, and that young blighter Travers as well. Were they going to take all that trouble merely to provide an understudy for a film, especially before they knew whether Sir Edward could act or not? Now you know the plot of the film roughly, and, from what you've told me, Hardcastle gave you some more details. A millionaire is kidnapped, and while he is held prisoner on board a yacht his enemies so manipulate the markets by means of information purporting to come from him that they make a pot of money. Thus the film, and thus what they proposed to do in real life, with only one difference – the yacht. In a film it was easy to have all the yacht's crew villains as

Hardcastle said: in real life it was impossible. Something else would have to be thought of. And don't forget that the film was going to be taken quite genuinely: the cameramen, the producer, were all absolutely honest. So the problem they had to face was how to make Sir Edward a prisoner under the very noses of a bunch of people who were not in the plot, and then hide him in a place where no one would dream of looking for him.

"The second part was easy: Glensham House, with its secret passages, was an ideal spot, especially as everyone believed he was at sea. It was getting him there that was the difficulty. And then they saw how it could be done, with Marton's help. There was a scene in the film where Sir Edward had to drink a glass of what was supposed to be drugged sherry. Then he was bound and gagged and bunged into the cupboard with the idea of later on being abducted in the lorry. And since there might be a little rough-house about it, it was decided that the understudy should do the second part. And everybody at the time, myself included, believed that he had done the second part.

"And then that night I got you out of bed, Algy, it dawned on me – the whole rich plot. It *was* drugged sherry that Sir Edward drank. He *was* unconscious when he was bound and gagged and bunged into the cupboard, behind which our one and only Irma, screened by a partition, erected on a thoroughly flimsy excuse, was waiting to see that nothing went amiss. But what could go amiss? Had he shouted – cried 'I'm drugged' – applause would have greeted his fine piece of acting."

"By Gosh! Hugh – now I come to think of it – he did shout," cried Algy.

"Let's go on. Two hours elapse, during which the still-unconscious Sir Edward is guarded in the office. Then the final abduction scene is played. It is dark, and Marton, talking to two of the gang, stands in the shadow, while Sir Edward is replaced in the cupboard. Naturally everyone thought it was the other way round, and that Marton was bound in the cupboard while

Sir Edward looked on. It was all over in a flash: Sir Edward was rushed into the lorry by two innocent actors who thought they were carrying Marton – there was a handkerchief over most of his face – and the lorry went off in the darkness pursued by the camera and the arcs. In the meantime Marton had left for London in his car, which halted a little way from the studio. The ticklish bit was now coming. Marton must show himself again as Marton, or the whole thing would be given away. So he removes his beard, comes back as himself, and is seen by everyone. Then once more he returns to the car, resumes his role of Sir Edward, and is driven to the Ritz Carlton with Gardini in attendance.

"Feeling a little chilly, he is muffled up, and so passes the commissionaire at the door easily. He spends the night in Sir Edward's suite, and leaves the next morning for a yachting cruise, where more of the film is going to be taken. He is still muffled up, and again completely deceives the man at the door. And now comes the subtle part. The secretary goes straight to Plymouth and boards the yacht. Marton, on the other hand, goes round the corner, boards his small two-seater, removes his beard, and arrives in due course at the studio as himself.

"That was their scheme, and then at the last moment Marton jibbed. Perhaps he lost his nerve – that we shall never know. And even though they thought they'd got him completely under their thumb by getting him into such debt that he stole five thousand pounds – a theft which I believe made his old father, who found it out, kill himself – he proved intractable. And so they did him in, and managed to get Travers as the substitute instead.

"Then came their doubts about me. All the way through, the one thing they had not been sure about was how much Marton told me that afternoon he was here. And so they decided to make sure I was out of the way when the actual abduction took place. If you remember, Algy, I said to you at the time that I wondered why they had selected that night instead of the next.

"It all fitted in, you see, as one looked back on it: I was convinced that Penton driving the lorry in the film had brought Sir Edward straight to Glensham House. The world thought he was on board the yacht: the yacht's crew knew nothing about it all, since the paragraph in the papers saying he was there had appeared *after* the yacht had sailed. But I had no proof: I had to find out for certain.

"So I toddled round to Dick Newall, and through him got in touch with Glensham, who luckily was in London. And he put me wise as to the secret passages, one of which fortunately led to an underground vault outside. I got in through that, and there, sure enough, I found my bird, in a pitiful condition.

"However, I cheered him up, warned him not to say a word, and then I ran Travers to ground. And with that young man I had a merry half-hour. He tried to bluster at first, and pitched me some cock-and-bull yarn about the whole thing being a joke. But I soon put the fear of God into him, and told him what he had to do. He had impersonated Sir Edward once, and he was damned well going to do it again.

"Then I got Sir Edward out of it the night before last, warned him still not to say a word until he'd queered their pitch over their next deal, and left Travers in his place. I knew they'd got to move quickly, for the yacht would have to put back to refuel, when the thing must come out. Of course I knew Travers wouldn't pass a close inspection, but it was dark down there, and he managed it for a day. Moreover, I was on hand as the ghost to prevent anyone lingering there, while Joseph kindly held the fort above, and incidentally found out some useful information.

"We were only just in time," Drummond continued thoughtfully. "Hardcastle was a bit oiled last night, but he was speaking the truth all right when he thought Sir Edward was his audience. Without the slightest doubt, they intended to kill him, and as far as one can see they'd have got away with it. Lapse of memory, nervous breakdown, and another convenient accident in Grimstone Mire."

The door opened, and the butler entered with the evening mail. And a few moments later a bellow of laughter from Drummond shook the house.

"Listen to this, chaps," he said weakly.

DEAR CAPTAIN DRUMMOND,

I feel sure you would like to have your chauffeur's insolent behaviour brought to your notice. We stopped on the way up to London for an early lunch, and to my pained amazement I found on receiving the bill that an item of eightpence for beer was included. I at once demanded an explanation, and on discovering that your man had drunk it, I struck it out and told the waiter to obtain the money from him. It is a matter of principle with me never to pay for alcohol consumed by servants.

On explaining this to your chauffeur, instead of his realising the high moral point at issue, he stared at me very rudely. Then he turned away and made an incomprehensible remark about a perishing, flat-footed, knock-kneed, yellow beaver. What he meant I have no idea: surely beavers are not yellow? And a flat-footed, knock-kneed one must in any event perish. It was his manner I took exception to – his tone of voice. You would do well to take him to task for it.

Yours very truly,
EDWARD GREATOREX.

"That's torn it," sobbed Drummond. "What is it, Jennings?"

"Your letter, sir," said the butler, "was not stamped. The postman is demanding threepence."

SAPPER

THE FINAL COUNT

When Robin Gaunt, inventor of a terrifyingly powerful weapon of chemical warfare, goes missing, the police suspect that he has 'sold out' to the other side. But Bulldog Drummond is convinced of his innocence, and can think of only one man brutal enough to use the weapon to hold the world to ransom. Drummond receives an invitation to a sumptuous dinner-dance aboard an airship that is to mark the beginning of his final battle for triumph.

THE THIRD ROUND

The death of Professor Goodman is officially recorded as a tragic accident, but at the inquest, no mention is made of his latest discovery – a miraculous new formula for manufacturing flawless diamonds at negligible cost, which strikes Captain Hugh 'Bulldog' Drummond as rather strange. His suspicions are further aroused when he spots a member of the Metropolitan Diamond Syndicate at the inquest. Gradually, he untangles a sinister plot of greed and murder, which climaxes in a dramatic motorboat chase at Cowes and brings him face to face with his arch-enemy.

S A P P E R

BULLDOG DRUMMOND AT BAY

While Hugh 'Bulldog' Drummond is staying in an old cottage for a peaceful few days' duck-shooting, he is disturbed one night by the sound of men shouting, followed by a large stone that comes crashing through the window. When he goes outside to investigate, he finds a patch of blood in the road, and is questioned by two men who tell him that they are chasing a lunatic who has escaped from the nearby asylum. Drummond plays dumb, but is determined to investigate in his inimitable style when he discovers a cryptic message.

THE FEMALE OF THE SPECIES

Bulldog Drummond has slain his arch-enemy, Carl Peterson, but Peterson's mistress lives on and is intent on revenge. Drummond's wife vanishes, followed by a series of vicious traps set by a malicious adversary, which lead to a hair-raising chase across England, to a sinister house and a fantastic torture-chamber modelled on Stonehenge, with its legend of human sacrifice.

SAPPER

THE BLACK GANG

Although the First World War is over, it seems that the hostilities are not, and when Captain Hugh 'Bulldog' Drummond discovers that a stint of bribery and blackmail is undermining England's democratic tradition, he forms the Black Gang, bent on tracking down the perpetrators of such plots. They set a trap to lure the criminal mastermind behind these subversive attacks to England, and all is going to plan until Bulldog Drummond accepts an invitation to tea at the Ritz with a charming American clergyman and his dowdy daughter.

BULLDOG DRUMMOND

'Demobilised officer, finding peace incredibly tedious, would welcome diversion. Legitimate, if possible; but crime, if of a comparatively humorous description, no objection. Excitement essential... Reply at once Box X10.'

Hungry for adventure following the First World War, Captain Hugh 'Bulldog' Drummond begins a career as the invincible protectorate of his country. His first reply comes from a beautiful young woman, who sends him racing off to investigate what at first looks like blackmail but turns out to be far more complicated and dangerous. The rescue of a kidnapped millionaire, found with his thumbs horribly mangled, leads Drummond to the discovery of a political conspiracy of awesome scope and villainy, masterminded by the ruthless Carl Peterson.